"Whoa!"

Storm's eyebrows shot up and he quickly lowered the binoculars, his astonishment turning to amusement. His smile slowly grew.

Once before he'd watched Donetta Presley strip off her underwear out in the open beneath Bertha, the old cottonwood tree—the day before her high-school graduation. Like now, she hadn't known he was there.

Man alive, that had been twelve years ago, but the image in his mind was still clear. It had been broad daylight, and she *hadn't* been wearing a granny gown. That day she'd had on denim shorts and a little shirt that left at least five inches of her belly exposed. And she'd had to take the shorts all the way off in order to remove the panties.

Although he was no longer cold—was pretty damn hot, to be honest—he went back inside, stowed the binoculars and made his way to his bedroom to listen for her return.

One way or another he was going to prove to her that love didn't need a crystal ball.

Love. His heart raced wildly, the speed brought on by a panic he couldn't name.

By God, the chances of getting any sleep were zip to none. And the blame rested squarely with the tall, stubborn, redheaded woman who was turning his life upside down.

SURPRISED BY A BABY

Mindy Neff

TORONTO • NEW YORK • LONDON
AMSTERDAM • PARIS • SYDNEY • HAMBURG
STOCKHOLM • ATHENS • TOKYO • MILAN • MADRID
PRAGUE • WARSAW • BUDAPEST • AUCKLAND

ISBN 0-373-75002-1

SURPRISED BY A BABY

This edition published by arrangement with Harlequin Books S.A.

Visit us at www.eHarlequin.com

Printed in U.S.A.

ABOUT THE AUTHOR

Originally from Louisiana, Mindy Neff settled in Southern California, where she married a really romantic guy and raised five kids. Family, friends, writing and reading are her passions. When she's not writing, Mindy's ideal getaway is a good book, hot sunshine and a chair at the river's edge with water lapping at her toes.

Books by Mindy Neff

HARLEQUIN AMERICAN ROMANCE

809—A PREGNANCY AND A PROPOSAL
830—THE RANCHER'S MAIL-ORDER BRIDE
834—THE PLAYBOY'S OWN MISS PRIM
838—THE HORSEMAN'S CONVENIENT WIFE
857—THE SECRETARY GETS HER MAN
898—CHEYENNE'S LADY
906—PREACHER'S IN-NAME-ONLY WIFE
925—IN THE ENEMY'S EMBRACE
946—THE INCONVENIENTLY ENGAGED PRINCE
998—SURPRISED BY A BABY

Chapter One

Donetta Presley's nerves were flat-out wrecked. And no wonder! She'd had another run-in with the town's new fire marshal; the contractor who'd renovated her trendy hair salon and her upstairs apartment wasn't returning her phone calls; and despite feeling like road kill and hugging the porcelain throne more times than she cared to remember, she'd actually given a haircut to a toy poodle named Debbie!

On top of that, she'd had to drive clear over to Austin just to buy a home pregnancy test. Hope Valley had the fastest gossip mill in Texas and she did *not* want the whole town discussing the nature of her purchase before she could even get home and remove the cellophane from the box.

She could have saved herself the trouble.

Pretty soon everyone would know anyway.

She wiped her clammy forehead with the back of her wrist, tempted to lower the thermostat on the salon's air conditioner another notch. That probably wouldn't be a good idea. Her clients were shivering as it was.

Trying to take shallow breaths, praying the nausea would pass, she removed the last few bobby pins and rollers from Millicent Lloyd's blue hair and tossed them into an open drawer. The pink-and-gray perm rods she'd used on a client who'd left more than an hour ago were still scattered in the shampoo bowl. Too bad the scent hadn't gone with the woman, because the acrid smell of ammonia that wafted from the shiny black sink bowl made Donetta's stomach revolt anew.

Wasn't that a hoot? The owner and operator of Donetta's Secret, the only hair salon in Hope Valley, Texas, couldn't bear the smell of permanent wave lotion.

Lordy, she didn't need this grief. Her schedule was so messed up she was now juggling three clients at once. And Miz Lloyd expected to leave here at two-forty-five on the dot—same as every Friday.

She patted the woman on the shoulder. ''Be patient with me, okay, Miz Lloyd? I'm tryin' my best to get you out of here on time.''

She reached for a bottle of finishing spray and gave Millicent's short barrel curls a squirt, then pumped a couple of aromatic spurts into the air.

Millicent's blue-tinted eyebrows shot up. ''Did you just blast me with air freshener?''

Donetta forced a smile and retrieved her small teasing brush from the top drawer of the laminate workstation. ''No, silly. It's finishing spray. It sets the curl and gives your hair more body. Don't you just love the way it smells?''

''You've never used it on me before,'' Millicent said, her light-blue eyes narrowing.

Donetta looked down at the sectioned curls. ''It's a new product. Just came in this week.''

''Expensive, I bet. Ought to have a care about wasting it.'' She sniffed, still clutching her taupe gloves in her age-spotted fist. Millicent Lloyd never went to town without matching gloves, shoes and pocketbook. ''Squirting it all over the place like it was toilet water perfume from the dime store. Why, if I wasn't trussed up in this cape, I'd be needing a bath.''

''You're fine,'' Donetta soothed. ''It's not sticky.''

As she backcombed Millicent's hair into a temporary Phyllis Diller look, she glanced at the chrome clock above the front door and checked the minute hands, shaped as neon-red scissors. Barring any more interruptions, she could probably finish these last three clients within the hour and close up early.

Then again, maybe not.

Her hand tightened around the red plastic handle of the brush when she saw the sheriff's car wheel into a diagonal parking space in front of her salon.

Storm Carmichael.

He was her best friend's brother—an ex-Texas Ranger who was now the sheriff of Hope Valley.

And he was the last person Donetta wanted to see today.

"I declare, Donetta. You're about to snatch me baldheaded."

She jolted and quickly smoothed out the two-inch-long section of hair she'd just teased into a ball of frizz.

"Sorry, Miz Lloyd. My mind wandered."

"Good thing you didn't have a pair of scissors in your hand. No telling what I'd look like." She cut her eyes toward the front window, then back to Donetta's reflection in the mirror. "That Carmichael boy is heading this way. Is that what's got you in such a tizzy?"

Storm Carmichael wasn't anybody's idea of a *boy,* Donetta thought, which was partly the reason her knees were shaking. Thank God she hadn't worn her miniskirt today. The man was more observant than a hawk, and Donetta had learned a hard lesson about showing vulnerability.

"Just running behind schedule is all that's wrong with me," Donetta said.

The door swished open, sucking out precious degrees of the salon's cool air. And there he stood, Sheriff Storm Carmichael, six feet five inches of sinfully delicious masculinity in boots, jeans, a khaki uniform shirt with a sheriff's star pinned above his breast pocket, and a Stetson sporting a cattleman's crease.

The very man responsible for this god-awful, debilitating morning sickness.

His gaze locked onto hers and never wavered, yet she knew he could probably give a detailed description of every customer in the salon, as well as the hairstyle models in the photos on the walls. Despite her outward control, her heart galloped like a thoroughbred on an open range.

She'd had a major crush on him when she was a dreamy ten-year-old and he was sixteen. But that was twenty years ago—and at this particular moment, puppy love was *not* the emotion she was feeling.

"Excuse me just a minute, Miz Lloyd." She set the brush on her station, then strolled toward the reception desk to head him off in case he had any ideas of coming in and getting comfortable. Not that he'd ever hung out in the salon, but he looked like a man with something on his mind, a man willing to wait until she was finished with her clients.

That was all she needed, she thought with a mental sigh. To have Storm's eyes trained on her backside while she worked. She'd likely give Darla Pam Kirkwell a mohawk.

She stopped at the reception desk, realizing she'd almost walked right up to Storm to automatically give him a hug.

That was what happened when a person had sex with a friend. Normal, lifelong habits became awkward. She'd *always* greeted him with a hug—even if she was miffed at him. Now she was afraid the simple gesture would give away more than she wanted him to know.

Wishing she could sit down for about five hours, she leaned against the red laminate counter, instead, and put on her polite, welcome-the-customer face. It took a Herculean effort. She felt about as sociable as a she-bear in satin.

''Afternoon, Sheriff. What can I do for you?''

His eyes blatantly lowered to her V-neck tank top, embroidered with a large, dramatic face of a cat, then to her slim khaki pants and open-toed platform shoes. Although it was October, a warm front had moved in from the Gulf, making it feel like the middle of summer. Storm Carmichael's visual caress cranked up her internal thermostat to triple digits.

''I guess you didn't see that red tag on the door,'' he said in his perfectly charming Texas drawl. He was one of those men whose smooth baritone voice had an innately sensual, teasing tone.

His thumbs were hooked in the front pockets of his jeans, a purely masculine gesture that drew the eye and put a woman in danger of losing her good sense.

''Now, don't you start in on me, too, Storm. As soon as I get ahold of my contractor, he'll take care of everything. And park those eyeballs back in your head, why don't you. I'm not in the mood to deal with one more condescending male today.'' She'd couched her annoyance in her trademark sultry tone, but for once, she wasn't quite certain she'd pulled it off.

She knew just how to flirt with a guy, to let him down easy without making him feel as though he'd struck out. It was her means of holding men at bay.

The trait was pretty much the only useful lesson she'd learned from a mother she hadn't seen in eight years.

''Can't blame a man for admiring. All these bold colors in here, and you still stand out like a million-dollar supermodel.''

She arched a brow. ''Flattery, Sheriff? My goodness, you must want something.''

''Oh, I want a lot of things,'' he said softly, making her shiver even though she was burning up. ''Right now, though, I'll stick to business. That citation on your door isn't part of a beautification project, it doesn't say 'Pretty please' and it doesn't mention a thing about phoning your contractor. It's an official injunction mandating you to vacate these premises until the issues that have been itemized for you—more than once, I'm told—are corrected and in compliance with county and state building codes.''

At the formality of his words, Donetta's heart pounded with a mounting sense of dread. This was Storm Carmichael the cop. Not Storm Carmichael the friend she'd slept with, the man who held her heart and didn't even know it.

''Now, I don't know how these infractions slipped through the cracks for two years, but the improvements on this unit have been declared unsafe by the fire marshal—''

''Would you just hush?'' she whispered fiercely. ''I know what the damn thing says.'' She looked around to see if any of the customers were listening. Of course they were. The three elderly women were practically leaning forward in their chairs, not even trying to disguise that they were exercising what they clearly viewed as their God-given right to eavesdrop.

''Listen, Storm, this will just have to wait.'' He wasn't wearing a gun belt and she didn't see any handcuffs, so it was a safe bet that he wouldn't actually arrest her for violating a court order. Hope Valley was a relaxed small town. The judicial system was naturally a bit more laid-back. And she wasn't ignoring the stupid paper—even though she'd flipped it the bird as she'd unlocked the front door this morning to open for business.

''I intend to take care of everything,'' she said, ''but first I need to finish styling Miz Lloyd and rinse Darla Pam before the bleach fries her hair. And I promised Cora I'd have her out of here before three o'clock. She has errands to run and has to be home before dark—you know she can't drive at night.''

Glancing down, she skimmed a fingertip over her appointment book, noticed that her acrylic nail was chipped at the very tip. Swell. One more thing she could add to her to-do list. She swallowed back the queasiness again working its way up her esophagus. She really, *really* didn't feel good.

''Why don't you give me a call around five,'' she said, fully aware she wouldn't be here. Millicent, Darla Pam and Cora were her last three clients for the day. ''I should have a break by then. Meanwhile...'' She stepped back and fixed a phony smile on her face. ''You have yourself a real nice afternoon, Sheriff, ya hear?''

STORM WATCHED DONETTA'S long cinnamon-red hair swish across her shoulders as she calmly turned around. That he'd been dismissed took a second to sink in. His eyebrows shot up, raising his Stetson a good inch, he was sure.

Without an ounce of respect for the badge pinned to his shirt, the confounding woman had left him cooling his heels beside the small reception desk. He was both astounded and aroused by her cheekiness...and seriously annoyed at himself because of the reaction.

His gaze naturally fastened on her sexy derriere as she sashayed across the red-and-black linoleum. Long and lean, she stood nearly five-foot-ten in her bare feet. He'd never once seen her slouch to minimize her height. Hell, she accented it with four-inch-platform shoes that would cause a less coordinated person to end up in traction.

His lips twitched when she breezed by the wall and flipped the air-conditioning switch without even looking. The domed hair dryers would likely have icicles hanging from the rims in a few minutes. Ms. Donetta Presley wasn't so calm after all.

Ignoring him, she went back to work on Millicent Lloyd's blue hair. In Storm's opinion, that attention-getting shade wasn't the best advertising for the beauty shop. Hell, the woman even had her eyebrows painted blue.

He shifted his gaze back to Donetta, and just that quickly, his groin tightened. He couldn't believe how he was responding to her after all these years. She'd always been just his kid sister's friend. Now he couldn't look at her without thinking about mind-blowing sex.

She frustrated the hell out of him, though. As a lawman, a big part of his job involved reading people. Yet he'd be damned if he could figure out what made Donetta Presley tick.

She was sexy, flirty and in-your-face sassy, but there was a vulnerability in her exotic amber eyes that worried him, made him want to wrap her in silk and slay her demons. She'd probably belt him if he tried—provided he could get close enough for her to take a swing.

She'd been holding him at an arm's distance for the past month, ever since she'd driven out to his ranch on an errand for his mother. He'd invited her to stay for dinner. God knows he hadn't planned it, but between drinks and friendly conversation an explosive chemistry had taken them both by surprise and culminated in a night of stunningly carnal sex.

Now she was determined to act as though they'd never seen each other naked, as though she hadn't rocked his world right off its axis. And it was making him nuts.

Donetta Presley was not a forgettable kind of woman.

Talk about straining a relationship—what he was about to do could well snap it altogether.

He moved up behind her as she emptied half a can of hair spray on Millicent's hairdo.

"Afternoon, Miz Lloyd," he said.

"It's polite to take off your hat indoors, young man. I know your mother taught you better manners." She sniffed and worked her birdlike hands into a pair of lacy brown gloves when Donetta stripped off the cape.

Storm removed his hat and combed his fingers through his hair. "Yes, ma'am."

Donetta shook out the vinyl drape and folded it over the chair Millicent had vacated, nearly butting against him when she stepped back. "I thought you were leaving."

"Not without you, darlin'."

She merely scowled at him. "Same time next Friday, Miz Lloyd?"

"I imagine if you don't find me dead in my bed, I'll be here."

A nearly imperceptible look of distress flashed in Donetta's eyes, yet she hardly missed a beat as she said, "Now, don't you be talking like that." She fixed the collar on Millicent's dress and brushed away a couple of stray hairs.

"You take care, Miz Lloyd. I've got to go shampoo Darla Pam. Think about letting me cancel out some of the blue tones when you come in next week."

Storm's jaw went slack. Hadn't he just explained to this irritating woman that she wouldn't be using the salon until the fire marshal gave his approval?

"I've told you time and again," Millicent said, her neck rising like a rooster ready to crow, "this is exactly the way Harold liked my hair, and that's how I intend to keep it."

Donetta patted her on the shoulder. "I'm betting he would have loved the softer blue, too. You give it some thought. I'll see you next Friday."

Without so much as an "excuse me," Donetta

headed across the salon, straining his patience to the max. Her delicate vanilla perfume lingered in her wake.

Millicent placed money on Donetta's station. "Don't you have work, Sheriff?"

"As a matter of fact, I do. Thank you for reminding me. You have a nice day, Miz Lloyd. And be careful not to trip on that extension cord." The cord was safely secured to the floor with black electrical tape, but he was annoyed enough to comment. Damn Blane Pyke for forcing him to come here in the first place.

"My eyes are fine, young man. I can still see to pick up my feet. You, on the other hand, had better watch your step. You were off chasing hooligans for twelve years, and just because you were raised here in Hope Valley, that don't mean you know everything. If you did, you wouldn't be standing here now, trying to enforce rules that new Yankee fire marshal ought to have the gumption to handle himself."

Millicent Lloyd didn't miss too much that went on in this town. For as long as he'd known her, Storm had never had a conversation with her that he'd fully understood. The undertones in this puzzling discourse clearly had something to do with Donetta, and the fact that he didn't know what it was gave him a jolt of unease.

"My hands are tied, Miz Lloyd. I have to follow the law."

"Things aren't always black and white, young man. What you see isn't necessarily the whole picture. You ought to know that better than most."

Direct hit. She was referring to his suspension several years back, allegedly due to excessive use of force on an obstruction-of-justice arrest involving a woman named Shantelle Kingsley. The fiasco had turned into a media circus, splashed across the news and carefully edited to show only what the television and cable stations wanted people to see—regardless of the accuracy. The reminder twisted his gut into knots.

But what did that have to do with Donetta?

"If there's something I should know about Donetta, why don't you just say it?" Great. Interview 101. Non-accusatory. Gain the subject's confidence and make him—or her—*want* to tell his story. He'd just blown this one like a rookie right out of the police academy.

As expected, Millicent took a step back from him. "If you're smart, you'll stop thinking with what's in your pants and look a little deeper than skin."

She hugged her purse to her side as though expecting a mugger to accost her on the way to the door and left him standing by Donetta's empty station, stunned.

What the hell did that mean? The woman almost seemed to know that he'd slept with Donetta. Millicent Lloyd clung to a personal standard of what was and was not proper. He was pretty sure her parting words put him in the *improper* category.

He felt as though he'd just been chastised by his mother. And he had no idea what he'd done wrong. Maybe she'd seen him checking out Donetta's backside a few minutes ago. It might have looked crass, but by God she didn't have all the facts. The woman ought to be paying a little more attention to her own riddles.

As far as the building-code violations went, he'd taken an oath to uphold the laws of the court. He might not *like* the assignments that crossed his desk, but rules were made to be followed.

There was one thing, though, that he was fast learning: dealing with hardened criminals was a damned sight easier than going up against the women of Hope Valley. Between his mother and her pals, his sister, Sunny, and her Texas Sweethearts group—which included Donetta, Tracy Lynn Randolph and Becca Sue Ellsworth—he'd be lucky to survive the next few days without blood being spilled. Namely *his* blood.

He shoved his Stetson back on his head and stalked across the salon. The hat was part of his uniform and he could wear the thing indoors if he felt like it.

He was tired of being ignored. He had better things to do than follow Donetta Presley around like an adoring puppy.

Folding his arms, he waited while she shut off the water in the shampoo bowl and wrapped a towel around Darla Pam's hair.

''Oh, my land, Storm Carmichael. Shame on you for catching us girls lookin' like a mess.'' Darla Pam, not a day under sixty, twittered and held the towel in place on her head, thrusting her chest out in the process.

Storm glanced away and saw Donetta roll her eyes in disgust. He wanted to mimic the gesture, but he'd probably hear about it from the mayor.

''You still look real fine, Miz Kirkwell.''

This time Donetta didn't bother rolling her eyes. They snapped to his. If the sparks shooting from them had been packed with gunpowder, his mama would be pressing his burial suit right about now.

Before Darla Pam could reply, Donetta aimed a falsely sweet smile at the woman. ''No flirting until everybody has her hair done. We allow only *genuine* compliments in here. I think I'll put you under the dryer for a few minutes, Darla, while I start on Cora.''

Storm was smart enough to stand back as she ushered Darla Pam to the red vinyl chair, dropped the dryer dome and cranked the blower on high with a vicious twist of her wrist. Darla didn't seem to notice anything was amiss.

Side stepping, she lifted the dryer hood from Cora Harris—who was Jackson Slade's housekeeper, and Sunny's, too, now that his sister had married the rancher. Cora wiggled her fingers at Storm and giggled.

''Cora, go ahead and have a seat in my chair.''

Storm cleared his throat. ''Sorry, ladies. Cora. Darla

Pam.'' He looked at each woman, lifted Darla's dryer hood and shut off the blower.

''Donetta's Secret is closed for business until further notice—fire marshal's orders. I'll have to ask you both to gather up your belongings and exit the building.''

Chapter Two

''For crying out loud, Storm.'' Donetta glared and marched right up to him. Survival instincts almost convinced him to retreat a step.

Thank God he didn't follow through. It would be a sad day in Houston if the men in his former Texas Ranger company got wind of Storm Carmichael shaking in his boots at the advance of a beautiful, ticked-off redhead. With her chest practically brushing his, he barely had to tilt his head to meet her seriously annoyed eyes.

''I will not let a customer walk out of here with wet hair!'' Darla Pam looked relieved to hear that, he noted. ''And you can't just come in here and start bossing everyone around,'' Donetta added.

''The court order in my pocket says otherwise.'' He'd tried to discuss this away from gossiping ears, but she'd been too stubborn to budge. ''You're holding a pair of threes against a full house, darlin'. You either close up this shop, or I'll have to arrest you.''

Donetta's jaw dropped. The two older ladies gasped and moved right up beside her. At least, Cora did. Darla Pam stood half a pace behind, clutching Cora's arm, her wet hair clearly forgotten since she was about to snag a juicy morsel of gossip to share at her ladies' club.

"Storm Carmichael," Cora snapped. "I'll have you know I have the ear of your mama *and* your sister. And they would *not* want to hear about your behavior. If you've any notion of arresting Donetta, you'll have to arrest all of us."

Ah hell. He'd predicted something like this would happen. "If that's the way you want it, Miz Harris," he said quietly, deliberately.

Darla Pam let go of Cora's arm and scuttled backward. Cora stood her ground. Storm had to admire her courage and loyalty. As the live-in housekeeper out at the Slade ranch, Cora often took care of his niece, Tori. He didn't have a single doubt that this was a woman he'd want at his back—and watching over his sister and her family.

Donetta quickly removed the curlers from Cora's hair and tossed them on a dryer chair. She finger-combed the curls, then slid her arm around the older woman.

"Cora," she said softly. "Storm's not going to take anyone to jail. But I think it'd be best if you both do as he asked and go. There'll be no charge for my services." She reached in the drawer of the station closest to her and pulled out two scarves, then retrieved purses and passed the items to the women.

Darla Pam lit out the door as though a posse were on her tail. That was when it sank into Donetta's brain that she was well and truly in a fix.

Her skin turned clammy as the nausea she'd been battling signaled a final, critical warning. The room grew hotter by the second, as if someone had switched on the furnace.

Giving Cora a quick hug, she said, "I'll call you. Later." Then she bolted for the bathroom.

SOME JOKER MUST HAVE HAD himself a good laugh when he named this pregnancy malady *morning* sickness, Donetta thought. The past week, it had been morning, afternoon and night sickness.

How could anything so tiny make her this miserable? If she'd been a horse, some kind Samaritan would have taken one look at her and put her out of her misery.

When she was fairly certain the worst of the bout was over, she sank onto the cold tile floor and leaned back against the wall—right next to the ridiculously expensive handicapped toilet that the contractor hadn't installed according to code.

This salon was her dream, her means of security. Hadn't she learned a good-enough lesson from her ex-husband about the consequences of allowing someone else to control what was most important to a person?

Yet that was exactly what she'd done. She'd trusted her contractor, Judd Quentin, to take care of paperwork she herself should have followed up on.

Her throat ached all the way up to her ears, and the need to cry nearly overpowered her. She'd been on the verge of tears all week and hadn't understood why. Well, this morning she'd gotten some answers—two pink stripes on a white stick.

And a red tag on her salon's glass door.

She swallowed hard, tried to go inside herself to that secret place where carefully erected walls formed a dam, safely holding back the rivers of silent tears she'd collected but never shed.

For almost twenty-two years, she'd been able to find protection at a moment's notice, find the place where vulnerability no longer existed and will replaced weeping.

Why was it suddenly so difficult?

She remembered when she'd first discovered the power of escape.

Her family had lived in a trailer park not too far from the elementary school. Mom was drinking—she always drank. That was why she couldn't get a job. Cybil Presley had wanted Donetta to *be* someone, to get them out of the dump they were living in. To her mother, having a pretty face was more important than getting good grades or joining after-school sports programs. To Donetta's regret, even as a little girl she'd had the type of looks that drew automatic compliments.

Cybil had begged Donetta to enter beauty contests like the ones that Tracy Lynn did, but Donetta had stubbornly resisted, for once glad that they didn't have money.

Her dad had been a partyer, as well, but his drinking and gambling had made him seem adventurous. Donetta had loved that man with every fiber of her being.

''Who's my girl?'' he would ask.

''I am!'' And he'd hoist her onto his shoulders and run down the narrow, barren streets of the trailer park, their laughter echoing off the aluminum siding of the dented mobile homes.

And then one day he left and never came back. Donetta had been sure her heart was broken, and she'd cried for days.

Until Cybil got sick and tired of the tears. The vicious slap had stunned Donetta. But it was the nasty words that had made her bleed.

''You silly brat. Crybaby. He's not coming back for you. He isn't even your father!''

That day was the last time Donetta had allowed anyone to see her cry, the day she'd learned to close off the tears—

Her first lesson in not trusting anyone or anything at face value.

Too bad she'd had to learn the painful lesson twice—with the man she'd thought was her father and with her ex-husband.

She'd never found out who her true biological father was. Perhaps that was why the Carmichael family had become such an important entity in her life. They'd accepted her constant presence in their home, opened their arms and their hearts without reservation, made her feel as though she mattered. They'd given her a place where she could at least pretend to belong when her young world had been so sadly adrift.

There were only a handful of people Donetta trusted completely. Storm's mother, Anna, was one. Sunny Carmichael, Tracy Lynn Randolph and Becca Sue Ellsworth were the others—three girlfriends of hers since elementary school, who were closer to her than true sisters. The Texas Sweethearts, they called themselves.

They didn't know about the pregnancy, yet. Oh, she would tell them. Just as she would tell Storm.

After she at least had a free moment to get used to the idea herself, to think things through.

The staccato rap of knuckles against the bathroom door made her jump. Without having the decency to wait for a response, Storm walked right into the ladies' room as though he had an engraved invitation.

She didn't even have the energy to yell at him. Was it normal to be heaving up her toenails every hour? At this rate, she'd have to be dead three days to start feeling better.

She wanted to go upstairs and crawl under the bed, pretend this day had never happened. She wanted to find her backbone, for pity's sake.

"Staring daggers at the pot won't budge it, Slim." He angled his head, stepped closer. "You sick?"

"No," she drawled, deadpan. "I'm having tea with Lady Bird Johnson." She reached up and flushed the toilet. "I bet if you look real hard in your precious penal code book you'll find that it's illegal for a man to come barging into the ladies' room."

"I knocked."

She gave an indelicate snort.

"And the law doesn't apply when there's only one bathroom," he added. "Then the facility is coed."

''Great. Ally McBeal comes to Hope Valley.''

He ignored her flippant remark, frowned and shoved one hand in his pocket. ''So, what's wrong with you?''

''Stress, probably. It's been a train wreck of a day.'' She pinched the bridge of her nose to staunch the burn in her tear ducts.

''That dog won't hunt, darlin'. The Donetta Dawn Presley I know would eat an armadillo before she'd admit to hugging the porcelain over a bad-hair day.''

''Well, maybe you don't know me as well as you think you do...*darlin'*. Or maybe I've just got the flu.''

She had to head this conversation in a different direction. She wasn't in any shape to spar with him, to hold her own. She fully intended to tell him about the baby—she would never keep that information from him. Right now was not a good time to inform him of his impending fatherhood: *Guess what, pal? You've just put the mother of your child out of business!*

Before she could stop them, tears welled in her eyes. *Oh, God, Donetta. You've made it this far. Hold it together. Don't do this. Please, please, don't do this.*

All these years...not even her ex-husband's fists could draw tears.

Yet even as she looked up at Storm's stunned face, fought like mad to find the strength that had served her well for almost twenty-two years, the dam broke.

STORM JERKED HIS HAND out of his pocket. He felt as though he'd been sucker-punched by a ham-fisted nun collecting donations for her parish. Shock, confusion and a sudden illogical longing for code-three backup slammed through him.

Donetta Presley *never* cried.

In two steps he was squatting in front of her. ''Hey,'' he said softly. ''Come on, now, darlin'. We'll make it right.''

Evidently, that had been the wrong thing to say.

Tears the likes of which he'd never seen spilled down her cheeks.

Utter panic clawed deep in his gut. For a split second, her eyes were as startled as he was certain his own were, and for the life of him he couldn't determine whether he was witnessing mortal embarrassment or heartrending anguish.

Before he could even begin to analyze, she slapped her hands over her face, locking him out.

He'd known Donetta since she was a little girl hanging out at his family's house with his sister and the other three girls in the Sweethearts group they'd formed. Donetta was the tough one. She had the clichéd redhead's temper, led with her chin, and despite her innate siren looks, she'd been the tomboy who was rarely without her prized basketball and who'd just as soon slug you if you dared feel sorry for her. Adding a little more confusion to her mix of contradictory traits, she'd also been the peacemaker and mediator of the foursome.

But damn it, he was dealing with the grown woman now.

And as far as his own behavior was concerned, he'd only been taking his cue from her.

Ever since they'd spent the night together, she'd given him major hands-off signals, *told* him flat-out, "Thanks, but no thanks. Be a pal and back off." He didn't like it, but he'd obliged her.

So how the devil was he supposed to know how to act when she kept changing the rules of conduct on him?

She had her knees drawn to her chest, her hands covering her face, and damn it all, her neck was turning red.

"Take a breath, Slim." He gently held her wrists, his fingers completely circling her slender bones, but she resisted his careful attempts to lower her hands.

Tears dripped down her wrists, soaking his fingers. Man alive, she had to have been storing these up for a good long while.

He still didn't know what to do for her, what she needed, how to stop the copious tears. But now that he'd allowed himself to touch her, now that he'd felt her erratic pulse where his fingers rested, he knew what *he* needed.

He needed to hold her. To wrap her up tight and protect her from any threat, shield her from pain, sweep her life free of bad guys—which at the moment, he realized, happened to be him.

"Ah, the hell with it." Abandoning his tug-of-war with her wrists, he scooped her up, took her place on the floor and settled her on his lap. She put up an immediate struggle, which he'd known she would. "Damn it, Donetta. Don't fight me. I'm fragile."

Her shoulders jerked as she sucked in a breath and held it.

Startled, Storm did the same, bracing himself as her head whipped up and her hands fell to her lap.

Utterly still, stunned and disbelieving, she stared at him out of amber eyes that had turned the most awesome shade of gold, with tiny starbursts the color of fine whiskey drizzled around the pupils.

He didn't know if she'd drawn him into some crazy spell or if he was simply afraid to take his eyes off hers in case she did something else to knock his senses for a loop. When he felt the first buzz in his head, the kind of black-out warning a chokehold produced, he blinked.

That was when he realized that he, too, was holding his breath.

Irritated with himself and the whole world in general, he exhaled in a huff. When had he turned into such a sappy fool?

And who the hell had taught her to suppress perfectly natural emotions? Because that was what she was doing—desperately trying to gain control, determined not to let the slightest sob escape. By damn, that just wasn't right.

"Woman, you're making me crazy. Would you please breathe?" He hadn't known it was possible to feel annoyed clear to the bone and tender at the same time. "I promise I won't let you drown in the flood, Slim. It's just us here. You don't have to hold back in front of me."

He meant the words, even though his insides made him feel like Humpty-Dumpty clinging to the wall by his big toe—one hiccup and he'd be history.

Strands of fiery red hair clung to her wet cheeks, stuck to his forearms. She didn't move, continued to stare at him while tears dripped off her chin, but for the first time since she'd begun spouting like a watering can, her breath hitched audibly.

Oddly enough, that made him feel better. She shouldn't have to suffer in silence.

The unblinking stare, however, was getting to him. She had him so shook up he probably looked like *he* was going to cry.

"Quit looking at me like I'm a two-headed catfish," he muttered. This whole experience was so surreal. Here he was with a beautiful redhead in his lap, and he was sitting on a hard tile floor two feet away from the toilet. At least the place was clean. China bowls held scented soaps and potpourri, while a discreet, automatic air freshener above the door puffed little blasts of vanilla at timed intervals.

It was a decent-size bathroom, about eight-feet square, decorated in shiny black and chrome, with splashes of red. An antique cabinet and crystal light fixture gave the room an eclectic blend of old and new—an intriguing contradiction just like the woman who'd decorated it.

She shifted in his lap, snagged the trailing end of the toilet paper anchored to the wall just above his shoulder and yanked. The roller spun like a well-oiled cylinder on a .38 pistol. A good seven feet draped over his shoulder before he could reach up and halt the revolutions.

He held the tissue steady until it tore. Unable to stand the torment a moment longer, he thumbed a tear from her cheek. She countered by blocking his hand, and blotted her own tears with a crumpled wad of the toilet paper, then pressed it over her eyes. Her withdrawal was subtle, the message loud and clear.

Don't touch.

If she thought he was going to heed that message, she'd just have to get over herself.

He'd tried it her way for the past month, kept his distance, respected her wishes, let her pretend that they were merely casual acquaintances who'd never tangled the sheets right off his mattress.

He'd known this woman over half his life, and by God, if he wanted to hold her, he damn well would!

She finally gave a watery chuckle. "Well, that was pretty mortifying—"

"Don't do that, Slim. Not with me."

She shrugged and sniffed. "You mounted a sneak attack, Carmichael. Is that how you get your crime suspects to sing? Feed them a lie so absurd their confession spills out when their jaw drops open?"

"You're not a suspect." He brushed another damp strand of hair from her cheek. "And I don't lie in interrogations. I tell stories, encourage a little feedback. You never know, I might decide to write a crime novel someday. Nothing wrong with bouncing a few creative ideas off another party."

Because she gave him a pitying look of disbelief that was so Donetta-like, and because her unique eyes still held a veiled anguish that was so *un*-Donetta-like, he snagged her nape and gently but firmly pulled her head against his chest. Wrapping his other arm around her stiff, resisting body, he kept her close.

"As far as a sneak attack on you, darlin', I'm glad it worked, but I have no idea what I did. I wish you'd tell me so I could at least analyze the playback later."

She sniffed again, gave his chest a tap with her fist and relaxed into him just a bit. "You said you were fragile, bozo."

He stroked her hair, rested his cheek on the top of her head. "That was no lie." Not where Donetta was concerned.

He tightened his arm when she shifted. He liked her just where she was. With her head tucked beneath his chin, her cheek resting over his heart, he could watch her, but she couldn't return the favor. Those unpredictable amber eyes easily sent him into a tailspin, and if he didn't get a few minute's reprieve to steady himself, he'd crash and burn for sure.

"I've never seen you cry. And you were dead determined to tuck in your chin and do it all by yourself. I know how to track a suspect and bring him down. *Most* of the time I can dodge a bullet—"

"Don't you even joke about that, Storm Carmichael." She gave his chest another tap with her fist. "Thank God a body can function with only one kidney."

"Makes you wonder why we came with two of them, hmm?"

"It's so excitement junkies like you have a spare when they don't have sense enough not to walk into a crack house and get ambushed. And if you make me cry again, I'm striking you off my Christmas list. I haven't made such an embarrassing fool out of myself since I was nine."

"Shh." He stroked her hair. "There's no shame in tears."

"Tears aren't going to fix my code violations or make Judd Quentin return my phone calls." She pushed against his chest, sat up and scooted off his lap.

This time he didn't stop her. But he drew up his leg so she wouldn't see the result her wiggling derriere had wrought on his body. "Your contractor is avoiding you?"

She shrugged. The few feet of tissue she hadn't yet scrunched in her hand floated like the tail of a kite, part of it still trailing over his shoulder. "He might be out of town."

"Doubt it. I saw his truck out at the Barberrys' place this morning."

"Then I suppose he *is* ducking me." She dabbed at her neck and chest, which were still damp. "Phyllis Barberry wants a new kitchen. I guess Allan finally gave in and let her get a bid."

Trust a beauty-shop owner to know the skinny on the townsfolk. "Why would she need his permission to get a quote? It doesn't cost anything to have a company work you up a price."

"I didn't mean that literally. It was just automatic phrasing."

"Hmm. Maybe you should give the Barberrys a heads-up. They might want to think twice about using J.Q. Construction."

"I'm not going to pass out unsolicited warnings about Judd. Especially since I haven't even talked to him." She turned her head and looked at him, her hair shifting against the tile wall at her back. "And I don't see why you can't just be a pal and let me stay open. I—"

"I'm being a pal by *not* letting you stay open. Donetta, according to that list of corrections Blane Pyke slapped on my desk this morning, this place is a powder keg waiting for a spark. You're missing smoke detectors in crucial areas, you don't have a big-enough electrical service to handle the load in a place like this, and there isn't a single ground-fault interrupter plug in the building that works. That means you could scoot the toe of those sassy shoes in a splash of water on the floor and end up electrocuting yourself or one of your clients. This is serious business, darlin'. And… Ah, hell.'' What little color she'd regained had just drained away.

He shot to his knees. ''Are you going to be sick again?''

She took several deep breaths, shook her head. ''I'm fine.''

''Are you sure?'' He hovered, poised for action. They were still within two feet of the toilet. ''You want a wet towel or something?''

''Don't fuss,'' she snapped.

He didn't take offense. He was too busy feeling relieved that the Donetta he was *used* to—the steady, unflappable, stubborn woman—appeared to be emerging. Now he could safely tuck away these uncomfortable sappy emotions he hardly recognized and rarely used.

Dealing with a weeping woman in a bathroom that smelled like a giant vanilla sugar cookie had his stomach balled up in a knot and he wasn't too proud to admit it.

Butting heads with a *stubborn* woman was another matter. One he could handle.

''I don't know why you have such a problem letting people in.'' He stood and extended a hand to her. ''What do you say we abandon the bathroom floor and take another look at the fire marshal's list. Put a plan together. Unless, of course, you think that would be fussing too much. You'll remember that I helped my dad build the extra bedroom and bath when Grandma Birdie came to live with us, so I happen to know a bit about construction. I've raised a few barns in my time, as well.''

''A man of many talents. What else do you do that I don't know about?''

He grinned. ''A smart man never gives away all his secrets on the first official bathroom date. If you're curious, you'll just have to stick around and let me surprise you with my...talents.'' He wiggled his fingers at her. ''Come on.''

''This isn't a bathroom date.'' She put her hand in his and let him help her up. ''Did everyone leave?''

''Yes. I imagine Cora Harris went straight over to my mother to lodge a complaint against me. I'm definitely on Cora's black list.''

''I've heard that's not a great position to be in.'' She turned on the faucet at the sink and leaned down to rinse her mouth.

Storm automatically gathered her hair to keep it out of the sink. ''I imagine my sister'll put in a good word for me.''

''Ha!'' Without looking in the mirror, she splashed water on her face. ''Don't count on it.'' Still bending at the waist, she reached blindly toward the chrome towel dispenser.

He leaned around her, pulled out two paper towels and stuck them in her palm.

''Thanks,'' she mumbled.

When she straightened, he let go of her hair, watched as she wadded the damp paper and tossed it into the trash. She hadn't once glanced in the mirror, and Storm decided not to mention the mascara smeared beneath her eyes.

He'd made that dire mistake with his sister once and learned his lesson well. God knows, if he sent Donetta into tears again, he'd probably join her. And that wasn't high on his list of fun things to do.

"Well?" she asked when he just continued to stand there. "Are you ready?"

"If you are."

In answer, she snagged his sleeve and tugged him around. He held the door open for her, and when she ducked under his arm, he fell into step beside her. She was nearly shoulder-to-shoulder with him, and he liked that, found it sexy. She had the tall, slender body of a sleek greyhound, graceful and athletic, with enough flash and dash to make a man plow through a stump or run his car into the ditch.

Her arm brushed against him, and for an instant he experienced an odd sense of déjà vu, as though an elusive memory shimmered just out of reach. A warm sensation flowed through his body, a sensation of peace, as though he'd found all he could ever imagine or want. With it came a flash of clarity. He saw himself walking with Donetta exactly like this—past or future, he wasn't sure which—down this same hallway of leopard-print carpet, lipstick-red walls, sparkling mirrors and gleaming Sputnik light fixtures reaching out to pull in the stars.

He shook away the spooky image and shivered. What the hell was that?

He waited a minute to see if any other weird images were going to launch an invasion, did a mental recon of his brain. Part of him wanted another look, because he was a man who liked to stand face-to-face with his opponent.

The other part of him wanted a stiff drink and his memory wiped clean of this foolishness.

Still on guard, he concentrated on putting one foot in front of the other, noted that Donetta didn't look as if she'd been juiced by anything strange, yet he imagined he could still feel that vague sensation of peace, hear an old Eagles song about contentment playing in his mind.

He'd forgotten about that tape. The Eagles. It was an eight-track. They didn't even make eight-tracks anymore….

Hell on fire, now he was fixating on old songs. This was so ridiculous he could hardly stand himself. He banged his hip against one of the salon chairs, maneuvered around it and pretended he didn't feel a twinge of embarrassment when Donetta glanced at him.

"Are you all right?" she asked.

"Fine." They were fifteen feet from the reception desk. He should have been thinking about a plan that would keep Donetta's building closed for the least amount of time.

Instead, he was driving himself nuts. The damn song was going to be humming in his brain all night—and he couldn't even remember the words. All he needed now was for some haywire short circuit in his brain to burst into song about perfect harmony, and by God, he was going to check himself into the booby hatch.

If somebody upstairs was trying to tell him something, he would have to beg to differ. Because there wasn't one thing that was peaceful or easy about Donetta Presley. Two minutes in her company and his emotions were all over hell and half of Texas.

And his mind—well, that was just flat-out gone. One redhead shedding a bucket of tears had caused him to lose it, and now he couldn't trust himself alone with his own thoughts.

Man alive, he needed a vacation. And he seriously needed to get a grip here. Next thing, he'd be holding a séance and playing chess with Gramps.

Chapter Three

"Storm, is something wrong with your hat?"

"Why?" he asked and tugged the brim lower. His single-word reply was full of accusation and suspicion.

Donetta retreated a step. "I don't know! That's why I'm asking you. Ever since we left the rest room you've been glancing up at it like you expect it to fess up to a crime. Either that or you've eaten a bug."

"Thank you so much, Donetta. I'm happy to see that you're feeling so universally peaceful."

"Univers— What is the matter with you?" She reached up and snatched off his hat. His forehead didn't have a red indentation so the hat wasn't squashing his brain. But he was still looking at her with a faint expression of accusation, as though she'd tripped him and was now standing there denying it.

"Woman, don't you know you're not supposed to mess with a man's hat?" He glowered and Donetta could clearly see that the annoyance was as fake as all get out.

She sighed. She didn't have the energy to analyze Storm Carmichael. What she desperately wanted was for this day to be over so she could go upstairs, lock the door, sink into a cool bath and give herself the room to think, to process, to have a well-deserved pity party, then to plan. Learning she was pregnant had knocked her for a loop. She couldn't even consider sharing the news with Storm until her emotions steadied.

She plopped the hat back on his head and gave the brim a tug. "Just checking your hat size. You might need a new one for Christmas."

"So, what size are you going to get me?"

She really ought to think through her prevarications a little better. "I haven't decided if I'm going to get you one at all. If we're plotting against my contractor, I need to sit."

She might as well have said "Ready, set, go!" Because the second she took a step, so did he, and a body slam was inevitable. The area at the reception desk was fairly small, yes, but two people shouldn't find entering the horseshoe opening and hopping onto stools difficult.

The impromptu waltz was a cop thing, she knew. He had certain positions and places he liked to stand and sit. An automatic habit to protect his back and his gun side. And Donetta could never remember if she was supposed to yield left or right. Finally, she had sense enough to stand still and wait for him to get where he intended to go.

He perched on the high stool on the right, swiveling so that his right hip was toward the desk—not hanging out for someone to snatch the gun he was *not* wearing. The desk was already facing the door, thank goodness, so she was fairly satisfied that there would be no future skirmishes.

"Are you all settled now?" she asked politely. "Good and comfy?"

"Perfectly, thanks." He merely looked at her as though she'd asked him a legitimate question and patted the stool next to him. "Come sit."

Donetta seated herself on the stool to the left, which is where she would've chosen to sit, anyway, because she was left-handed. As she was sitting down, a smear of blue hair dye on the countertop caught her eye.

Panic did a hit-and-run on her system. It was gone so quickly she almost questioned what she'd felt. Obviously, her brain had had sense enough to realize that Storm was not Tim, and the blue hair dye in her own beauty salon was *not* the red marinara sauce she'd neglected to wipe from the kitchen counter in her house. Lord, she hadn't had one of these flashes in a long time.

So when Storm swore, jerking up his palm and frowning at the smudge of blue, Donetta didn't even blink. She snagged a tissue out of the box in front of her and passed it to him.

"Watch that you don't get that under your nails," she cautioned when he started to scrape with his finger. "It'll be all over town by morning that you were running your fingers through Millicent Lloyd's hair."

He looked up. "That's not funny, Donetta."

Actually, it was pretty hilarious. And so was his frowning expression.

"You can't tell me Harold really liked his wife's hair blue." With the dye mostly off his hand, he wiped the desktop.

"I doubt it was on his top-ten favorites list at first," Donetta said. "But people get used to bold things once the shock wears off. Besides, Harold loved that woman beyond reason, and she was just as crazy about him. You ought to remember. You saw the way they were together when Harold was alive."

Storm smiled. "He and my dad belonged to the Elks club. Dad said the men used to rib Harold about being henpecked because Millicent was so bold and bossy, but Harold would just laugh and wink at them. Never commented beyond that. Drove those old guys nuts."

"Oh, how sweet. Maybe I better not give out his secret."

"You know what the wink meant? Does it have to

do with her hair?'' He leaned in so quickly his elbow nearly slid off the counter.

''If I tell you, I'll have your word that no other man will hear this from your lips. Especially those old boys over at the Elks lodge.''

His lips twitched and he raised his hand. ''I'm a peace officer. We're right up there with the pope when it comes to zipped lips.''

''Mmm-hmm. Let me see your other hand. I want to make sure you're not crossing your fingers.''

He laid both hands on the reception desk. ''It kills my soul that my dad's not here to listen. There was one hell of a betting pool going on over at the Elks about the Lloyds' private life. Especially after she started wearing blue hair.''

''She's wearing her own hair,'' Donetta corrected. ''But when it turned gray, she followed the instructions she found in a magazine for a do-it-yourself color at home—which she put on her brows, too—and ended up looking like a Smurf.''

Amused, he asked, ''Is that your description?''

''No. Millicent's. She's a cartoon buff. Watches them every day. That's why she doesn't answer the door on Saturday mornings if folks happen to come call on her—'' She stopped. ''You're still the pope, remember? Miz Lloyd's TV-viewing preference isn't part of the blue-hair wink story.''

He raised his right hand again to signal his oath. ''I'm having some trouble, though, picturing Millicent Lloyd talking to you—or anyone—about her personal business.''

''Funny thing about doing hair. You slide your fingers along people's scalps and they seem compelled to share all their secrets—totally unsolicited.''

''I'll have to remember that.'' His eyes danced with sensual amusement. ''Is that why you named this place Donetta's Secret?''

She shook her head, unwilling to discuss that subject—because it really was a secret she was keeping. Instead, she gave her standard grin and flippant answer. "It's my secret. Anyway, Millicent hated what she'd done to her hair, but Harold told her she looked so sexy it drove him buck wild, and to prove it, he whisked her off to bed right there in the middle of the day."

"Must have been some afternoon."

"Evidently it was. He did such a good job convincing her that she decided she liked it, too. She's always been a trailblazer. So there's your wink. And as long as I'm her hairdresser, her hair color will be blue because every day she looks in the mirror, she has a reminder of her Harold. I'd just like to tone it so she won't be the butt of jokes. I tried once, but before I could blow-dry her and show her I'd only taken the color down one level, she had a fit and made me redo the process. I'm telling you, Storm, to see that feisty woman's eyes tear up and her chin quiver sent me right into a tailspin."

"I can surely relate to that," he mumbled.

Donetta poked him lightly on the shoulder. "That was a one-time shot, Carmichael, so don't go blabbing it all over town. You're the pope, remember?"

"Let's leave it at peace officer. I'm having some trouble visualizing myself as the other. Or," he said, his eyes steady on hers, "you could do something really crazy and trust Storm Carmichael, the man. Seems to me when two people go back as far as we do, it ought to count for something."

"Isn't that interesting. I was thinking the same thing before my customers were railroaded out the door."

"That's like comparing a squirt gun to a deer rifle. I'm talking about trust and you're talking about aiding and abetting. If I break the law or shirk my duty, I wouldn't be someone you'd want to trust. So, don't shoot the messenger, darlin'. Especially when he's trying to help you.'' He pulled a slip of paper out of his pocket. ''You should have received a copy of this.''

Aiding and abetting? She hadn't considered that. Getting the father of her baby tossed in the hoosegow was certainly *not* part of her plans.

From beneath the counter of the small reception desk, she retrieved the punch list of required improvements. ''Right here, Sheriff. Blane-the-Pain was helpful enough to personally deliver a copy.''

''Blane-the-Pain?'' A smile lit his eyes. ''Is that any way to talk about a man who only has your welfare in mind?''

''I've been open for business for two years and I haven't electrocuted a single client or burned down Main Street. I don't understand why I can't stay open while the work's being done.''

''Why should Blane trust you now when you've ignored all the other inspection reports for the past two years?''

''I didn't ignore them! I was *told* there wasn't a problem with the workmanship, and that the notices were merely a clerical error.''

''Told that by your contractor, I imagine,'' he said. ''The inspector who was here at the start of this job didn't retire. Did you know that? Duke Matheson was fired for dipping his hands in the county till. And guess who was his bosom buddy. Your pal, Judd Quentin. There's an ongoing investigation. And since Blane's taken over, the more he gets into the job, the more he finds out. Now, maybe it's my skeptical nature, but it seems odd that right about the time Matheson found himself up to his armpits in alligators, your paperwork ran into a snag.''

''I don't get it.'' Donetta scooted the appointment book out of the way and leaned her arm on the desktop. ''My salon was finished two years ago. Matheson was still here. If Judd was asking for favors like you suspect, then why aren't all my documents in order?''

''Matheson was smart enough not to sign his name and perjure himself. He just filed whatever Quentin turned in. Regardless, Donetta, this situation would have come up one way or another, either because of a major catastrophe here at the salon or because of another fire inspector. Duke Matheson wasn't a spring chicken, and someone new was bound to take over sooner or later. They'd cite you in a minute. Hell, *I'd* cite you if I'd discovered some of this stuff.'' He picked up the paper and waved it between them.

''Well, that makes me feel all warm and fuzzy. And despite your dire warnings—which I'm not discounting or taking lightly—I still think Blane should try to work with me a little here. Now that I know the papers were for real and not just clerical errors, I'll take care of it—which is exactly why he should trust me. Because *this* time, *I'll* be driving the bus.''

He frowned. ''That should be a comfort to the new fire marshal?''

''Absolutely. Roosters crow, sugar. Hens deliver.'' And wasn't Storm going to be surprised when he learned that electrical panels and handicap rails weren't the only thing this hen was going to deliver.

He'd started to look away, but his head snapped back. ''That's a damn sexist remark to make.''

''Oh, don't get your tail feathers in a twist. I've got my sights aimed at a rooster who's shorter, heavier, older and uglier than you.''

''If that was a backhanded compliment, I'll take it.''

She automatically slipped into her seductress role, the one she consciously—and sometimes *unconsciously*—employed to keep a man off balance. The playful angle of her head, the sultry pitch of her voice...being a flirt came so easily. ''I figured you would, sugar.''

Most men looked away, laughed and made some silly comment meant to sound macho, which totally gave away their bluff. With her feet steady on the ground, Donetta could hold men at a distance and they never even realized she was doing it.

But Storm wasn't most men.

His green eyes zeroed right in on hers, and the utter, deliberately seductive intensity turned her knees to water. With an unhurried, easygoing confidence that made her fight-or-flight instincts scream in alarm, he hooked his boot heels over the bottom rung of the stool, his knees spread wide, and laid the building department form over his thigh. It might as well have been a glowing neon arrow pointing front and center below his belt.

The position he'd shifted into was a blatantly sensual invitation that made a woman just *know* he could show her a good time. The fact that Donetta could attest to that made her palms go damp and her insides tremble like mad.

The corner of his lips tipped in a bad-boy smile. "I'm game, darlin', for whatever you've got in mind. You can either put some words to what that sexy tone implies, or I can start guessing." His deep Texas drawl could tempt a saint to sin without batting an eyelash.

Donetta was in over her head.

She affected a look of innocent confusion, but knew in an instant the pretense had failed. She gave it a shot, anyway. "What I thought we *both* had in mind was discussing this punch list."

"Don't ever take up poker, Slim." His eyes remained unnervingly steady on hers. "You don't bluff *or* lie worth a damn."

At least she knew when to fold. "Fine. Do you want to get back to business now, or what?" She crossed her arms and lifted her chin.

"I wouldn't mind trying out the 'or what.'" He scooped the paper off his thigh and laid it on top of the reception counter. "But I'll wait since it looks like you're back in business mode."

Donetta let out a carefully masked, shaky breath. This was one man she couldn't manipulate with her deliberate subterfuge.

"I took a look at your electrical panel before I had to rescue you from the ladies' room. Not a whole lot's been done to it in the past hundred years."

"I didn't need rescuing," she said.

"Right. It was the toilet I saved from annihilation. And it's a good thing I intervened, because the fixture is fine—your contractor *did* install a handicapped toilet. The *problem* is that he merely parked it back over the existing opening. Call me a skeptic, but I'd put my money on laziness and greed. What you *paid* for, darlin', was to tear up most of that concrete floor, reroute the plumbing and shift the seating arrangement a bit to accommodate a wheelchair."

"Instead, I got a fancy new throne that sits you down several inches before you expect it to—which is actually a nice feature for long-legged women," she said, forgetting for a moment who she was talking to.

"There is that," he agreed, for once bypassing an opportunity ripe for his sensual brand of teasing. "This isn't going to be a half-day job. It's pretty major."

She rubbed her forehead, wished she felt more up to fighting. "Judd's not returning my calls. I don't have the money to sue him *or* to hire another contractor and get all this stuff done if he refuses to make things right. Unless the sky suddenly rains thousand-dollar bills down my chimney, I'm up a creek. And I won't have *any* money if I can't book any clients."

"If you need cash, I can help you out—"

"Don't make me mad, Storm."

He studied her for a long moment. "You know, you're the only woman who could say that to me—besides my mother—and actually make me shake."

"Oh, for pity's sake, I—"

He leaned forward on his stool, put a finger over her lips. "Friendly advice. *Never* reveal your bluff until your opponent surrenders his weapon. Even then, it's best to holster your revolver, let him always wonder whether you've fired five rounds or all six."

The touch of his finger against her lips wiped every thought from her mind. Why were they talking about guns?

"As long as you signed a contract with Judd Quentin," he said, lowering his hand, "there's no reason you should incur any out-of-pocket expense."

She could still feel the warm imprint of his finger. As she stared down at the county form on her desk, images shimmered in her mind of twisted sheets and slick bodies, of hot green eyes locked onto hers while she straddled his naked thighs, opened her mouth over his index finger and slowly, sensually, worked her lips from knuckle to tip.

"Donetta? You *did* sign a contract, didn't you?"

Her gaze snapped up. She cleared her throat. "Of course."

"And you've paid him up tight?"

She blinked. "Yes."

"Then unless the architect made a whopper of a miscalculation, somebody's been enjoying steaks off your grocery bill. Because it looks like you paid for a whole lot of material and labor you didn't receive. How do you feel about taking a ride with me out to Judd Quentin's place?"

"Can I hold the gun?"

He laughed and stood up. "I'm trying to keep you *out* of jail, Slim." He rubbed his thumb over the skin at the corner of her eye. "Give me fifteen minutes to go change my shirt and get my truck."

"Your truck? Won't it have more impact if we show up in your patrol car?"

"That's against the rules, darlin'. I'm not going out there on police business. This is personal." He moved toward the front door and paused. "In the meantime, you might want to go have a closer look in the mirror. I imagine I'm already in enough trouble with my mama. If she gets word that we were riding through town in my truck and somebody'd blacked your eyes, she'll have my tombstone carved and planted out there at the cemetery before we even make it past Gorley's dairy farm."

Her hands flew to her face and she immediately fled to a mirror. She nearly screamed when she got a good gander at herself.

"Oh, my God. How could you let me walk around looking like…like a raccoon with a hangover?"

He held up his hands and inched closer to the door. "Now, Donetta, *you* said that, not me. Besides, you never asked for my critique on your makeup, and, darlin', a smart man learns early which subjects are best left alone unless they're *clearly* unavoidable. Driving down the center of Main Street is like posing for the front cover of the *National Enquirer,* and *that* is what categorizes this instance as 'unavoidable.' Otherwise I wouldn't have made a peep. And the black stuff's not even that bad," he added. "It's only—"

"You better just quit." She licked her finger and rubbed at the black mascara with little thought for the delicate skin around her eyes. "For a guy who grew up with a sister and three extra females underfoot half the time, you're not very smart at all. And if somebody's told you different, that person's an idiot!" She knocked over a can of mousse as she snatched up two facial tissues. "Talk about categories," she griped. "There's a mandatory, unwritten code about honor among friends and family. Sunny would skin you alive if you sat around lookin' at her half the day and didn't tell her she had spinach in her teeth or lipstick on her chin."

"She would not. Where do you think I learned my tact? I thought I was being helpful one summer when it was humid as all get out, and I told her that her eye paint had slid down to her cheeks. She *cried.* I mean, *really* cried. I felt lower than a basement cockroach."

"She cried because Jerry Willick cheated on her with Patti Sandalsteen!"

"I know my own memories of my sister, Donetta. Besides, when I went up to her room to apologize, she was scrubbing her whole face with the washrag and cryin' her eyes out."

"It was the Independence Day barbecue, for heaven's sake. Sunny and Jerry were going steady. You didn't notice she was wearing her cutest halter top, and that her boyfriend was conspicuously missing?"

"She was in the eighth grade, damn it. She had a whole closetful of tops. And how do you know so much about this? You weren't even there!"

"I," she stressed, "was delivering a brilliantly scathing 'Dear Jerry' letter over at the Sandalsteens' pool party and ratting Patti out to her parents. Sunny was supposed to go with me, but your mama made her stay home because *you* were home and she didn't think y'all spent enough time together. So, Sunny was counting on me to go over to the Sandalsteens and shove the little two-timer and his hussy into the pool." She dipped a tissue in a jar of petroleum jelly before she ended up creating real bruises by rubbing so hard with only spit and her fingers.

"But when I got there the little cruds were out by her daddy's shed, and Jerry Willick had his hand up Patti's top. Naturally, I was forced to explain to Mrs. Sandalsteen that I couldn't stay, and I asked her to give Jerry the note when he and Patti came up from the shed—where I assumed we were all supposed to be putting our clothes. In eighth grade and all, I told her, you don't want your peers to think you're a loser because your grammy won't let you go to a naked swimming party. Especially when there's parental supervision. By the time I got over to your parents' house, *you* had already flitted off somewhere.'' She resisted tacking on ''So there.'' Gloating was unladylike, Grammy had always told her.

Amusement and admiration danced in his eyes. ''It might have been nice if someone had clued me in on all of this. I've spent the past twenty-some-odd years half traumatized, thinking *I* had scarred my sister for life. Hell, after that, every time she came in the house all dirty from helping Dad out in the barn or tending to some animal, and Mama would say something about fixing herself up like a girl, Sunny would glare at *me.*''

Donetta straightened away from the mirror and faced him. ''Are you doing this on purpose, just to irritate me?'' She realized that girlfriends understood one another in ways guys never could or even cared to. That was fine. But brothers were supposed to be different, exempt from the ''guy'' category.

''Didn't it occur to you that your sister might have been glaring at you because you were just sitting there like a log, instead of standing up for her?''

''No. Damn it.'' He ran his hand down his face. ''It *wouldn't* have occurred to me because for all that time I thought I was the one who'd hurt her, made her cry by pointing out her makeup, you know? See how that single incident affected me? And that was nothing compared with what you put me through today. No way in hell I was going to take a chance on making you cry again.''

''That has got to be the most pitifully ridiculous excuse for an explanation I've ever heard. How can you stand there like a fox with feathers sticking out of his mouth and tell me you didn't eat the chicken?''

His mouth twitched. "To be slightly more factual, we were going with raccoons."

"There you go. That's twice now you've blown your own excuse. If you'd been so worried about me bawling like an idiot again, you'd have kept your mouth shut. Huh! Scared, my foot. Calling me a raccoon and saying you're embarrassed to let me ride in your truck until I wash my face sounds pretty doggone chancy to me."

"Damn straight, it is. Why do you think I waited until I was within sprinting distance of the door before I said anything?" He pushed open one of the glass panels enough to get his foot out on the sidewalk.

"Hell, *most* women *look* in the mirror when there's one right in front of their face. And I stalled as long as I could, figured you'd get around to fussing with your hair or something and let me off the hook."

Avoiding the mirror had been deliberate. She'd been disgusted and mortified enough over her lack of control. She didn't need to *see* it staring back at her.

"As far as I was concerned you looked fine. But, honest to God, Donetta, your tears about tore my heart out. Please don't do that again."

She didn't know how the irritating man managed it, but he made her want to smile. She was surprised she still could, given that her brain had gone numb hours ago. Massive overload, she imagined.

She was pregnant; her business had been closed until further notice; nausea gnawed at her without respite; and she'd bawled her eyes out in front of the very man who was tangled in her life tighter than a rubber band in matted hair. And the day wasn't even over yet.

Grammy was fond of reminding her that trials built character. That was a good thing, Donetta decided. But it felt a whole lot like she'd started at the advanced level and was working from there. At this rate, she'd be singing with the angels before she ever had a chance to practice with the choir.

Storm was almost out the door when he poked his head back in. "Hey, Donetta?"

She sighed because she was standing ten feet away from him with two coats of black mascara still smeared under one of her eyes. "Yes?"

"You *do* scare me something fierce."

She watched him jog to the curb and ease his six-foot-five frame into the county patrol car.

Hold on to your hat, pal. Pretty soon I'm going to ratchet that fear right up to ring the bell.

Chapter Four

Late-afternoon sunlight filtered through a stand of evergreens, casting long shadows across the two-lane road as Storm drove them out of town toward Judd Quentin's place. Donetta still clutched at a strand of hope that Storm was wrong about the contractor, that by tomorrow everything would be straightened out and it would be business as usual.

Maybe she was a fool, but hope was better than the alternative—trying to get a loan at the only bank in town, the bank where her ex-husband sat on his God-like throne and decided who would and who would not get lucky that day.

She didn't have doubts about which category she'd fit into.

She groaned, battling a wave a nausea that heated her skin from the inside out. Whenever she got excited or upset, the sickness seemed to grow worse. She pressed her hand to her stomach. Poor little baby. Was she making it have an ulcer?

"You okay over there, Slim?"

"I suppose."

He reached across the cab and laid a hand over hers. "I can go talk to Quentin by myself, if you want."

Donetta wondered if there was anything Storm wouldn't jump in and do. What affected this man's fortitude besides a woman's tears? He exuded confidence. Even though he had his wrist hooked over the steering wheel and his attention was divided between her and the road, she didn't worry about him running them into a ditch.

"I need to deal with this, Storm. I was so caught up in the excitement of having my own salon...I got lax about things I should have seen to myself. I love the creative part of the business—doing hair and trying out new styles, sending my clients out transformed or refreshed and feeling good about themselves." She smiled at him, wishing her queasy stomach didn't feel as though it were sitting in her throat.

"I'm like a happy pill. People come to me and share their secrets, their pain and their joy. They get things off their chests, tell me what their kids and grandkids are up to—"

"Sounds a lot like going to a shrink, if you ask me."

"Only a man would consider that a bad thing. What I provide is even better. Think about it. Where can you get therapy for the price of a hair color and cut and come out looking like dynamite to boot? That's the fun part. So, I didn't think twice about delegating time-eating chores like dealing with the county. Out of sight, out of mind, and I'd go happily along with my day."

"Do you know how lucky you are?" He removed his hand from hers and signaled before turning onto Valley Way. "Not many people can get up every morning excited to start their day because they love their job."

"Did you feel that way with the Texas Rangers?"

He nodded. "That was my dream. From the minute I came out of the police academy and made every rookie mistake in the book, I'd set my sights on being a Texas Ranger. I single-mindedly maneuvered my career toward that goal and I reached it. It was a great feeling."

She watched him talk about the job he'd loved, felt a flutter in her chest just looking at him. He'd exchanged his uniform shirt for a plain black T-shirt, which he'd tucked into his jeans, but he still wore the sexy black Stetson that seemed as much a part of him as his onyx hair. His shoulders were as wide as a linebacker's, his waist and hips lean. The stainless-steel watch on his wrist was large and masculine, just like the man.

With an odd sting of sadness, she tracked the second hand as it clicked each beat on the white dial, and remembered how close they'd all come to losing him several years ago, and what that horror had cost him. When he'd been shot during an undercover assignment, the bullet had destroyed one of his kidneys. According to the rules of the Texas Rangers, a missing body part, even if you could function just fine without it, constituted an automatic retirement.

"You miss being part of the Rangers, don't you?"

"Sometimes." He flashed a smile. "I'll probably always be an excitement junkie, as you called it. But I love the job I have here, too. I didn't realize how much ugliness and violence I was exposed to as a Ranger until I came home. Good thing I let Jerome Randolph talk me into running for sheriff."

"Running, my foot. Tracy Lynn's daddy was going to put you in that office come hell or high water."

He frowned. "I can't quite decide whether or not I've just been insulted. You don't believe I won the election on my merits?"

Donetta laughed. "Cradle your ego, Carmichael. With your charm, you could snag the governor's seat without half trying."

"No way. I'd shrivel up and die in a job like that. The governor's safe from me." He pressed a little harder on the accelerator and the white Chevy truck responded with a healthy growl. "I need speed and a little danger."

Donetta laughed, because at one time she'd been the same way, a tomboy determined to climb the tallest tree, dribble a basketball around a court and body-slam the opposing guard who tried to block her perfect shot.

She'd been thinking about that a lot lately, ever since she and Storm had made love with a fervor that had not only given her out-of-this-world pleasure, but had given her the high of athletic competition, the thrill of pitting her agility against an equal opponent. Their lovemaking had been erotic, physical and fun.

And it had made her wonder how she could have surrendered that part of herself—the thrill-seeking, game-for-anything woman who'd also needed speed and a little danger.

At the moment, though, thoughts of her night with Storm were a bit *too* dangerous. She needed to quit wandering in that direction.

"I imagine this truck'll not only keep you on your toes," she said, "it'll stand you on your head if you're not careful. I'd bet money some hot-rod mechanic has tinkered with the motor. The muscle under this hood is definitely not standard equipment or a factory add-on. At least not from any dealership I've ever been to."

He grinned and turned down a pigtail road that was hardly more than two ruts in the dirt. "You'd win that bet. A guy in Houston did the work. He's an ace at pulling every drop of extra horsepower out of an engine. The DPS—Department of Public Safety," he clarified, "keeps him on retainer. Donovan makes sure our rides will outrun anything the bad guys are pushing. So how do you know whether or not a motor's stock has been 'tinkered' with?"

She gave her hair a sexy toss and shot him a look that was purely feminine. She didn't do it deliberately, didn't even realize it until she *felt* it. The heady excitement of knowing she'd impressed him, that they had something else in common besides the baby in her womb, had simply engulfed her and taken over. The admiration in his deep voice and sharp green eyes had brought on an intoxicating confidence that had naturally manifested itself in the kind of sultry look every woman possesses, the kind she can feel right down to her soul and knows will get a man's attention.

Instead of resisting, she went with it. Because anything that pleasantly distracted her from the ever-lurking queasiness, even if it was for two seconds, was welcome. "I took auto shop in high school. Better watch out, pal. Not only can I mop a basketball court with your butt, I can fix your blown manifold when you get a little overeager chasing bad guys."

"Since I don't plan to blow the manifold any time soon, I'll let that challenge go. But I'm calling you on the basketball match. My place. We'll see who mops whose behind."

Her heart and stomach lurched at the same time. She'd just instigated a challenge she wasn't sure she could accept. Since she'd only learned of her pregnancy today, and with all the other blows she'd had to deal with, there hadn't been time to make an appointment with the doctor. What if the game was off limits during pregnancy?

The nausea that had been coming in waves all day again crested. She took several deep breaths to settle herself. Maybe she was right that elevated adrenaline or heightened emotions caused the baby sickness. *That* would definitely be adding insult to injury. With hormones flooding, keeping her on a roller coaster temperamentally, this could end up an around-the-clock misery.

She'd never been to Judd Quentin's house and had no idea where they were. She'd thought she knew every road in Hope Valley, but right now, if she had to get out and walk, it would probably be days before she found her way home.

"How much farther?"

"Just a few miles." He glanced over at her. "You doing okay?"

"Actually, no." Lord have mercy, how many times today was she going to embarrass herself in front of this man? She sat erect in the seat, reached for the clasp on the seat belt. "I need you to pull over."

He looked as though she'd just told him there was a bucket of rattlesnakes under his feet. "Right now?" He checked the rearview mirror and braked. Gently.

Way too gently for Donetta's peace of mind. She nodded, afraid to speak, her hand on the door handle.

"We've got a mushroom cloud of dust tailing us. It'll cover the whole truck if we stop fast."

She jerked her head and glared at him, ready to tell him what he could do with his precious truck—or what she was fixing to do *inside* it. He must have read her expression.

"Damn it! It's not the truck I'm worried about—it's you. Hang on, darlin'."

Donetta snatched up her purse and dumped the entire contents on the floorboard at the same time that Storm jerked the wheel to the left and bumped outside the ruts to bring the truck to a halt in the patchy clumps of crabgrass. As she yanked the door handle, he grabbed the purse from her hands and shoved the little trash bucket in its place.

She didn't have the time or the option to object, or to figure out how he'd managed to work the steering wheel, the brake pedal, spare a thought to save the ruination of her purse and accomplish the exchange with the trash bucket simultaneously. She jumped out of the truck, wishing there were a place to hide, feeling so miserable she just wanted to crawl into a bed with a fan blowing on high speed and stay there for a solid week. Her stomach muscles ached from being sick so often these past few days.

He'd covered all the bases in a matter of seconds. His thoughtfulness pressed at her chest and squeezed. That was some brain he had. Would her child inherit the best of his traits?

She glanced down and realized she'd forgotten about the little trash bucket in her hand, having availed herself of a handy sagebrush behind the tailgate of the truck instead. Her eyes were tearing from the dust and from the spasms that had gripped her stomach seconds ago. She tried swiping the corners of her eyes with the backs of her wrists, but grit clung to her skin. Evidently, she and mascara were not destined to get along today. She should have known better than to reapply it after she'd gotten rid of those smudges.

One thing was for sure. She was going to look in the side mirror before she got into the truck. No sense scaring Storm and Judd, too.

She walked the few feet back to the truck. Dust coated the pristine white paint job. So much for the shiny black polish on the beefy tires and the flashy chrome rims, she thought.

Donetta leaned against the fender of the truck, hoping her eyes would dry on their own, grateful that Storm hadn't come over to hover, was giving her as much privacy as possible.

Looking out across the field, she tried to get her bearings. She could see a brown ranch house in the distance, guessed maybe sixty or seventy acres away, and realized they were probably parked on part of Judd Quentin's front yard. Squatty scrub oaks dotted the land that was still patchy green with devil grass. On the other side of the crude dirt road, a stand of maple trees still held on to their fiery leaves in a brilliant tribute to autumn.

Halloween was only a few weeks away, and time

would slip by fast after that with the festive rush of Thanksgiving and Christmas.

Except for the autumn of her engagement to Tim and the two years of their marriage, she and Grammy had always spent the holidays with the Carmichaels. Anna loved to cook, and loved it even more when a whole bunch of people gathered to appreciate it. She'd drag in every stray, and those without loved ones nearby. Next year, there would be one more at the dinner table.

Donetta's hand automatically gravitated to her still-flat stomach. Her insides felt shaky and her nerves were well past frayed.

How long did morning-noon-and-night sickness last? she wondered.

And how much longer would Storm buy her story of stress or the flu?

Tomorrow, she promised herself. She would tell him tomorrow. She just wanted one evening alone to think; then she'd sit down with him and outline a plan.

Because Donetta knew all too well what it was like to lose a treasured friendship. She'd grown close to her ex-sister-in-law, formed a bond they'd both thought would last a lifetime. But Cindy had been forced to choose sides during the divorce.

And she'd chosen Tim's. By comparison, Donetta's feelings for Cindy and her feelings for the Carmichaels weren't even on the same page, but the experience reminded her what *could* happen when friendships were caught up in the middle of strife.

The Carmichaels were a thousand times more important in her life. Way too important to chance causing a rift. Storm would surely understand that.

She'd *make* him understand—as soon as she figured out exactly how to do it.

She jumped when a blue towel dangled over her shoulder. Heat flooded her cheeks when she realized

Storm was standing behind her. She took the towel, surprised and elated to find it blessedly cool and damp.

"My gallant knight," she said, and wiped her face. "Thank you." Even though she'd been mostly out of the dust's path, particles still clung to her skin. She rubbed the cloth over her arms and hands.

She hadn't turned around and Storm hadn't spoken, but a bottle of water appeared over her shoulder next. She accepted it, felt the icy condensation slide over her palm.

"You're spoiling me." He must have an ice chest in his fancy truck. She drank deeply, felt the cool water travel all the way from her throat to her stomach, was almost surprised there wasn't an audible splash as liquid hit an empty cavern.

How could she keep getting sick when she didn't have anything in her tummy?

"Not so fast," Storm murmured close to her ear. "It's best if you let it sneak up on your stomach."

She lowered the bottle and turned around to face him. "Sorry about that. You surely haven't seen me at my best today, have you?"

He studied her through solemn, worried eyes. "You're just getting it out of the way in one fell swoop, darlin'. Like ripping off a tape bandage. Maybe when we're through with Quentin, you can put some curlers in your hair and smear some of that green mud stuff on your face. I'll have a quick gander." He shrugged. "That'd pretty much cover all the bases and you wouldn't have to worry about it anymore."

"Well, I don't wear curlers, and at least once a month Tracy, Becca, me and now Sunny get together and give one another facials." She fished a piece of gum out of her pocket, slipped it out of the wrapper and bit off half, offering the other half to him. He shook his head, so she popped it, too, into her mouth.

"It's one of those hen parties. No boys allowed." She stuffed the wadded wrapper in her pocket.

He nodded. "Let me see that towel."

When she passed it to him, he cupped her chin and gently ran the tip of the cloth beneath her eyes and at the outer corners, dabbed at her cheeks.

Spellbound, she didn't move, hardly dared to breathe. She hadn't realized he'd meant to use it on her. He was so close, his hands so large, so gentle. His gaze was still solemn, alternating between the skin he was carefully cleaning and her eyes.

This was an expression she didn't understand, couldn't read. His usual teasing was absent. There was no anger. Just a vague curiosity and a quiet worry. His demeanor made her nervous, yet it also somehow made her feel soft inside.

He stepped back a half a pace and offered her the towel. She shook her head. "I'm good, thanks. I take it I don't have the raccoon-eyed look going on anymore?"

"Even if you had a ring of charcoal around your eyes, you couldn't look like a coon. There's something about your face..." He stopped, still studying her, then shook his head and shrugged. "You know how you look."

No, she wanted to say. *Tell me what you see.* The thought surprised her. She'd hated it when her mother had constantly talked about beauty and what it could get a girl, been embarrassed by the attention she'd drawn. So why did she suddenly want to hear the words from Storm?

He was staring at the cat face on the front of her tank top now. Two large eyes slanted just below each of her breasts where the hidden band of the built-in bra rested. A large, embroidered pink nose and turned-down mouth rested at the center of her stomach, and six beaded whiskers fanned out from each side of the nose, spanning her waist to the side seams.

"You like cats?" he asked.

"Yes." Lord, he was in a funny mood. "I have one. She's a very spoiled Persian-and-you-name-it mix. Because of her long hair, she insists she's a purebred and she gets highly insulted if you try to tell her different. To keep peace in the family, I just avoid the subject altogether."

His lips quirked and a hint of the old Storm returned to his eyes. "Don't tell me you talk to your cat the way my sister does with that goofy hound of hers."

That made her smile. "I'm not as bad as Sunny. And I don't think Simba's a hound. Oh, wait, I guess he is—Irish wolfhound and Labrador. Scooby-Doo with an attitude."

"I thought it was Marmaduke."

"Old news. Tori convinced him Scooby-Doo was much more handsome." Each time Donetta saw the little girl she was amazed at the change Sunny had brought about in the child's life.

Before Sunny had come back to Texas, Jack's little girl had been a shy, overly polite child who hardly spoke and always did her best to be perfect, for fear that her daddy would get tired of her—as her horrible witch of a mother had—and send her away.

"I think Simba's shifted his loyalties," Storm said. "He seldom leaves Tori's side—my sister's jealous."

"Oh, she is not. There's enough of Simba to share. And since Tori rarely leaves *Sunny's* side, they're all a happy clan."

"That kid's got a talent with animals. She wants to become a veterinarian, like Sunny."

Donetta felt her heart melt. "I like to think I had a hand in her transformation. You know, it was in my shop that her awakening began. Of course, your sister and Tracy Lynn were the ones who got in a tug-of-war over the sprayer hose at the shampoo bowl and ended up drenching everyone in the salon. Including Millicent Lloyd.''

''Sunny and Tracy Lynn got in a water fight?'' His smile was wide and delighted, and Donetta realized that whatever had come over him earlier had finally passed. Regretfully, he hadn't told her what he'd seen in her face. Not really. ''Who won?'' he asked.

''Would you believe it if I told you Tracy Lynn?''

''No.''

''Well, she did. They were both trying to wash Tori's hair—we had to put peanut butter in it to get the gum out. And you know Sunny's never been one to mess with hair—would just as soon stick a hat on her head as take the time to style it.''

''Sounds like my sister.''

''Mmm. They had words, and it seems to me that Tracy said Sunny ought to stick to shampooing animals—'' She paused while Storm laughed.

''And my sister was insulted—like your Persian, right?''

''Bingo. Next thing I knew, Tracy Lynn tucked in her shoulder, led with her elbow and dealt Sunny a body slam worthy of the Dallas Cowboys' center. That's when the hose whipped around like a wild snake and gave everyone a shower bath. And Tori giggled.''

''Who wouldn't around the four of you girls? Hell, I've probably giggled at you.''

''Oh, I think that's a big fat lie. But if you ever feel compelled to, let me know so I can bear witness.'' She gazed across at the dusty field. ''I imagine we ought to head on over to Judd's before he sees us and goes out the back way. I really want my salon open again.''

''That might take a while.''

''It better not. You were worried about being on a few people's bad list—you'll probably have to add Tori, as well. She's partial to Donetta's Secret. That's where we held our whipped-cream-and-chocolate-chip ceremony officially declaring Tori Slade a Texas Sweetheart.''

He blinked. ''Whipped cream? Darlin' if you ever need to practice up for one of those ceremonies, I'd be obliged if you'd give me a call.''

The image of Storm licking whipped cream and chocolate off her body made Donetta groan. ''Um... I'll, uh, try to remember that.''

His smile was slow and sensual. And then he winked at her. ''You do that, darlin'.''

She was *not* a woman who was so easily taken with a man that she found herself having to pry her tongue off the tips of her four-inch platform shoes. For pity's sake, she hadn't even dated in two years, had no intention of doing so in the future—despite that life-altering night a month ago with this very man.

So what was the deal here? It was as though he'd turned up the wattage of his charm and done something to her with that unreadable, mesmerizing stare.

She busied herself brushing the dust off her tank top and the front of her pants. ''Okay, I'm ready.''

''Not quite.''

Before she had time to think or object, his arm was across her chest, setting her breasts on fire as he held her steady and whisked his hand over her body from shoulder blade to calves, then worked his way up again.

When he let go, she nearly fell face first into the dirt. His lips quirked. ''Now we're ready.''

He helped her into the truck and closed the door. Her gaze followed him as he rounded the hood. He was the epitome of tall, dark and handsome, a virile male who made a woman want to climb right up his body, *inside* his body, and just stay.

How had her life turned to disarray just when she'd finally smoothed out most of the wrinkles?

She and Storm were a volatile mix. One minute she

wanted to love him, could almost imagine the two of them sitting in wooden rocking chairs on the porch, bouncing their grandbabies on their knees, happily growing old together. And then the next she'd want to pinch his head off and pitch it in the lake behind Bertha—the old cottonwood tree that had on more than one occasion sported girls' underpants from its branches.

How ironic to finally realize that she'd loved him all her life, and she didn't even know him. Not really. She mainly knew what she saw on the surface—and experience had taught her that surfaces could be deceiving.

Anyone looking at her beautiful salon would see a perfectly functioning beauty shop decorated with breathtaking flair. But behind the boldly crimson walls in Donetta's Secret, where no one could see, were faulty electrical wires, waiting for the opportune time to electrocute someone or cause a fire.

Maybe the wiring wouldn't malfunction. Maybe it would operate perfectly for years, never give her a problem.

Then again, maybe the flaws *would* prove to be serious and dangerous. The possibility was truly there. Hidden.

Everyone hid a piece of themselves. She did—a fairly substantial piece. It was human nature.

For her, hiding was self-defense. She couldn't allow herself to lead with her heart again. The outcome had been disastrous the first time around.

When Storm slid into the driver's seat and started the engine, Donetta still hadn't found her voice. Why had fate practically handed this man to her like a gift, when the package was way too risky for her to hold?

Storm Carmichael was the one man in the world for whom she might have tried dipping her toes back into the waters of trust.

He was also the one man she could *never* allow herself to take that chance with.

Because he was part of a surrogate family that meant the world to her. *His* family. The Carmichaels.

Theirs was a friendship and love she would not—*could* not—compromise or risk.

Chapter Five

Judd Quentin was arranging tools in the bed of his diesel pickup when Storm and Donetta parked behind him, neatly hemming him into his own driveway. He was a stocky man in his late fifties, with ash-blond hair shot through with gray. A leather belt held up his denims, the buckle all but disappearing beneath a belly distended by his love affair with beer.

Storm climbed down out of the cab, tugged his hat lower on his brow and came around to her side of the truck. Donetta already had the door open but wasn't quick enough to escape his hands at her waist as he helped her down from the higher-than-standard truck. "Let me handle this, okay, Slim?"

"He's my contractor," she whispered, trying to ignore the way her heart skittered at how easily he'd lifted her out of the truck. She wasn't wholly comfortable having him touch her waist—which was ridiculous. He couldn't *feel* the baby. "I can do my own—"

"I know you can, tiger." He winked. "Don't be a killjoy. Let me have a little fun, will you?"

"Maybe you better let me hold the gun after all." She glanced toward his belt, then jerked her gaze back up. "Did you bring it?"

He grinned. "I brought it. Come on."

He didn't bother to tell her where he'd put it, and it

certainly wasn't visible, so Donetta left the subject alone. Surely Storm would conduct himself in a professional manner—even if he wasn't on duty.

They walked toward Judd, who had moved to rest a hip against the tailgate of his pickup. He took a drag off a cigarette and blew smoke into the evening air as though he didn't have a care in the world.

Uh-oh. That wasn't a good smell, Donetta thought, wary of the noxious odor. If she got sick again, her body would turn itself inside out like a rubber glove yanked off a colorist's hand.

"Evening," Storm said. "Judd Quentin, right?"

"I reckon you're a man who knows who he's walkin' up on, Sheriff."

Storm smiled. "I have an advantage." He indicated Donetta. "Your client. And it's 'Storm' tonight. I left the badge at the station." His lips curved in a friendly smile, but his deep, quiet tone was a blatantly dangerous challenge.

Judd paused with his cigarette halfway to his mouth, and Donetta whipped around to look at Storm.

His calm demeanor was deceptive. She knew it, and Judd knew it, too. Donetta glanced between the two men as the air snapped with tension. This was not the kind of party she liked to attend.

Judd puffed on his cigarette and blew smoke in Storm's face. Donetta decided she'd had about enough of this pissing contest. She was perfectly happy to be a killjoy.

"Judd," she said. "The fire marshal shut me down today." She passed him the list of violations, ignoring Storm's look of aggravation because she'd interrupted his king-of-the-sandbox display. "Did you get a copy of this?"

Judd pitched his cigarette in the dirt, glanced at the form and passed it back. "Don't know what to tell you, doll. I built that building exactly according to the plans.''

''Do you have a copy of those plans?'' Storm asked. ''Maybe we could clear up a couple of these discrepancies.''

Judd smirked and leaned back against the fender of his truck. ''Well, I tell you, Sheriff—''

''Storm,'' he corrected. ''I'm off duty tonight.''

''That give you special freedoms or something?''

''Or something.'' The slight pause was just enough of a threat to scatter a person's nerves.

Judd's focus sharpened as he acknowledged the obvious antagonism. ''Looks like you wasted a long trip from town. I'm a busy man. Got a lot of jobs going around these parts. Ain't no way I could keep every set of blueprints on every project. The beauty shop was put to bed a couple years ago. Sorry. Wish I could help you, but I done my job.''

Donetta wanted to scream. Storm had provoked the contractor, and now the man was clamming up and they wouldn't get anywhere. Why were men so pigheaded? Why couldn't they just come right out and ask a damn question instead of dancing around barely veiled threats and innuendo, waiting to trip up the other guy?

''Judd, the ground-fault interrupting plugs aren't working, and Blane Pyke is having a fit over that. Might there be a part or a wire missing or something?'' Donetta asked.

''Honey bun, that building was built back in 1850. The electrical has been updated over the years, but not since 1965, when the code started requiring a ground-fault wire. I'm thinking your architect figured the system was just fine the way it was, because he didn't call out for a bigger service.''

''If that was the case,'' Storm said, ''why did you

put in the GFI plugs? Seems strange...if the plans didn't call for the new electrical service, I mean."

Judd tapped out another cigarette from a crumpled soft pack. "I'd already bought the plugs, figured no harm in putting them in. Make it easy if someone down the road wanted to overhaul the system."

"It'd be a pretty serious offense if a person deliberately bypassed the ground on one of those circuits, wouldn't it?" Storm asked conversationally.

"Imagine it would. Wasting our breath speculating 'bout it, though. Cain't tell if that old boy who done the drawings fouled it up or not. Heard tell he had a fire out at his place 'bout a year back. Him and me were the only two that had a set of blueprints and specs for the job."

"I have a set of drawings," Donetta said, frowning. "The originals that were approved by the county."

Judd took the cigarette out of his mouth without lighting it, his gaze going from Donetta's to Storm's. "In that case, I suppose I might swing by and have a look-see."

"Oh, I think you'll have a little more than a look-see," Storm said pleasantly. He advanced a step. "You'll be out at the salon first thing in the morning with a full labor crew. And you will have the additional material that Ms. Presley has already paid for...two years ago, I believe." He moved closer still, his chest almost touching the contractor's.

"Material that I'm sure the original blueprints will show is curiously absent from the job. If I were wearing a badge right now, Quentin, I might be mentioning words like *fraud* and *felony.* But this here's just a friendly social call. You sat down in your own coyote trap this time, buddy, and you're going to make it right."

The corner of Judd's left eye twitched, and his jaw

went rigid. ''I got no problem standin' behind my work.''

Storm stepped back. ''Good. Then I'll expect you at the salon at eight o'clock in the morning. That gives you a little leeway to contact any supply houses you need to. Oh, by the way. I just signed on as your foreman.''

STORM WAS DETERMINED to feed Donetta. He'd had to stop the truck again on the way back to town because she was ill. He hated to see her suffer. They needed to go back to the salon, get the drawings and collect the files with all the invoices and receipts for the remodel, but by damn, she was going to eat something first.

And then there was the matter of where she was going to stay. God, he was feeling worse by the minute for his part in making her life so difficult, but it couldn't be helped. Still, no one should have to be away from his or her comfortable environment when not feeling well.

He parked in front of Anna's Café. His mother had bought Wanda's Diner and had finally changed the name and spruced up the decor. Having his mama work after all these years of her being a stay-at-home mom still felt weird.

''I'm really not all that hungry,'' Donetta said.

''Tough. I don't remember if you're supposed to starve a cold and feed the flu or the other way around, but Mama will know. You've got to get something back in your stomach.'' Anna Carmichael wasn't a doctor, but she was a mom. And she considered Donetta one of her own.

''It's starve a *fever.*''

''Whatever. It's probably just an old wives' tale, anyway.'' He helped her out of the truck and ushered her inside the café. ''Mama! Donetta's sick!''

Donetta nearly socked him. "Good one, Carmichael. Since when did you become the tattletale?"

"Since I watched you turn green and go weak as a kitten...*three* times."

"I told you—I'll be fine."

"Right. Every time we stand still for more than five minutes, you run for the bathroom or make me pull over to the side of the road. That sounds real fine to me. And don't tell me it's something you ate, because you haven't eaten anything since I've been with you and—"

"You two hush up." Anna bustled out from behind the counter, the backs of her fingers already at Donetta's forehead. "You kids bicker worse than two crows in a pecan tree. What's wrong, honey?" Anna asked.

Donetta looked into the woman's soft eyes and felt ridiculously wimpy sobs back up in her throat. Honestly, she'd never been so emotional in her life. But she loved Anna Carmichael like a mother. "I'll be fine, Mrs. C. I'm having an off day is all."

"Translated," Storm said, "that means she's been throwing up all day."

"I'll bet you didn't go get that flu shot like I told you to. There you are, working around all those people, Donetta. They come in coughing and sniffling—you need to inoculate yourself against those germs."

Her arms around Donetta's shoulders, Anna led her to a padded stool at the counter. "You need a mother's care is what you need. And decent food. You look like you're about to dry up and blow away. I'll just stand in for your grandma Betty, why don't I? She and Birdie are quite the gadabouts these days." As Anna spoke, she rubbed Donetta's back.

The glance she directed at Storm, though, didn't bode well for the meal Donetta knew he was anticipating. No doubt word had already reached Anna about

Storm's part in closing down the salon, and his mother wasn't all that happy with him. He'd be lucky if he was allowed to stay inside the brightly lit café long enough to have a glass of sweet tea.

Donetta would have smiled, but she didn't want Storm's mother mad at him. That type of dissention was the very thing she was determined to avoid, the very reason she'd stayed away from him for the past month.

"It does seem funny that Grandma Birdie and my grammy are cruising to Mexico," Donetta said to Anna. The back rub felt heavenly. Anna was a woman who touched often and well. It was part of her nature, a trait she was rarely conscious of. A total stranger could board an elevator with the woman and find himself the blissfully startled recipient of conversation, unsolicited advice and an impromptu neck massage.

"I thought they were visiting your sister in Florida," she continued. "Next thing I knew Grammy said she'd loaned out her house for a couple of weeks to some woman *I've* never met, and she was hopping on a ship to see if she could get some action."

Anna's hand paused between Donetta's shoulder blades. "Oh, dear. That doesn't sound like Betty. That sounds more like something *my* mother would say. If your grandmother comes home with a man…oh, I hope Birdie doesn't influence Betty in an illicit manner."

Donetta grinned when she saw Storm's raised eyebrows. Picturing either of their grandmothers in an "illicit" anything was a challenge. "Grammy can hold her own, Mrs. C. I'd worry more about Grandma Birdie bringing a man home."

"You're right. I don't even want to think about the possibility. Who's staying in Betty's house?"

"Patty Winger and her family. She's in Grammy's quilt guild. They had a small fire out at their house and needed someplace to stay while the damages are being repaired.''

''Oh. I remember now. I don't know how Patty puts up with two grown daughters and three grandchildren living with her. I'd have thought twice about lending my home, but it's none of my concern. Now, you need some soup, and I've got just the thing to fix you right up.'' She patted Donetta's shoulder, then moved back behind the counter.

''You'll not get bad food in here—I'll see to that. You should be taking better care of yourself.'' Anna shook her head as she bustled around, lifting a lid off a steaming kettle on the stove and ladling mostly broth into an oversize cup.

''You girls. Standing on your feet all day, eating like a bird. Men like curves on a woman. How do you expect to land a husband looking like—oh, my gosh! I did it again. I am so sorry, dear!''

''I'm not interested in landing a husband, Mrs. C. And what did you do again?''

''I'm working on curbing my tendencies to give unsolicited advice—critiquing in a hurtful manner.''

''You didn't hurt me.''

Just then, Sunny Carmichael came in through the back door. She smiled gently at her mother, obviously having heard the exchange. ''Donetta's smarter than me, Mama. She knows your advice is given out of love. It just took one of us—'' she pointed to herself ''—a little longer to see that.'' Sunny kissed her mother on the cheek, hugged Donetta and glared at Storm.

Storm elbowed his sister. ''Netta's got an advantage, Pip. She didn't have Mom full-time.''

Donetta was horrified. She quickly glanced at Anna to see if her feelings were hurt. Then she realized that Storm was teasing, and that Anna had already figured that and didn't take offense.

Growing up, Sunny had often been at odds with her

mother, which Donetta had never understood. She would have given anything to have what Storm and Sunny had, to be a true part of the Carmichael family, to claim Anna as her own mother.

Donetta had secretly been thrilled when Anna lectured, interfered and scolded, or offered opinions and advice. Sunny, on the other hand, had chafed, silently hurting, viewing Anna's comments to her as criticism.

Thankfully they'd worked out their discord and misunderstandings.

Things were different since Sunny had come back home. She'd been gone for ten years, yet her return seemed to have changed the town and everyone's life in it. Donetta couldn't explain it, but she knew it felt darned odd.

Now, however, Sunny was clearly upset with her brother. "How could you?" Sunny demanded of Storm. "Where is your sense of decency? Of loyalty?"

"And we would be talking about...?" He let the sentence trail off, apparently hoping she would fill in the blank.

"We're talking about you being a traitor and closing Donetta's Secret. I know darn well you could have pulled some strings and let her salon stay open."

"Maybe. But that building is dangerous the way it is, Pip. This is for Donetta's own good. She'll be staying with me for a while."

Donetta's jaw dropped open. Sunny gave her brother a pitying look. "Stay with the enemy? I hardly think so."

"I'm not the enemy, damn it. And you're my sister. You're supposed to be on my side."

"I am on your side. But Donetta's my sister, too, and my friend. We girls are naturally going to stick together."

Donetta listened to the altercation. It wasn't by any means out of hand, but it was an example of what *could* happen. Already, Storm expected Sunny to side with him, and his sister was put in the middle. Just as Cindy had been during the divorce.

Donetta couldn't bear it if history repeated itself. What if the argument was serious? The decision impossible to make? This was a prime example of why she and Storm couldn't form a lasting relationship beyond casual friendship.

Instead of passing the food across the counter, Anna came around, shooing everyone out of her way. She set the mug of chicken broth in front of Donetta, along with a plate of crackers and a small bottle of Coca-Cola, which she opened and poured into an ice-filled glass. ''Now, you just sip and nibble, and let your tummy get accustomed to the nourishment.''

''Thanks, Mrs. C.'' She didn't have the heart to tell her the broth didn't even smell appetizing. Her attention was on Storm and Sunny's sniping.

''Storm,'' she said. ''I'm not staying with you. I have a perfectly good apartment and I can take care of myself.''

''Let's talk about this later,'' he murmured close to her ear, lifting the mug she had her hand wrapped around and guiding it to her mouth. ''You need to eat.''

She sipped, then took a bite of cracker when he pushed it past her lips. Before she could hardly chew, the mug was being tipped again. She balked.

''I can feed myself, thank you.''

''Then do it,'' he said softly. After brushing a strand of hair off her cheek, he arranged her long mane of curls over her shoulder and slid onto a stool at her right, swiveling so that he had a view of the door. ''Drink some of your Coke. Mama used to give it to us all the time to settle our stomach.''

It was as though they were the only two people in the café. His attention was solely on her, and being the recipient of that type of behavior was so foreign to Donetta that she found herself utterly mesmerized.

He surrounded her with both his size and his presence. One arm draped over the back of her bar stool and the other resting on the counter, he enclosed her in the half circle of his personal space.

After endless minutes where he bullied her into eating and drinking, she noticed that both Anna and Sunny had retreated and were watching with curious smiles on their faces. Oh, no, Donetta thought. She'd have to run some damage control in that area. She didn't want them building hopes over something that wasn't going to happen.

She held up a hand. ''That's it. I'm good for now. Why don't you sweet-talk your mama into fixing you something to eat?''

''She's likely to poison me.''

Donetta patted his leg and winked. ''I'll taste it for you. If she pounces, we'll know you should go home and make a sandwich.''

''You're a real pal, Slim.''

''That I am.'' And she wanted to stay that way. Despite the occasional times they got a little crossways with each other, the Carmichael family had always had one another to turn to. But Donetta hadn't been gifted by birth with that sense of family and unconditional love—and she could *not* afford to lose the love and friendship of this surrogate family she had claimed as her own.

STORM DROVE AROUND BEHIND the salon, where the back entrance opened to the staircase leading to Donetta's small balcony and apartment. He knew in an instant something was wrong. This was his town. He patrolled every inch of it—especially the square that housed his mother's café and Donetta's shop.

He cut the lights and drove the truck right up to the rear door of the salon.

Donetta slammed her palm on the dash. ''Storm! Are you going to drive right through the wall?''

He flicked on the police radio he kept in the truck and lifted the mike. ''Dispatch, one-Adam-one. I need backup for a possible break-in at Donetta's Secret—2132 Main Street. I'm parked by the rear entrance. Advise the deputy to meet me inside.''

''Copy that, Sheriff.''

He shut off the radio, knowing Margo would dispatch the closest deputy. No sense having radio chatter announcing his presence.

''Stay put,'' he said to Donetta. He slid the .38 out of his boot and palmed a flashlight as he got out of the truck, then pushed the door closed just enough to shut off the dome light.

The wood doorjamb was splintered and the strike plate was bent. It had been a flimsy setup to begin with. A kid could pry his way in.

The slight shift of gravel beneath the sole of a shoe sent every one of his senses on alert. For an instant, he was back at that warehouse in Houston, experiencing the flash of awareness that comes too late—recognition that you're about to get your gut pumped full of lead and there isn't a damn thing you can do about it.

But this wasn't Houston. His muscles strained as he held his body perfectly still, as though he was preoccupied examining the broken lock. Another pebble crunched. He held his breath. *One. Two. Three!*

He whirled. ''Freeze.''

Donetta screamed.

Storm jerked his weapon skyward and flicked the safety. ''Hell, Donetta!'' His heart drummed so hard small wonder it didn't knock a hole in his chest.

''Are you trying to get yourself killed? I *told* you to stay put. I could have shot your ass!''

She had her hand over her heart, and it wasn't looking too good for his mother's famous chicken broth to stay down much longer.

She sucked in a deep breath. "You can't just tell me to stay put and then hop out without waiting for my input." Her voice was a shaky, fierce whisper, proving she was upset but was still mindful that someone might be inside her salon.

"How do you expect me to stay all by myself in the truck when you're sneaking around with your gun drawn? Forget it. No way. I'm holding on to the back of your shirt and that's all there is to it. So deal with it. Do you want my shop key?"

Storm's adrenaline dropped only slightly. This woman was going to be the death of him. "Not necessary. The lock's busted. You want to stand here talking all night and wait for somebody to swing open the door and say 'Boo,' or shall we go see what's going on?"

"Do you think someone's still in there?"

"No. I didn't see any movement when we drove by out front, but I don't want to take any chances."

"Maybe I should go check my apartment." She whirled toward the outdoor stairs, but Storm snagged her with an arm around her waist and hauled her right back.

"I want to feel some part of your body touching some part of mine at all times, got it?" He glared at her, deliberately trying to intimidate her. She gave him a "la-di-da" shake of her head, demonstrating that he'd failed miserably. "Got it?" he repeated.

"Yes," she said in exasperation. "But I think we should wait until your backup gets here. We don't need to be going in there by ourselves."

"Right. So, why don't you get back in the truck, and *we* won't be doing *anything* by ourselves."

"Oh, just shut up and turn around. Someone's probably stealing me blind and running out the front door.''

Donetta stepped behind him, hooked her hand in the waistband of his jeans and eased up against his back. His body was warm and the evening mugginess was starting to carry a little chill, which was welcome after the soaring temperatures earlier.

He carefully opened the door, and Donetta matched her steps to his as he slipped inside. Despite her brave talk, she slammed her eyes shut and ducked her head behind his back. The width of his body hid hers just fine, but with her platform shoes on, her head would look like an extra target sitting on Storm's shoulders. She wasn't all that crazy about impersonating a duck in a carnival booth.

And then she remembered something. Releasing her hold on his pants, she ran her hands over his back and sides, then up around his chest.

Storm reached over and flicked on the lights, nearly blinding her, making her jump.

''Whoever was in here is gone,'' he announced, glancing back at her. ''Can I help *you* find something, darlin'?''

Donetta rolled her eyes, even though she could feel her face heat. ''I was checking to see if you were wearing your bulletproof vest.'' The only thing she'd felt beneath his snug black T-shirt had been nicely sculpted muscles. ''And you're not. So what possessed you to burst in here without waiting for backup?''

She was more upset with him than she'd expected to be, and the feeling was escalating, right along with the queasiness in her stomach.

''Hope Valley isn't the type of town where peace officers feel compelled to suit up,'' he said. ''As for 'bursting' in—'' he flashed her a grin and winked ''—thanks for worrying about me, darlin', but I'm damn good at what I do.''

''Oh, I feel ever so much more reassured.'' She

didn't know why she wanted to clobber him. Probably because of the memories bombarding her of the night she'd spent at a Houston hospital as Storm had fought for his life after a bullet had torn through flesh unguarded by body armor.

"Come on, Slim. Stop walking through graveyards. I'm 99.9 percent sure our guy's gone, but I need to clear the back room anyway. Then we'll see what's missing. Although I've got a pretty good idea. This job was fast and messy. Definitely not the work of a pro." He headed toward the office at the rear of the salon, his gun still drawn.

Donetta glanced around to satisfy herself that no one was in the salon, despite Storm's assurance. The place was messier than she'd left it, and her spirits sank. She didn't feel well, and now she had extra cleaning and straightening to do. She dreaded even going into her small office. But she didn't intend to be left standing by herself.

She caught up with Storm in three strides, gripped the back of his shirt and peeked around his shoulder. The door was open. Light from the main salon illuminated enough of the room to suspend Donetta's breath. It was worse than she'd expected. Files strewn everywhere, product lockers emptied, cabinet doors flung open.

Suddenly, she found herself sandwiched between Storm's body and the wall.

"Would you *please* let go of my shirt and stay put?" He said the words over his shoulder, his voice barely audible. "Three seconds is all I'm asking for. If I haven't shot anybody by then, feel free to grab hold of any part of me you like."

She flicked back her bangs, lifted her chin. "Fine," she whispered. "You always were a loner. If you don't want any backup, then go on and play the hero. And I wish you'd make up your mind. *You're* the one who *insisted* on body contact.''

The irritating man had the nerve to grin at her. Then he did a credible imitation of James Bond and disappeared into the shadowy room. If he had let *her* carry the gun she wouldn't have been forced to creep behind him like a fraidy cat.

''All clear, darlin'.'' The lights clicked on as he spoke.

She peeled herself off the wall and tugged at her tank top, then rounded the corner as though the situation didn't bother her a bit. She kept her computer and filing cabinets in the break room, which also served as a kitchen, mixing bar and storage area. Her second look at the disaster didn't ease the shock.

''You think Judd did this?'' she asked.

''Do you have any other enemies who might be interested in a set of blueprints?'' he asked.

''I didn't think *Judd* was an enemy. Besides, the blueprints are upstairs in my apartment. So are the work orders and receipts.''

''Then we ought to go check on them.'' He looked up as two of his deputies came in with their guns drawn. ''All clear, Skeeter,'' Storm said. ''I'd like for you and Steve to dust the place for fingerprints, though. I'll bring you in a set of prints later and see if we can get a match.''

''You have an idea who took a dislike to Ms. Presley's filing system?'' Skeeter asked.

''Judd Quentin would be my hunch—the contractor who originally did the remodel on this building. I'll catch you up to speed later. Keep an eye out, though. Let me know if you see him hanging around. Right now I'm going to check out Donetta's apartment and get her settled. The lock on the back door's busted. Board up the rear entrance when you're finished here, okay?''

''Will do, Sheriff.''

Donetta was eager to get upstairs. The idea of someone pawing through her personal things, touching clothing that she wore next to her body, made her feel violated. She could only hope the culprit had been interrupted before he'd had an opportunity to rifle her apartment.

''I wasn't hiding the blueprints,'' she said, hardly aware that she'd automatically accepted Storm's hand as they went up the outside staircase. ''The cupboard in my bathroom was the only storage space tall enough that they'd fit in.'' Which wasn't totally accurate. Her bedroom closet was tall enough, but shoes took up every square inch of available floor and shelf space.

Using the flashlight to guide their way, Storm reached for the doorknob. When it turned easily, his arm shot out, grazing her stomach. She jumped.

''It's unlocked. Stand back.''

''I left it unlocked.''

He swung around with the flashlight aimed at her. She didn't need to see his frown. She could hear it. ''You had a memory lapse.'' Part statement, part question, total rhetoric.

''No. I live in Hope Valley, remember? No call for body armor or locked doors—usually.'' She was about to open the door, but he pushed it wide, then stretched an arm in to flick on the light switch.

''Holy smoke. This is purely malicious and uncalled-for.''

Donetta sidled past him. She should have been embarrassed by the mess, but to her the laundry scattered on the sofa waiting to be folded, the magazines spilling off the coffee table and the newspapers she'd read and tossed on the floor beside her favorite chair were a chaos that spelled *freedom.*

She didn't need a shrink to tell her the disorder was a form of rebellion, a reminder that she was in control now and could do whatever she pleased. Tim had been adamant about keeping a perfectly clean and organized house. For the past two years, Donetta often left her wet towels on the floor just because she *could.*

"No one's been in here."

His brows shot up. "Did you throw a fit?"

"Cute. I'm not the best housekeeper. Beneath the clutter, though, it's clean."

She glanced at her unmade bed on her way through to the master bathroom, wishing she could detour and curl up on the soft sheets, forget about this nightmare of a day.

Storm followed her into the small bathroom, where she opened the wood cabinet door that had a tendency to stick due to fifty-plus years of paint layers. By the time she'd finished remodeling the salon and most of the apartment she'd exhausted her funds and had had to skimp on bathroom improvements.

"I guess lack of storage space in the salon turned out to be a good thing. The drawings are still here, thank—"

She broke off when she heard Storm draw in a swift, ragged breath.

"Donetta? Are you *pregnant?*"

Chapter Six

Donetta whirled around, adrenaline blasting through her system with a scorching heat that slicked her hands and closed her throat. Pinpoints of light flickered before her eyes.

Storm stared at her, holding the pregnancy test strip as if it were crucial evidence in a volatile, unsolved case.

Oh, God. She'd completely forgotten about the home test kit. Just as she'd never expected the city would lock her out of her business, she'd never dreamed Storm Carmichael would end up standing in her master bathroom.

"Donetta? I asked you a question." His voice was deadly quiet.

She snatched the plastic strip away from him. "That's none of your business." She could hardly draw in enough breath to get the words out.

"Try again, darlin'. You left it sitting out in plain sight. According to the information on the box, two lines indicate positive results."

"Well, at least we know your college education didn't go to waste. You can read. And you've answered your own question. I guess that means you got high marks for cognitive skills." In light of the muscle working in his jaw and the barely leashed anger in his eyes, she was a little surprised at herself for going head-to-head with him.

"If you're through evaluating my intelligence, I think we should discuss this baby. I can't believe it didn't occur to me sooner. The timing's right—the sickness..."

"There's nothing to discuss, Storm. So just drop it, okay? I've got everything covered."

"Like hell you do. I have a say in this."

"What makes you so sure?"

In a move so swift it left her dizzy, he had her backed against the wall, his hand firmly cupping her face so she couldn't turn away. Everything inside her froze, trapped in the icy shock of an all-too-familiar dread.

The look, feel and taste of a man's anger hung in the air, and she found herself without the safety net she counted on. The tiny sea-green-and-pink-tiled bathroom suddenly took on the personality and feel of the elegant marble bathroom from her nightmares. She was unsafe in the haven of rebellion she'd created to signify freedom. Unsafe with the friend she'd known for more than twenty years.

"I'm a detail man, and I don't miss many. I know damn well it was a good long time since you'd made love. *That*'s how I'm sure." His voice was so low it might have been a caress if not for the vibration of anger. "You try to hide beneath that seductress front, but it doesn't work with me. Your body gives you away—which I can prove in two seconds flat. Now, do you really want to play this game with me, Donetta?"

She shook her head, swallowed hard. Her heart hammered as fear clawed its way up her throat. She reminded herself this was Storm. The guy she'd known since she was in kindergarten. "No."

"Good. Now, I want you to pack a bag. You're coming home with me. And we *will* discuss my child."

"Coming home...? You're nuts. You can't order me around. I'm not—"

"I didn't ask. If I have to carry you out of here, Donetta, I will. I want you where I know you—and my baby—will be safe."

She'd been bombarded with one thing after another today, and she was teetering on the verge of a major meltdown. His aggression threatened to tip the balance, but she fought to remain steady.

"I'll go stay with Sunny and Jack. Or—"

"And take a chance on putting them at risk? I don't know enough about this contractor you more or less handed the keys to, but a first-year rookie could figure out that the guy's been feeding you a pack of lies and you've been swallowing them like candy. I didn't like his cocky attitude, and I sure don't trust him, especially now that his house of cards is collapsing."

"My salon's collapsing, too."

"Which leads us back to an obvious trail. Until I get a positive ID on your burglary and determine intent, Judd Quentin is at the top of my list of suspects. You have something he wants and that makes him unpredictable. I don't like it when somebody has an agenda I don't know about." He paused, letting the beat of silence weight his words. "Especially when it involves the safety of people I care about."

Donetta wanted to scream. *She* didn't *have* an agenda regarding the baby. Not yet, anyway. Maybe his cop antenna was overly sensitive about Judd, but that didn't matter. He was right. There was no way on earth she'd ever put one of her friends at risk.

Grammy's house wasn't an option since the Wingers were staying there. She could take a room at the motel, but she needed every spare penny she owned to bring her shop up to code. Despite Storm's bullying, she didn't wholly trust Judd Quentin to show up in the morning, and that would mean hiring another contractor. Plus, every day she was shut down meant lost income, which would likely make her mortgage check bounce like a Super Ball.

Anxiety billowed in her chest, squeezed her lungs. With Storm on a tear about the baby and nefarious suspects, she could pretty much guarantee he'd want to park himself in her motel room—at least to guard his child. And wouldn't that just delight Darla Pam Kirkwell to no end. By morning, it would be all over town that Storm Carmichael and Donetta Presley were shacking up at the Hope Valley Motel. That was all she needed. Shades of her mother all over again.

"You know I'm right," he said.

He was still crowding her against the bathroom wall. She felt like a wild animal trapped in a snare. She couldn't think. Her hard-won independence was slipping through her fingers. The scream inside her churned, ramming against the restraints of dignity.

"You've got ten seconds. After that, you'll have to make do with what *I* pack."

Sound rushed in her head, buzzed in her ears. She'd sworn never again to give a man power over her, never again to obey a command like a sad-eyed mutt.

"Give in, Donetta."

Emotion erupted like spewing lava. "No! I can't! I won't. Don't you see? It's the same as being beaten into submission! And I won't ever let—" She clapped a hand over her mouth. She hadn't meant to blurt that. *Oh, God.*

An instant of deafening silence exploded between them.

As shock turned his bones to chalk, Storm jumped back, giving her plenty of room, his gut clenching, his mind whirling, his emotions all over the place. He wondered why he couldn't fill his lungs, why he felt as though a bullet had slammed into his Kevlar vest. Why was he still standing when the force of impact had knocked the breath out of him?

She's afraid of me.

In the maelstrom of learning Donetta was pregnant, he hadn't been paying attention to her signals. What he'd thought was her usual stubbornness was actually masking sheer fear.

He'd had her pinned against the wall, for God's sake, concentrating on his own sense of betrayal because she hadn't told him about his child.

And she'd been terrified.

It's the same as being beaten into submission.

God, he wanted to tear her ex-husband apart. He decided right then that he didn't want the likes of Tim Dilday in his town.

He reached for her, intending to soothe, to apologize, and he saw her flinch. He made a Herculean effort to tamp down his anger—not only at her ex, but also at her for even thinking he could be lumped in the same category as Dilday.

Keeping his hands gentle, he cupped her bare shoulders and drew her against his chest.

"I had no idea, Netta." His palm swept over her spine, down and up, then rested between her shoulder blades, his fingers splayed beneath the fall of her thick red hair as he held her close. After a moment, her resistance eased and she laid her head against his collarbone.

"I swore I'd never be controlled by a man again," she whispered.

"Shh. I know. I'm sorry. Why didn't you tell me what was going on? You know you could have called me."

"You were in Houston."

"So? I'd have come home and kicked his sorry ass from here to China."

Just thinking about that time in her life made Donetta's insides knot. ''I was ashamed that I'd allowed it to happen.'' She shifted so his metal sheriff's star wouldn't imprint itself in her chest, kept her head tucked against his neck. It wasn't often that she could comfortably lay her head on a man's shoulder while wearing four-inch platforms. Ironic that their bodies fit so well, when their lives were so hopelessly out of sync. ''I told Sunny.''

She felt his chin shift against her hair as he nodded. Then he eased her back so he could look in her eyes.

''My sister is definitely loyal. She never breathed a word. Did my mom know?''

She shook her head. ''Just Sunny. I went to stay with her in California for a couple of months.''

He kissed the arch of an eyebrow. ''Let me start over, okay? Please come home with me. I'm worried about you, and I only want to make sure you're safe. We've got blueprints that I'm ninety-nine percent sure will spell out a larger electrical panel and GFI plugs. That proof could land Quentin in deep trouble. Not only fraud for taking your money and not providing the proper materials, but he could face felony charges if he willfully bypassed the ground on those breakers. He knows that.''

''If you think he's so dangerous, why did you insist he man the job in the morning?''

''There hadn't been a break-in then. I still want him on the job, though. That way I can keep an eye on him. He owes you material and labor. Plus, we've got the blueprints now. If he skips town, he knows I'll track him down. I wasn't here to help you two years ago.'' His fingertips feathered over her bangs.''Let me be here for you now. For the baby, too. I'm due some time off. I'll make sure your salon gets open again with the least amount of delay I can manage. But I can't do that if I'm worrying about you being alone. I can stick like glue to Quentin during the day, assign a deputy to watch him at night, but I'll go nuts worrying about you. If you're at my place, at least I can get a little sleep. Please."

Donetta rested her forehead against him, then lifted her head and let it drop a couple of times as though she was banging her head against the wall. "Why don't you just give me a gun and let me shoot the bastard."

"Because then I might have to put you in jail. And I've spent most of today making sure you stayed *out* of jail." He raised her face and kissed her, his lips tender, unhurried. "Please."

She swallowed hard, acknowledged her surrender. "If you do that again, you're going to scare me off. I'm not ready for…for more." Even though they'd done much, *much* more than kiss.

"Okay. Whatever you say. You call the shots. As long as it's from my place."

She laughed. "That was a boomerang compromise. I get to call the shots as long as it's according to your wishes."

He grinned. "What can I say? It's ingrained behavior."

"Well, it's going to butt heads with *my* ingrained behavior."

"Might be fun," he said, giving her a suggestive wink. "Need help packing?"

Her shoulders settled and she relaxed—marginally. "I think I can manage. And I wouldn't be so quick to gloat if I was you, Carmichael. Pandora and I are *not* ideal roommates."

DONETTA KEPT HER EYES on the taillights of Storm's truck as he turned down a private road that wound around for a good eighth of a mile before ending at the large white farmhouse he called home.

Her insides were jittery and she could feel the nausea taking hold again as she parked her SUV next to

Storm's pickup. Gosh, what in the world had she agreed to?

Only the dome light glowed in the pitch-black night as Donetta coaxed Pandora off the floorboard of the truck, where the Persian had wedged herself between a shoe tree and makeup case. The cat wasn't the only one reluctant to make a temporary move to Storm Carmichael's house.

She got the cat in her arms and stood beside the truck, breathing in the night air. The cicadas and crickets droned in harmony with the deeper voices of the frogs. The smell of the lake drifted on the breeze, as water lapped the banks at the edges of Storm's ten-acre property.

She felt awkward, didn't know how to act, couldn't help but remember how they'd ended up the last time she'd been here. And now she was carrying his baby. Worse, she didn't have a clue what kind of compromise would work for her.

"Let's get you inside before the mosquitoes eat you alive," Storm said from beside her.

"If you hand me a suitcase, I can manage it along with this spoiled girl."

He gave Pandora's ears a quick scratch. "I'll unload. You shouldn't be lifting anything heavy."

Donetta fired him a look that was completely lost in the dark of night. "Don't start bossing me around and treating me like a weakling. It's bad enough that I let you talk me into coming here."

He astonished her by hooking his hand around the back of her neck, dragging her head forward and pecking a kiss on her forehead.

"And I appreciate you doing that for me, Slim."

She couldn't very well object to the kiss on the forehead. It was something he'd done before as a friend. But darn it, her heart wasn't supposed to skip around over a friendly gesture.

He grabbed two suitcases and a large trash bag out of the back of his truck. Donetta's apartment had been so messy, Storm had just started scooping stuff into big trash bags and told her she could sort it out later.

"Get the front door, would you?" he said. "It's open. We might as well see if the three ladies are going to get along or do some hair pulling."

"And you fussed at me about leaving doors unlocked?"

"I don't live smack-dab in the middle of town on Main Street, darlin'."

She abandoned the argument, because she was met at the door by two of the enthusiastic ladies Storm had mentioned—Sneak, a tiny white-and-brown rat terrier, and Dixie, a retired K-9 shepherd. The third lady, of course, was her Persian-mix cat. As Donetta pushed open the door, Pandora's ears flattened and she hissed out a warning that seemed to thrill Sneak and Dixie. Sneak barked and scampered in circles, her nails clicking on the hardwood floor. Dixie politely wagged her whole body—head to rump, her tail swinging almost as an afterthought.

"Look, Pandora, a welcoming committee."

Spitting, her hair standing on end, Pandora struggled right out of Donetta's arms, shot across the hardwood floors and dove underneath the sofa in the living room.

The cat could have saved the dramatics, because the dogs were interested only in the humans. Sneak bounced straight up as though she had springs attached to her paws. Storm set down the suitcases and caught the excited little dog. She had the sweetest brown face. Soft ears stood at attention as she listened to Storm's greeting, then they flopped and dangled when she whipped her head around. She licked his chin, sniffing and vibrating with excitement. When Storm attempted to put the dog down, Sneak cuddled right into his neck.

He looked up and grinned. "She's crazy about me."

''I can tell.'' Seeing this big masculine guy, the sheriff, cuddling a little dog made Donetta's insides turn to mush. Since Pandora had abandoned her, Donetta buried her fingers in Dixie's fur. The shepherd had been at the vet's office—the practice Sunny had taken over—when Donetta had been here last, so this was her first time meeting Dixie. ''Aren't you a sweetheart. She sure doesn't act like a police dog.''

''That's exactly why she's retired,'' Storm said, reaching down to give the shepherd a pat. ''She didn't have the heart to be aggressive. She did fine in training, then promptly forgot everything they taught her by the next day.''

''Well, that's okay,'' Donetta said, patting the dog and burying her fingers in Dixie's fur. ''Sometimes we girls need a little more femininity to balance out the rough stuff. Huh, Dixie? Your life was simply unbalanced.''

''Don't go ruining my dogs, Donetta. You start talking to her, and she'll expect me to keep it up.''

Donetta looked up. ''Why don't you say that to me again when you don't have a little dog all snuggled against your neck. Don't think I didn't hear that baby talk.''

The words fell between them like hailstones on a tin roof. *Baby.* And *talk*—which was exactly what they needed to have. Storm lowered Sneak to the floor and snapped his fingers. Both dogs trotted into the living room and curled up on separate pillows in front of the fireplace.

''What are your thoughts about the baby?'' Storm asked.

''My thoughts?'' Her hand went to her stomach in an unconscious protective gesture. Only those who were very close to her would even notice the signs of pregnancy—a slightly bloated abdomen that had always been blessedly flat. ''I'm having it, of course.''

"I know that." He raked a hand through his hair, seemed to just now realize they were still standing in the entry hall. He closed the door, then ushered her across the hardwood foyer and into the step-down living room. "When were you going to tell me?"

"Soon. When the opportunity was right."

He raised a brow. "My answering machine isn't exactly overflowing with messages, darlin'. And I've spent a good six hours with you today. Most of it alone. You didn't find an opportunity that suited you?"

"Storm, I just took the test today. I don't know what I'm feeling—other than sick as a dog. And angry that I'm in this position." *And scared.* "I don't think the reality has totally sunk in yet. When it does, things could go one of two ways. In either case, you'd be well advised to keep a cautious distance until I come to terms."

The corner of his mouth tilted for a bare instant, dimpling his cheek. "Meaning you'll either clobber me or fall apart?"

She glanced at him, annoyed that he'd guessed so accurately, embarrassed that she'd shown her vulnerability. "I *don't* fall apart."

He ignored her protest. "Technically, that's only one way. Anger and tears are in the same emotional family."

She heaved a deep sigh. "Fine. You want to split hairs, I'll spell it out for you. In anger, I'm going to slug you. That affects you directly. Tears, I have to deal with on my own. You won't suffer directly from that again, but I'm not a barrel of laughs to be around when that battle is taking place."

"Hell, you wouldn't even let me kill a spider back when you were twelve, so your threat to do bodily harm is a pretty sorry bluff. I had Tracy Lynn grabbing one of my arms, screaming for the death penalty, and you were yanking my other arm out of the socket, begging for the poor little thing's parole.''

''If Tracy Lynn had her way, the world would be absent of all insects. She even shrieks if a fly lands in her hair.'' Donetta remembered the incident he'd cited, though. Sunny's parents had taken Grandma Birdie to Austin for some minor surgery and had planned to stay the night, leaving Storm in charge of his sister and the house.

Donetta, Sunny, Tracy and Becca had been camping out in the Carmichaels' backyard, their sleeping bags laid out like the petals of a daisy so that their heads all met in the center. They'd been shining a flashlight in the tent, giggling about whatever twelve-year-old girls giggle about, when Tracy Lynn spotted a fat spider.

In a bout of pure histrionics, she'd knocked the tent down around them with her screaming and thrashing. Storm, whose open bedroom window faced the backyard, had raced out, wearing only his light blue boxer shorts, gripping a shotgun as though he expected to encounter a wild animal or some madman preying on the four young girls.

Not until the spider was shooed on its way had Donetta noticed his half-dressed state. Even at twelve, she'd nearly swallowed her tongue. Storm, at eighteen, had been a man well worth drooling over. Of course they'd all gone into the house to camp in the living room, because by that time Tracy Lynn had convinced herself they'd be attacked by tarantulas and June bugs the size of bats.

Storm had noticed Donetta's flaming red face, the curse of her red hair and pale skin. He'd mistaken the fiery blush for embarrassment and had made a teasing comment about guys in boxer shorts. Thank God he hadn't realized her heated face was the result of stupid puppy love.

''Second,'' Storm said, bringing her awareness back

to the present, "I've never seen you cry before today. And let me tell you, darlin', that *did* affect me. I'll gladly stand still for you to slug me if you promise not to cry again."

There wasn't a single thing about his words that should have choked her up, but the teary emotions were backing up in her throat again. Donetta was fed up with this nonsense. It was embarrassing, upsetting, made her feel out of control, and it turned her nose red and caused her mascara to run.

"I'll try to contain myself, but you might be out of luck. I just feel…I feel…" She wasn't sure quite how to describe it. For lack of a better word, she used one of his. "Fragile. And doggone it, I don't like that feeling."

He stepped toward her, reached out, but she backed away.

"I don't need to be cuddled." *Oh, God, yes I do.* "Or coddled. I'll deal with this."

"*We'll* deal with this." He studied her for a long moment. "You were always the independent one. I'm not feeling sorry for you, Slim—I'm in this as deep as you are. You might want to pay closer attention before you automatically bite a hand that's merely extended in friendship."

She closed her eyes and scooped her hair back off her face.

"So, when do you want to get married?" he asked.

That snapped her eyes open. "Never?" She made it sound like a question because she didn't want to argue with him again tonight.

"In my family, when two people are having a baby, they get married."

"That's ridiculous. Nobody in your family even *has* a baby!"

"My cousin Tara on my mom's side, and Brenda

Lee on Dad's side. Both got pregnant and both married their baby's father right away."

"Well, good for them. Tara was nineteen and Brenda Lee was twenty. They'd both been dating their boyfriends for more than a year, plus neither of them was self-supporting." Being an unofficial member of the Carmichael clan, Donetta knew the scoop on all the cousins, aunts, uncles and extended relations.

"Comparing them with us is like saying brunette is a shade away from platinum blond. Besides, I've been married, and I don't intend to do that again. Ever."

"I'm not Tim, damn it! And you're having my baby!"

She flinched at his raised voice.

His green eyes narrowed, hardened like icy emeralds. For Donetta to stand her ground, when her automatic reaction was to retreat and apologize, took every ounce of strength she possessed. Even now, ideas and excuses were flipping through her mind, ways to defuse the tension and smooth his mood so chaos wouldn't erupt.

For two years she'd lived without these reactions. Why were they blindsiding her now? With Storm of all people? Perhaps it was guilt. As a girl, she'd felt guilty for dreaming of the older boy. As a married woman, she'd been sure Tim could read her thoughts, see that she was superimposing another man's face over his at the breakfast table.

All her life Storm Carmichael had stirred her in some way or another. Even now, she still felt too much. That frightened her because she'd promised herself never to allow another man to steamroller her with his charm.

Whether he wanted to be or not, Storm *was* an authoritative man—with charm to spare.

Chapter Seven

Donetta squared her shoulders and lifted her chin. "I'm having *my* baby," she clarified. "And for all I know, once you forget to mind your p's and q's, you could be just like Tim."

He clenched his jaw. "I'm going to pretend you didn't say that."

"Why? Storm, what do I really know about you? We didn't exactly run in the same circle of friends. Plus, you were gone for twelve years. And what do you really know about me?"

"I know that you've been part of my life for close to twenty-five years—"

"During our childhoods," she interrupted. "I've spent more time actually talking to you today than all the time put together over the past twenty-five years."

"That's not so."

"Think about it. Holidays when you were older, you hung out with your dad. As a kid, you were in your room or with your pals. We were mostly visual acquaintances. You were *aware* of me because I was an extra body at your dinner table most of your life. But 'Pass the potatoes' isn't the kind of conversation that lets a person know the other."

"I was a hell of a lot more than *aware* of you, Donetta. I drove you home from school. I was there when you graduated—from junior high *and* high school. We played basketball—''

''Yeah, right. You call stealing my ball and lobbing it into the net on your way to the car playing basketball? You were at your *sister's* graduations, and I was graduating, too. You drove your *sister* home from school—I just happened to tag along. None of that's talking or getting to know someone, Storm.''

''I can't believe you're saying this. It's crazy. What about that night you all camped in the living room—when I found you sitting up by yourself after Tracy, Becca and Sunny had already crashed? We talked.''

Donetta ducked her head. That night had remained special in her heart. It had colored her fantasies, highlighted her imagination. The memory of a hunky eighteen-year-old boy on his way to the kitchen to make a ham sandwich, noticing his sister's twelve-year-old friend sitting in the dark with her basketball in her lap, staring out the window at the stars. Oh, how her heart had jumped when she'd heard his soft voice. *What're you doing sitting out here all by your lonesome, Slim?*

He'd caught her at a vulnerable moment, and it had made her mad. He'd just grinned and tugged her hair, then told her to come on out to the kitchen with him and have a midnight snack.

She'd sat on top of the table, her feet on the chair, and watched him fix sandwiches. He'd had on pajama bottoms over his boxers by then, and she'd sighed a bit over that, but his bare chest with its light sprinkling of dark hair in an intriguing triangle had kept her spellbound for several tongue-lolling moments.

Looking back now with the advantage of age, she imagined he'd noticed her crush—twelve-year-olds were rarely subtle, even a late bloomer as she'd been. All legs, bony butt and no boobs. But that didn't mean she'd been a slouch in the looks department. The muscle tone that had molded her skinny bones, and her mane of curly red hair, had turned plenty of heads, even then. She'd just pretended not to notice, because, frankly, it had bugged her.

He'd taken her outside and challenged her to a game of basketball at 2:00 a.m. He'd won, she remembered, but not by much—and she'd made him work for it. Something had changed between them that night. In the way he'd looked at her. More respect. Admiration. A special tenderness. Still…

"You were nice to me. But you're still talking about strictly surface things. People only show what they want others to see. The real truth hides deep down. Can you give me an ironclad guarantee that you'll never lose your temper? Never strike out of reflexive anger?" She shook her head, answering her own question. "It seems I recall a story splashed across the news *showing* you doing just that!"

Silence fell over the room. "You believed what you saw on the news?" he asked.

"That's not the point—"

"Answer the damn question, Donetta."

"No." She looked away.

"Liar." He said it softly, yet she heard.

"Sunny told me it was a setup. At the time, though, I was *living* male anger. What was I supposed to think? Everyone can be pushed. If you'd put a gun in my hand, maybe I would have used it on Tim. We'll never know. But sometimes 'what-ifs' come true. If there's any chance of that, I can't risk it."

"Damn, Donetta, why did you sleep with me if you thought I was a guy who got off on hurting women?"

"I didn't think that! I wasn't even *thinking* at all. I just…you made me feel desirable. Feminine. Excited. It had been so long since I'd experienced that—if ever. I got carried away."

"Ah, hell, Slim. How could you let him take that spark from you?"

The quietly spoken words, though she knew they were meant in compassion, might as well have been fists, because they knocked the wind right out of her. She hugged her arms to her chest and turned away, suddenly freezing, even though it was still a balmy seventy degrees.

He'd just asked the very question she'd struggled with for so long, the source and core of her shame.

And he'd phrased it right. She'd *let* Tim hurt her. With the first incident, she'd been a victim. The second time, she couldn't claim that excuse. *Fool me once, shame on you. Fool me twice, well…* The flashes of temper and heart-wrenching apologies had continued for two years. By not walking out, she'd allowed it to happen. And that was her own cross to bear.

For a while, she'd desperately searched her memory, trying to recall any hints she might have missed during the year they'd dated. A clue that Tim had the potential for violence. There weren't any. He'd seemed so perfect. So loving.

How could she ever again trust her judgment when life clearly offered no guarantees?

She couldn't. Which was why she'd vowed not to marry again, why she had to remain free.

She felt Storm's hand on her shoulder, would have moved away, but his hold was too firm. He tugged her around to face him, then let go.

"I feel like I'm dancing in a minefield. Tell me what I just said that would make your face go paler than it already is."

She rubbed her chilled arms and shook her head.

"Meet me halfway, Donetta." His tone was filled with frustration and genuine confusion.

"You just hit a hot button is all."

"I *know* that much," he snapped. "And damn it, you shouldn't have that kind of memory in the first place. I'm only a few rational seconds away from driving back into town and hanging that ex of yours by his balls.''

She knew he was serious, and capable of doing exactly as he threatened, but his aggression didn't raise her automatic shield of caution. Oddly enough, it jogged a memory, made her smile, gave her an excuse to veer from a subject she'd just as soon forget.

''When I was sixteen,'' she said, ''I went out with a guy who did an annoyingly credible job of impersonating an octopus. I finally got fed up and told him if he so much as breathed in my direction again, you were going to show up at his house, rip off that itty-bitty pride and joy tenting his thin sweatpants and feed it to his daddy's hog.''

Within the space of three seconds, Storm's expression went from one of frustration to one of astonishment. She could almost see his brain scrambling to catch up with her words. Then his eyes yielded to amusement as his slow, sexy smile banished the remnants of tension in the room.

''You told your date I was going to beat him up?''

''Sure. I'd passed the age where it was marginally acceptable for girls to fight. I could have easily taken him myself—Jimbo Nash only *thought* he was a tough guy because he'd made varsity quarterback—but I'd just given my newly acquired acrylic nails a killer French manicure, and I didn't want to mess them up. So I took the easy way out and threatened him with you. He drove me right home.''

Storm gave a resolute nod. ''Damn straight he drove you home. His mama didn't raise no idiot.''

''Oh, don't get all caught up in yourself. Jimbo would've wet his pants even if *Grammy* had shown up at his house.''

He shook his head and chuckled. ''Upstaged by your grandmother. I could almost feel sorry for ol' Jimbo. Maligning a man's Johnson is a seriously low blow.

It's especially rough when the words *itty* and *bitty* are involved.''

''I was only being truthful. It wasn't any bigger than a perm rod. And I'm talking the size I'd use in Drucilla Taggat's hair.''

''Dru Taggat doesn't have enough hair to wrap in a curler.''

''I can get anybody's hair wrapped in a curler. I'm good at what I do—which you wouldn't know about, since you've never let me cut your hair and now you've locked me out of my place of business.''

''Uh-uh. One thing at a time. We were talking about the size of Jimbo's goods.''

''You're the one making an issue of his size. I merely alluded to the particular body part you were going to relieve him of, and I was politely, *delicately,* letting you know it wouldn't have been all that difficult.''

He hooted with laughter. ''You're a piece of work, Slim. Might have been nice of you to tell me I'd threatened a man by proxy...hey, wait a minute. I was pushing a radiator around the mean streets of Houston when you were sixteen.''

''Pushing a...oh, the patrol car.'' She shrugged. ''I told Jimbo you were my boyfriend and came home on the weekends.''

His dark eyebrows lifted. ''If I was your boyfriend, what were you doing going out with another guy?''

She gave him a wicked smile. ''Keeping my options open?''

Storm reached out, intending to give her hair a playful tug the way he used to when she was a kid. If he hadn't been a trained observant, he would have missed the automatic flinch and block, which she quickly covered by fluffing her curls, lifting them off her neck as though hoping for a cool breeze.

His gut twisted into a boulder-size knot and his back

teeth snapped together. Damn it, he had to get out of here. He made himself calm down, speak pleasantly.

"Well, why don't you exercise your options and pick out a room. I'll go get the rest of your things out of our trucks. Then I have to go back to the station and mark myself off the schedule, switch some of the deputies around. I shouldn't be gone too long. Dixie might pretend to have amnesia, but you're safer with her by your side than you'd be with an armed guard."

"Thanks so much for scaring me to death."

"You're welcome. I want you to be careful until this whole Quentin code-violation mess is cleared up. You need anything from town?"

She shook her head. "Just my life back."

"I'm working on it."

STORM DIDN'T SHUT OFF his headlights or bother with stealth on his second arrival at Judd Quentin's house. Tires skidded in dirt and gravel, and dust particles rained in the halogen beams as the sudden stop sent a billowy cloud of brown grit over the cab in the dark night.

Judd opened his screen door and stepped out, a shotgun held in his hand. Good. Storm was in the mood for a fight.

Back in 1909, Ranger captain Bill McDonald had coined the phrase that had become the Texas Rangers' creed: *"No man in the wrong can stand up against a fellow that's in the right and keeps on a-comin."*

And that was exactly what Storm did: kept right on a-comin'. Slamming Judd's body up against the screen door, he rammed his forearm beneath the contractor's chin and pressed hard, shoving the head full of gray hair right through the mesh screen. He yanked the shotgun away, felt with his fingers for the safety, then tossed the weapon in the flower bed. After pinning one of Quentin's meaty hands to the brick wall beside the door, he slapped a strip of sticky fly-paper over the man's palm and fingertips.

His left hand on the palm and fingers of Judd's right hand, Storm looked him in the eyes and smiled.

"You a betting man, Quentin?" He drawled the words a little more quietly than usual. "What do you think the chances are that the fingerprints we've got here between us match the prints found in a big old mess over at a beauty salon in town?" Using his weight as leverage, Storm leaned in, then shoved himself back, taking the print evidence with him.

Judd rubbed his throat and coughed, sweat trickling down his temple. "I didn't steal anything," he said. "You got nothing on me. Besides, I have a key."

"To the front door. Guess you forgot it didn't work the back door, as well?" He held out his hand. "I'll take it, if you don't mind."

"It ain't on me."

Storm shook his head. "You'll understand that I don't exactly trust you, so I'll just have a look-see myself." He advanced, and Quentin jerked back, his elbow tearing another hole in the screen door.

"You might want to step away from that door, Judd. I'm in a real funny mood right now, and I'm just dying to cut loose on somebody. You're about to be it."

Judd snatched a single key out of his pocket and tossed it toward Storm. It hit him in the chest and fell to the ground. He didn't pick it up, but he did stop.

"When you packed up your tools two years ago, your entitlement to use this key ended." Keeping his gaze on Quentin's, he moved a few feet to the right and put his hand on the hood of the J.Q. Construction truck.

"Hmm. Engine's still pretty warm. Seeing as this is the back of the house, it's not *too* odd that the grill is practically nosed into the brick on the house. Could be you were out having a drink with the boys, misjudged a little. Maybe your brakes are starting to go?'' He shrugged. ''Some folks just get in an all-fired hurry to get home and get in the house.''

Judd wasn't saying a word, but in the porch light, Storm could see that the corner of his left eye still twitched.

''There's a pry bar in the back of your pickup. I have a funny habit of noticing things, you know? And I don't recall seeing it there this afternoon. The tool all by itself would give me cause to charge you with possession of a burglarious instrument…*if* I were here wearing a badge, that is. We could look at probable cause for unlawful entry, malicious trespass, vandalism, invasion of privacy…that's just the beginning. Mostly misdemeanor stuff a good lawyer can make go away—or at least make it not hurt so bad. But the felonies, now those will stick. No doubt about it.''

''Look,'' Judd said, folding his arms across his chest, his body shaking now. ''I cut some corners, okay? The electrical service was adequate for the load one hairdresser ought to put on it. I couldn't very well help it if she went out and beefed up the wattage of her hair dryers and stuff.''

''Man, every time you open your mouth, I'm convinced your IQ's about half your boot size. You know what the contract said, you know what you got paid for and you know what you installed—or *didn't* install. Granted, that's only *one* of the problems we're looking at, but it happens to be the biggest…and potentially deadly. How would you feel about murder charges added to fraud and…'' He shook his head.

''Damn. I keep forgetting I didn't come out here wearing my law-enforcement hat. But, pal, I've got to tell you, you're wading in a pool of quicksand over hell, and I'm the man who knows how to pull the plug.''

''I said I'd make it right. None of this would have

happened if Matheson—'' Quentin's mouth snapped shut, and he raked his fingers through his thick gray hair.

Storm grinned. ''Yeah. You're probably smart not to go there. I might have to put my badge back on for information about our former fire marshal and what type of deals the two of you teamed up on. Meanwhile, this here deal's between me and you. Donetta's salon is going to be your one and *only* priority for the next two weeks—''

''I can't get all that done in two weeks. You're talking saw-cutting concrete, tearing into walls—''

''Two weeks,'' Storm repeated. ''I don't care if you have to hire a crew of five hundred and work twenty-four/seven, you *will* have Blane Pyke's signature on a certificate of occupancy and the doors to that hair salon open in fourteen days or less. And two years' worth of interest on Ms. Presley's money should take the sting out of your checkbook when you reimburse her for each day her business is forced to stay closed—another incentive to hustle. Seeing as there are just the two of us civilians here, I'm making you a deal. If you stick to your half of the agreement, then as far as I'm concerned, you and I are square. Personally and legally.''

He didn't need to spell out the consequences of not sticking to the agreement. They were clearly implied. And whatever deal he made with Judd didn't have anything to do with Donetta. She could file against the man's contractor's license, take him to court, make things go pretty badly for him.

''Do we have a deal?''

Judd stuck out his hand, then let it drop when Storm deliberately kept his own hands in his pockets.

''I imagine we're seein' eye to eye,'' Judd said.

''Good. Just one more thing and I'll let you go on in and get your beauty rest. Stay away from Donetta Presley. If you so much as talk to her without me standing right there, you will find out in a hurry why I have a reputation for being a very good person not to mess with.''

Smiling, he tipped his hat and walked back to the truck, breaking the beams of the headlights as he passed in front of them. He climbed in, started up the engine, put it in gear and left a nice rooster tail of gravel as he peeled out of Quentin's yard.

He realized he hadn't actually gotten a chance to take a poke at the guy, but he felt better.

His high beams lighting the dark country road, Storm cruised at an easy speed. When he'd left the house, he'd been spitting mad and dying to unload on somebody.

The thought of what Donetta had gone through in her marriage made his blood boil, but how could she be uneasy around *him?* That was what he didn't get. And how could she suggest that they didn't *know* each other after all these years? Hell on fire, they were having a baby. If that wasn't knowing a person, what was?

And if he was such a shirttail acquaintance, why the hell would he be running up and down Old Bird Creek Road at ten o'clock at night, leaning on a sleazy contractor? And why would he have gone nose to nose with the damn fire marshal this morning?

When Blane Pyke had forced him to put duty over friendship it had galled him to the bone. The resentment had nearly burned a hole in his gut by the time he'd opened the door and stepped into Donetta's salon, looked into those amber eyes and fought to mask his dread and discomfort.

God knows, he'd stalled as long as he could, given her as much of the day as possible to finish her ladies. If he'd gone in there with his hat in his hand, let her see how badly he felt over having no choice, she wouldn't have budged.

And tonight she might have been sitting in a jail cell,

waiting for a judge to set bail or for her friends to come through for her. Hell, he would have posted the bail himself.

And she probably would've tossed it back in his face.

Damn it. The woman had knocked him right in the heart today with surprises that were bigger and more important than any that had ever come into his life.

She was having his baby. And she didn't trust him. He hadn't realized how much that would bother him, had never imagined it would ever be an issue between them to begin with.

He wanted his child, and he wanted Donetta's trust.

His headlights sliced through the dark and glanced off the barn as he navigated the last curve of his private drive. The final arc illuminated Donetta's fiery red Tahoe.

Flashy and bold, just like the woman.

Seeing her car parked in front of his house, knowing she was waiting inside, gave him a feeling of rightness he hadn't experienced in a long time, if ever. It was that same, weird, déjà vu sensation he'd had earlier at the salon.

She'd been part of his world for as long as he could remember. And now he understood. He wanted Donetta, the woman—all of her. Not just in his bed. He wanted her in his everyday life.

Man alive, he was scared to death.

DONETTA AWOKE EARLY the next morning, disoriented for a moment. It took mere seconds and the sickening revolt of her stomach to clarify her mind. She was at Storm's house, in the guest room across the hall from his bedroom.

The package of Saltine crackers was still next to her on the bed. With shaking fingers, she pulled out a square and nibbled. She'd talked to the doctor last night, and crackers, dry toast or ginger ale were Lily O'Rourke's suggestions, since Donetta was adamant about not taking prescription drugs.

She tried to focus on something, anything, besides the seething cauldron in her stomach, and quickly slapped the pillow over her face.

But the scent on the pillowcase distracted her. It smelled familiar. It wasn't the faint hint of her vanilla perfume. Something else. Storm had given her the pillow last night—from his bed. That was it. The familiar scent was Storm. Just Storm.

She remembered one time years ago when she'd spent the night with Sunny and had forgotten her pajamas. Sunny was too petite for anything of hers to fit, so Anna had given her one of Storm's old baseball jerseys to sleep in. It had still smelled like him, even though it had been washed. She'd pressed it to her face, imagined him, yearned. And felt totally stupid because of it. He was six years older than she was. She was a skinny giraffe who'd been sent to the principal's office more than once for getting in a fight. Why, she had asked herself, would a hunky, all-star college boy ever be interested in a kid?

Yet when she'd gone to his house six weeks ago, she was no longer a little girl, and she could *see* that he was interested.

Despite her deliberately flamboyant, sultry behavior—behavior that ensured *she* would be the one in control from now on—her confidence in herself as a woman had been badly bruised. That was only one of the many reasons she hadn't dated since her divorce. And didn't plan to travel that road again.

Not until Sunny had come home from California had Donetta's and Storm's paths begun to cross more frequently. The chemistry between them as adults was potent, but she'd told herself he was just a guy who knew how to play the teasing, flirting game, and she'd vowed to treat him the same as she did all the other men who were merely good friends.

She'd been relaxing with him on that late-summer's evening, laughing over the rim of her third glass of wine, and something had shifted. The intensity of his gaze. The stillness in the room. The leap of her heart. The trusted, familiar scent of his skin.

She'd felt desirable, sexy, truly wanted. And it had been the strongest aphrodisiac. The coalescing of all her secret dreams, dreams she'd hidden away and rarely thought about, had burst from the locked chambers of her soul like glittering fairy dust scattered by a magic wand.

Caught up in the wild, heady moment, she'd let down her guard, forgotten about the past, present or future. She'd known only desire: *Storm.*

It wasn't until the next morning, when she'd regained her wits, that she'd realized she was an idiot, that she should have never allowed that intimacy to happen.

Especially with this man. Her best friend's brother. If tension arose between them, it would bleed over onto her relationship with the rest of his family—and she would not risk her bonds with them. Ever.

She glanced toward the curtained window. The sun was barely lighting the horizon. The crackers weren't cutting it, and she couldn't ignore the horrible churning in her stomach a second longer. She flung back the blankets and raced to the connecting bathroom.

A few minutes later, she heard the door swing open and wanted to sink through the floor. Thankfully, the bouts of "baby fits," as she'd begun to call them, were quick. She just wished they weren't so darned often.

"Aw, darlin'." His baritone voice was even deeper from sleep and compassion. "You've hardly had any rest all night."

She made a shooing motion with her hand, but Storm

didn't pay any attention. He ran water over a washcloth and squatted to wipe her face. Donetta snatched it from him and flushed the toilet, burying her face in the cool cloth.

"Do you always have to come in and see me looking like a walking corpse?" Twice during the night she'd been sick. And both times Storm had appeared by her side with a wet cloth and gentle, soothing hands.

"I'm half responsible, Slim." His voice was soft, solemn.

"Yeah, you are. So, I vote that you take this half." She glanced at him. His feet were bare. So was his chest. All he wore was a pair of men's cotton pajama bottoms. She'd just had her stomach lining yanked inside out in the most jolting manner, and now butterflies were dancing there with giddy delight at the sight of Storm in his pajama bottoms. Not only was she sick in the stomach, she was sick in the head.

"Sorry, darlin'. I'd like to be noble and all, but I'm a big baby when it comes to the collywobbles." He smoothed her hair over her shoulder. "I'm taking you to the doctor today. This isn't right—you being so sick like this. It can't be good for you. Or the baby."

"I already have an appointment set up for Friday. That was the soonest I could get in with Dr. O'Rourke."

Storm frowned. "You need someone with more experience than Lily O'Rourke. I know of a good man in Houston, but that's too far away for convenience. I'll make some phone calls, find out who's the best OB-GYN in Austin. Don't worry. I'll make sure you get in today."

Donetta's jaw dropped open. Lily O'Rourke had been a classmate of Storm's—and she'd chosen to come back to Hope Valley to set up her practice after medical school.

"You're not calling another doctor! Lily has plenty

of experience. Do you think they just pass out medical certificates without giving doctors any hands-on training? Honestly, Storm. You can't just come into my life and expect to make decisions for me and—'' Her stomach pitched again.

She planted her hand in the middle of his chest and shoved. Hard. Tipped off balance, he slid backward across the tile floor, giving her precious seconds of semiprivacy.

Minutes ticked by until she at last pressed the damp washcloth to her swollen eyes and hot skin. The silence in the room made her much too aware that Storm was still sitting behind her and she was wearing pajamas that were hardly more than a see-through camisole and silky shorts.

''Can we at least go sit in Dr. O'Rourke's office?'' he asked quietly. ''Kind of like a standby passenger on an airline flight?''

Ridiculously, Donetta felt a bubble of laughter escape. Instead of answering him right away, she got up and brushed her teeth, then dried her face and sat back down on the floor.

''I don't think doctors' offices operate under the same principles airlines do.''

''I bet if you barfed in her waiting room she'd hustle us back to a room in a hurry.''

''What's with this 'us' stuff? I'm not planning to have an audience when my gynecologist examines me.'' She had an odd thought that they did a lot of visiting while sitting on bathroom floors. He had his back against the wall by the door, and she was propped against the oak vanity, facing him. If she stretched out her legs all the way, their feet would touch.

''Don't you think it's a little late in the game for modesty between us?''

''Have you ever been present during a female exam?''

"No."

She smiled. "Exactly. And you won't be, either—at least not mine—so deal with it." She held up her hand when his face darkened with irritation and challenge. "I should *not* have to paint you a picture here. Would you like me in the room when the doc sticks his finger in your rear end and invites you to cough?"

He opened his mouth, stared at her for a long, somewhat bewildered moment, then dropped his head back against the wall and laughed. "You're a holy terror. How can you be so sick one minute, then rally enough to put me in my place the next?"

"Talent. Pure and simple." She grinned. "It helps that the nausea leaves as quickly as it comes—well, that's not totally correct—"

"Come here."

She frowned at his interruption. "What?"

He sighed and got to his feet in one fluid motion. "Don't ever sign up for the military or police academy. You'd never make it." He bent down, scooped her up in his arms and strode to the bedroom.

"What…?" Her brain was having trouble keeping up. "Thankfully, I have no desire to join either service. And just because someone doesn't respond to an order doesn't mean you can gain compliance by…by manhandling them. I was in the middle of talking to you, but obviously you didn't care enough to listen." And damn it, that hurt her feelings. "So, you can just—"

His mouth covered hers. Utter surprise and flashpoint desire effectively shushed the rest of her tirade.

Chapter Eight

This second interruption took the sting out of his rudeness.

Storm Carmichael was a man who knew how to kiss.

She felt weightless, hardly aware that he'd carried her into the connecting bedroom. He sat on the edge of her bed and settled her bottom in his lap without ever lifting his head.

He kissed her slowly, elaborately, as though he'd invented the very act of kissing and this was the first trial run. She slid her arms around his neck and held on, knowing she shouldn't indulge, helpless to stop herself. The easy skill he brought to a kiss was something a woman wouldn't want to miss.

His tongue never entered her mouth to push for more or explore. With only his slightly parted lips, he nibbled, worshiped, soothed…and aroused. The tenderness was more arousing than she'd ever realized it could be.

Kisses like these didn't happen often.

Muscles flexed beneath the warmth of his skin as he twisted his body, lifted her from his lap and laid her on the bed in a single, effortless move. She was hardly petite—she could practically look him in the eye—yet he'd been carting her around and arranging her to his liking as though she *was*. Tucking her against his side, he cradled her head in one arm, holding his weight off of her, and placed his other hand on her stomach.

Somehow, the simple touch felt far more intimate than the kiss, and it gave her a jolt.

He lifted his head and gazed down at her as if he'd sensed her distraction, his palm still spanning her stomach.

"What's not totally correct about your being sick for short bursts at a time?" he asked.

She blinked. It took her a minute to realize he was picking up the thread of their conversation, proving he *had* been paying attention. She, however, couldn't remember a blessed thing about the point she'd wanted to make. "I have no idea."

His thumb idly stroked her cheek. "I didn't mean to interrupt you. I just…I needed to hold you. It tears me up to see you so miserable." His green eyes were earnest.

"This is going to sound really awful, but that actually makes me feel better." She smiled at his raised eyebrows. "I'm pretty sure I'm kidding. Maybe. Although it does seem a tad imbalanced that the woman goes through all the physical pain and indignities that come with pregnancy and childbirth, and all the man has to do is aim and fire."

"Darlin', if that's how you remember my part in this, I think you need a refresher course."

She slapped a hand on his bare chest, a stop sign, her heart racing. The heat of his arousal pressed against her hip, the thin cotton of his pajamas doing little to disguise shape, size and state of readiness. She definitely didn't need any reminders of Storm's clever skill in bed. Her memories were just fine, thank you very much.

"I was generalizing," she said, removing her hand now that he wasn't posing such a sensual threat. Her nipples were hard and clearly visible beneath the satiny camisole, but what could she do? Distraction was probably the best plan.

"I'd like to know what idiot came up with the cruelly misleading term *morning* sickness? Sneak attacks of baby fits twenty-four/seven—"

"Baby fits?"

She shrugged. "It sounds better than nausea, or throwing up, or collywobbles. You get up on mornings like this and think you've felt as close to dying as you're going to for the day, and soon find out how sadly you're mistaken."

"How long have you been feeling bad?"

"Close to a week. I just hope it's not going to last the whole nine months. I've heard of that happening, you know?"

"My ex-partner's wife had a rough go for the first few months." He lightly rubbed her abdomen, his palm and fingers nearly spanning her entire stomach.

Instead of soothing her, his touch made her tense. Maybe the unease was born of memories from the past. Perhaps it was merely an instinctive need to protect the child in her womb. She placed her hand over his, intending to casually move it away. Instead, she ended up lacing her fingers through his, holding his hand aloft between them, softly exploring the contours of his thumb.

"About that appointment…it's the whole feet-in-the-stirrups deal I object to. You can come when they do the ultrasound or check for the baby's heartbeat." She shrugged, not wanting to sound as if his presence was a big deal. "If you want."

He gave her a slow half smile. "That's where we get to look for extra body appendages and then pick out boy names or girl names?"

"I suppose. Unless I choose not to know the sex of the baby."

"Why would we choose that?"

She pretended not to notice his deliberate use of *we*. "For the surprise. Seems to me a person could get in trouble with some of these new tests. What if a woman wanted a boy, but the test showed a girl. Would she resent her daughter? Wonder how long it would be before she could try again for a boy? And what if the test showed a girl and she was prepared with pink *everything,* and out popped a little boy?"

"Yikes. What happened to his little peter?"

"I don't know! He was bashful and hiding it?" She couldn't believe he was being so literal. Yet one look at his curious "guy" expression told the tale.

"This is a hypothetical baby," she said. "The point is, the test would have encouraged the mother to bond with that child as a little girl the first eight months or so in the womb. To name her, to plan for her."

"We can tell the lab technician we don't want to know unless she's ninety-eight percent sure. How about twins—do they run in your family?"

Donetta stared at the open-beam ceiling and let go of his hand. "I haven't the faintest idea."

"Oh, man." He flopped over onto his back. Side by side, they gazed up at the ceiling fan, their legs bent at the knees and hanging over the side of the bed. "I wasn't thinking, Nett."

"It's okay." She didn't know who her father was, and she hadn't seen her mother in eight years. Cybil had no idea that her daughter had been married and divorced, or was now expecting a baby and had no intention of marrying the child's father.

That her life had been paralleling her mother's of late was a frightening thought. The big difference, though, was that her child would know his or her father. And Donetta would never get drunk and forget to pick up her daughter from her first day at kindergarten. Nor would she shack up with a different man every other month and stay gone for days at a time, leaving her child to fend for herself when she was barely in the second grade.

"I really wish you'd see a doctor sooner than Friday," Storm said. "That's three days away."

"I called Lily. She might not have enough hours in the day to squeeze everyone in, but she's always happy to talk to her favorite hairstylist on the phone. She said there are a couple of prescriptions she can give me for the nausea. But I don't want to take any drugs. I want everything that goes into my body to be as natural as possible."

She turned her head toward him, realized that he'd already abandoned his fascination with the ceiling fan and was watching her.

It dawned on her then that they were lying together and talking as though they were a young couple in love. She sat up.

"You seem to have formed an attachment with our baby last night and this morning," he went on.

She shrugged. "We've been awake together quite a bit this last week. It wasn't until last night that I knew who or what I was talking to. So, we've had a conversation or two."

"Did the two of you come to any conclusions?"

He was asking if she'd made any decisions about *him.* She shook her head, drew her knees up and rested her forehead on them. The mattress shifted, and wonderful chills raced over her skin when he began a spontaneous backrub.

"Mmm." The sound was a purely blissful moan. "I'll give you an hour to stop that."

He chuckled. "Lie down and I'll do it right."

"Uh-uh. Lying down and doing it right is what got us in this predicament in the first place."

His hand paused over her middle vertebrae, then resumed stroking. "I'm glad to know you think we did something right...the making-of-the-baby part."

He could have put the more blatantly sexual spin on her words. She was touched that he didn't.

"I always wanted children," she admitted.

"Have you noticed that these baby fits seem to be triggered by emotional highs and lows?" he asked.

"Yes. At least, I thought so, until I wore a path in your rug last night running for the bathroom. I don't think I was dreaming anything stressful."

"Have you ever considered hypnosis?"

"Sure. But I can't be hypnotized."

"Who told you that?"

"No one. It didn't work before. I'm not sure I can give up that kind of control in order to let the suggestions take hold."

"What about with me? I'm trained in hypnosis—compliments of the Texas Rangers. We used it in forensic investigations. I was the best in the department."

"You hypnotize people?" Odd that Sunny hadn't told her about that. Then again, during her marriage Donetta hadn't kept in close touch with her friends—and Sunny had lived out of state, anyway. She supposed there might have been opportunity when she'd stayed those two months in California with Sunny, but under the circumstances, their conversation had been more therapeutic than reminiscent.

He grinned. "Yep. It's amazing what the mind can do. You could look around this room and later on probably recall the colors, furniture pieces, stuff like that. You don't realize that at first glance your subconscious mind captured an intricately detailed picture—for instance, right down to the nick on the base of that lamp."

She leaned over to look for the flaw that she surely would have seen turning the bulb on and off as many times as she had last night. Sure enough, the lamp had a small crease in the metal base. "I'll be darned. But how is vivid recall supposed to get rid of baby fits?"

"That was just an example of what your brain is capable of." A dimple creased his cheek. "For your malady, we'd use a little different imagery."

"Can you make people lose weight and stop smoking or cussing and stuff?"

"A bar of soap'll do all three of those." He smiled. "I can't *make* a person do anything. But offering positive suggestions when someone is in a relaxed state of mind has unbelievably positive results. Roy's wife, Marnie—Roy's my ex-partner," he clarified, "didn't think she could be hypnotized, either, and she had a really bad case of morning—uh, baby fits. After three months, she gave in and asked me to help. It worked on her. Will you at least let me try to help you?"

"You wouldn't go into my thoughts and mess around with anything like…say, making me think I'd agreed to a wedding date or anything?"

A half smile kicked up at the corners of his mouth. "I hadn't thought of that." His devilish expression clearly said he was thinking about it now. "I have a strict standard of ethics. I would merely guide your subconscious to respond differently to the nausea. That's all."

"At this point, I'm willing to try anything. Even my rib cage is sore."

He sat up and pressed a kiss to her temple. "Tonight, when it's quiet and you're relaxed, we'll give it a shot. Think you can hold out that long?"

"I can hold out as long as it takes. The sooner things settle down, though, the happier I'll be."

"Me, too. Now, I better hit the shower so I can be at the salon to greet our contractor."

"Can we shower at the same time?"

His brows shot up, and his green eyes filled with instant joy, gratitude and desire.

"Whoa. Down boy. I meant, can your water heater handle it if I'm showering in here—" she pointed to the guest bathroom "—and you're showering in there—" she pointed across the hall to the master bedroom.

"That was very cruel, Slim." He shook his head, took a deep breath. "Yes, the water heater can handle two showers running at the same time. But you don't have to rush. You can go back to bed and rest if you want."

"Strangers are going to be messing with my salon and I want to know what's being done. Besides, you might need my input on something. And the phones will probably be ringing."

"You're not working, Donetta." His tone rang with warning.

"Of course I'm not, silly." She deliberately misunderstood him. "I'm fixing to take a shower. So, shoo. Go tend to your own business."

She intended to go into the salon and get an idea how extensive and messy the job was going to be—do a little planning of her own. Perhaps she'd have an opportunity to slip a client or two in for a quick haircut. Two weeks with no income, especially with a baby on the way, wasn't her idea of security. It made her a nervous wreck.

After she showered and blow-dried her hair, Donetta dug through her suitcases and plastic trash bags and came up with denim hip-hugger capris, a sleeveless white blouse and black slides that had a three-inch wedge sole. Since it was another warm day, she kept her makeup to a minimum—a tinted moisturizer, blush and lip gloss—then rummaged through her cosmetic bag for waterproof mascara. No raccoon eyes today. With a couple of twists and a few bobby pins, she fixed her hair in a quick up-do that would keep it off her face and out of the way.

Pandora was still hiding under the bed, forcing Donetta to get on her knees to fish the cat out.

"Come on, Pandora. I'm leaving, so you don't have to hold your bladder any longer or starve yourself. You know darn well where the litter box and food are." She managed to snag the cat. "When I get home tonight, you might try getting out and making friends instead of sulking. You're gonna be stuck here for a while, girl. So deal with it. Meantime, in you go."

She set the cat on the bathroom floor, checked the water and food dish, then grabbed her hobo bag, hoping she'd stuffed everything in it that she would need.

She was used to having her apartment right upstairs, and was always prepared for whatever came up. From the looks of the trash bags and suitcases strewn in Storm's guest bedroom and living room, she'd be lucky to find anything left at her apartment.

She shut the door to the hallway and closed the sliding pocket door leading to her bedroom, safely corralling Pandora in the bathroom. Her car keys in hand, Donetta headed down the sea of dark oak that flowed over the wide hallway. The way between the bedroom suites to the kitchen, which was at the far end of the house, was a straight shot. All the rooms off either side of the wide hallway were open and massive. Although the house had two levels, the upstairs was hardly used. It consisted of several bedrooms and a bonus room that housed the pool table.

She saw Storm heading toward her from the kitchen, his attention on the dogs. Dixie and Sneak were happily catching chunks of bread that he was tossing to them, nearly tripping him in their exuberance. She stopped in the entryway to wait for him.

"You're supposed to chew," he said to the dogs, "not swallow whole. Now, listen up. You two be good today, you hear? And don't mess with the cat. Yeah, I'm talking to you, Sneak. That cat's bigger than you are, buddy. And her name's Pandora. That ought to give you a clue right there to stay clear. Dixie, you're in charge, got it?''

He looked up when he reached the entryway, and Donetta grinned. ''Dixie and Sneak are off the hook. Pandora's spending the day in the bathroom. And after what I just witnessed, I'm thinking you'll want to retract that warning about me ruining your dogs. It would be pretty hard to top you.''

He gave her a mock scowl. ''If you tell anyone, I'll just deny it. I have a reputation to maintain, you know.'' He bit into a piece of toast spread with a thin layer of strawberry jam and passed her the extra slice he held in his hand.

''You made me breakfast?'' she asked. ''What a guy.''

''That's what I've been trying to tell you. So, do you want to set a wedding date? Snap me up quick? I even do breakfast in bed.''

She opened the front door and he followed her out onto the porch, offering the dogs a commiserating look as he closed the door behind him.

Lord, to keep things light between them when they both had different agendas was difficult. Stalling, she took a bite of toast, navigated the porch steps and headed toward her Tahoe. Hoping he would let the subject drop if she dazzled him a bit, she gave him a sassy smile full of mystery and gripped the driver's-side door handle.

He stopped her with a hand on her arm. She should have known when he followed her to her SUV instead of veering to his truck—which was parked right beside hers—that he wasn't going to let the subject of marriage slide.

''It's a little early to leave. Judd won't be at the salon until eight. Why don't you take a walk with me.''

The air smelled fresh, and the sun had already begun to warm the earth. Birds sang in the trees as though celebrating the gift of summer in October. It was a perfect morning for a walk. Too bad it was going to include a serious conversation.

After opening the Tahoe's door, she tossed her purse inside and grabbed a light sweater, then fell into step beside Storm as he headed around the side of the house toward the lake.

Grass that was still green from recent rains carpeted the land, gently sloping over Storm's backyard until it reached the banks of the lake. Morning dew clung to the verdant blades, making the toe grips on her slides practically useless as moisture worked its way between the soles of her feet and her sandals.

"So much for clean feet." She grabbed Storm's shoulder and pulled him to a halt. Bunching the soft cotton of his T-shirt to steady herself, she took off her shoes.

"I don't know why you wear those deathtrap stilts." He slid his arm around her waist and plucked the half-eaten toast out of her hand. "In your line of work, you ought to wear something with better support."

She tsked. "These shoes are cute. And they have three inches of cushion for support." She straightened, accepted the toast he passed back to her, took a small bite and breathed deep of the morning air. Shoes were her passion and her one major indulgence. There was nothing worse than putting on an outfit and not having the right shoes to go with it.

They started walking once more and she didn't bother to object when he took the sandals out of her hand as if they were a ten-pound weight she shouldn't be carrying. Let him be gallant, she thought. That would leave her hands free to feed the ducks if they were around.

"I love the smell of the lake. It's funny that you ended up buying the Anderleys' place, and now Bertha's practically in your backyard."

He glanced down at her, sensual amusement dancing in his eyes. ''That old cottonwood was the main draw. It used to be the talk of the town. Since I've lived here, though, not a single pair of panties has decorated its branches.''

That Texas Sweethearts ritual of hanging their panties on Bertha when one of them had made a faux pas or done something beyond the pale had cost Donetta a lot of underwear over the years.

''Not knowing who was flying their drawers right out there in front of God and everybody used to drive the gossips batty,'' she said with a smile. A couple of months ago, she'd found out from Sunny that Storm had known. He'd seen her depositing an atonement—all because she'd gone to the show with Tommy Drew and the two-timer had neglected to tell her he was dating Tracy Lynn.

''That's the thing with small towns. Folks always want to talk about your business.'' He stopped where the grass ended at the hard-packed dirt pathway that skirted the lake. Ten feet away from the gnarled cottonwood.

''We need to talk about ours, Donetta. Pretty soon people are going to find out—my mother, for one. What will we tell them? 'Yes, we're having a baby, but Donetta doesn't want to get married?'''

She didn't have an answer for him—or even for herself. And that was all she could say.

''I honestly don't know. The part of me that tries to greet each day with optimism and hope wants to say, 'Fine, let's give it a try.' But then the pragmatic side…'' She shook her head and gazed out at the sun's reflection off the still water of the lake, Cindy Dilday's words echoing in her mind.

I'm sorry, Donetta. This breaks my heart, but Tim's my brother. I have to ask you to leave now. And please, don't contact me anymore.

"I can't lose myself again, Storm. And I can't lose *you*. Or Sunny and your mom. That's what's at stake for me. I'm sorry."

"You're not going to lose us," Storm said as though she'd just told him Polar bears were going to water-ski on the lake.

"You can't guarantee that. Five years down the road, after you've lived with me twenty-four/seven and the kids are squabbling—what if you decide you're bored? That you made a mistake. What if I feel that way? What then?"

"Kids?" he asked, a smile beginning to tip his lips. "We're going to have more than just this one?"

"Are you even listening to me? Damn it, this isn't a joke! *I've* been married before, so I think I've got a little more knowledge on the subject than you do, pal."

Her short fuse lit his. "Fine. You're right. I've never lived with a woman. That said, don't you tar me with the same nasty brush as your ex. I don't abuse women."

For a moment, Donetta lost the thread of the conversation, didn't even respond to the banked anger in his voice. In all these years, he'd never had a live-in girlfriend? Why did that please her?

She picked up a smooth rock and tossed it in the water, the splash barely audible as smooth rings fanned out across the glassy surface.

"I'm not comparing you with Tim, and I don't expect you to understand my emotions on that subject."

"Donetta, you flinch when I reach out to touch your hair."

"Yeah, well, sometimes I catch myself aligning the silverware in the drawer with a ruler and level, too, and you're not even around." She blew out a breath, hadn't meant to fire that particular missile back at him.

He uttered a curse. "Netta—"

"It's not *you,* Storm. It's any man. An instinctive

reaction. I'm not afraid of you...." She batted at a stubborn fly, released a frustrated breath.

"Look, this isn't the time or the place to talk about deep issues. I don't know how to express myself to you so that I don't sound like a...a wimpy victim or something. I'm not, believe me. I *will not* put myself in that position again. But memories don't just go away. Look at some of the men over at the Veterans of Foreign Wars who still have flashbacks from the war. It just happens. And you don't need to be getting all touchy about it, okay?" A robin took flight from the cottonwood, startled by her rising voice. Darn it, she'd just decided she didn't want to have this conversation, yet obviously her mouth hadn't gotten the message.

"Okay." He picked up a fist-size rock and sent it sailing through the air like a baseball. It landed nearly in the middle of the lake.

That was it? No elaborating? Arguing? When he turned his head, all she needed was one look at his confident expression to know that he was already working on a strategy to overcome her objections. The problem was, her objections weren't one-dimensional. They were soul deep.

Her stomach was feeling a little iffy after eating half the toast. And from the conversation, she suspected.

"Storm, neither of us knows what the future holds. Most people can just take a chance and hope for the best. With us...all my life I've wished that your mother was my mom and your sister was my real sister...."

"And me?" he asked. "Where did I fit in? As the brother?"

She started to flick her hair back, then remembered that she'd put it up. So she straightened, giving herself enough height to almost meet him eye to eye. Which is exactly where you should look at another person when telling the truth—or at least, part of the truth.

"No. I never cast you in the role of a brother in my…family fantasy. Most of my young life I had a crush on you—which I'm sure you knew—but I haven't ever put a label on you. You're simply part of my family. When I think of the Carmichaels, your face is *always* right there in my mind. Someone I love." Her insides were shaking like mad. Saying the words to his face jolted her right down to her toes.

"Marriages break up, Storm, and the repercussions rip apart friendships and impact everyone involved. You're someone I'm not willing to risk losing even if the chances of 'what if?' are only minuscule. That gamble is just not an option."

"Ah, darlin'. Right now I feel humbled. And lucky. But at the same time, my gut is twisted in the biggest knot because I still don't get it. I'm at the opposite end of the fence from your way of thinking, and I don't know how to convince you that you're wrong."

"And I don't know how to convince you that I'm right. Face it, we're a bad match because we *both* want to be the leader. I told you our similar character traits were going to make us butt heads."

He slung his arm around her shoulders. "Then we'd best get to the salon and light a fire under that contractor."

"See there," she teased. "You're already wanting me out of your hair—and your house."

He tipped up her chin and kissed her. It was merely a three-second kiss, yet it was so potent, so deliberately sensual, it left her dazed.

"Don't start borrowing those 'what-ifs' just yet, darlin'."

Chapter Nine

By mid-morning, Donetta hardly recognized her salon. Huge sections of her scarlet-red walls had been ripped away in jagged chunks. The deafening noise of a jack-hammer pulverizing her bathroom floor made her ears throb.

She swept up a pile of drywall dust and dumped it into the trash can. Although she'd spent the morning trying to keep the construction debris corralled, clearly her attempt had been futile.

Judd Quentin and his crew had hit the ground running at 7:30 a.m.—half an hour early. The contractor avoided her as much as possible, which she found odd since he'd been almost cocky the previous night when they'd gone to his house. Probably had a guilty conscience, she thought. Especially since the fat set of blueprints lay draped over her guest chairs, mocking him, proving that all the code violations were the direct result of his cheating and greed.

"Watch my picture!" Power tools drowned out her voice. She raced across the salon and rescued the framed print teetering on a shelf as a guy wearing baggy jeans hauled off and clobbered the wall with his hammer, then reared back and let his arm fly again. The three men working with Judd hadn't been on the original job, and this one, Al, wasn't all that pleasant.

"Can't you at least wait until everything's off the walls?" she snapped, her nerves frayed.

Al glanced over at her. He was about Judd's age, late fifties, early sixties, maybe, with skinny hips and watermelon gut. He had no business wearing baggy pants that were about to fall off his butt, and a skintight tank shirt where tufts of gray hair frizzed out of every exposed opening. She wanted to get her buzzers and have a go at him.

"Ain't getting paid to take down the decorating," he said, about to deal the wall another blow. "Just told to hurry."

Donetta's temper went from simmer to boil in a flash. She snatched the hammer right out of his hand, so mad she could hardly take time to marvel at the slick maneuver or Fuzzpit's stunned face.

"You're working for *me,* buddy. And *I* say you are to treat every last decoration, piece of furniture, board or screw as if they're irreplaceable china."

"Problem, Slim?" Storm asked, plucking the hammer out of her hand as easily as she'd slid it from Al's.

Where the devil had he come from? Last she'd seen him, he'd been bird-dogging Judd in the back room.

"She's about to have a problem of one less man on the job," Al snarled.

Storm lifted the man's hammer. "Mind if she borrows this for a minute, Al?" He nodded at Donetta, then at the well-used tool, a good-ol'-boy smile on his face.

Al stepped back several paces, obviously not trusting her with a weapon, and shrugged.

Donetta didn't like the belligerent expression on Al's face, and was a little surprised at herself over her bold aggression. She also didn't have a clue why Storm was wrapping her fingers around the handle of Al's hammer.

"Darlin', I want you to take this and wail the devil

out of that wall, just like you saw Al do a few minutes ago.'' He pointed to the spot where several dents cratered the drywall. ''You just get a good picture in your head of anybody's face you'd like to rearrange a bit and have at it. Best stress reliever ever.''

Her blood still simmered, but she felt foolish beating up the very walls she was battling over. She felt even sillier doing it in front of an audience...until she saw Al's smirk. Oh, she knew that look, and by dog, the first hotshot who opened his mouth and uttered ''PMS'' was going to be in deep doo-doo.

Storm put his hands on her shoulders and leaned close to her ear. ''Trust me on this, Slim.'' The words were only loud enough for her to hear, but for Al's benefit, he said, ''Just make sure it's not my face you're imagining.''

She rolled her eyes. ''You wish.'' And then she gripped the wooden handle like a baseball bat and swung, stumbling forward with the momentum as the steel head went clear through the drywall.

''Whoa.'' Storm grabbed her waist and steadied her as she pulled back and ripped out a chunk of the wall. ''Looks like Ms. Presley won't have a problem with one less man on the job—she's better at it than you are, Al.''

He took the hammer from her and passed it to Al. ''You can pick up your tools and clear out now. We won't be needing your services anymore.''

Donetta opened her mouth to object, but the quiet danger in Storm's tone stopped her. Al responded to it, as well, and didn't waste any time gathering his tools. She watched as Storm escorted the seething man to the front door.

What had she done? They couldn't afford to lose workers. Even ones who were jerks. She felt stress rising again, and wondered whose hammer she could bor-

of them—except for Jack Slade—was single. Wouldn't you just know it. The only hunk out of the pack that she was attracted to was the one she couldn't have.

Her stomach flip-flopped, and just that quickly, her skin turned clammy, then fiery hot. Oh, no. The shrill, deafening concrete cutting saw and the pounding jackhammer reminded her that the bathroom wasn't usable. And the baby was about to throw a fit.

The men began to move inside, gearing up to go to work as Storm gave instructions. Donetta headed for an opening between broad shoulders and raced out. She didn't have time to stop and explain. She sprinted two doors down the sidewalk and shoved open the entrance to Becca's Attic.

Impressions registered subconsciously—the smell of fresh brewed coffee, the scent of books, old furniture and trinkets that put one in mind of one's grandmother's house. Becca Sue Ellsworth was behind the counter. The only customer in the shop was Tracy Lynn Randolph.

Both women jumped up, their eyes wide as Donetta burst through the door. She didn't stop to chat, barely paused.

"Please. Don't let Storm in here," she managed to say as she ran past them toward the rest room.

Minutes later, Donetta decided she ought to just give up trying to get some privacy for the more embarrassing indignities in her life. Granted, Storm wasn't hovering over her this time, but Tracy Lynn and Becca Sue were.

Tracy Lynn passed her a wet paper towel.

"At least in my salon I supply y'all with soft towels," Donetta complained as she ran the stiff paper over her face.

"Well, we're in *my* shop now," Becca said. "I'm not wealthy enough to buy the prissy throwaways and I'm sure not dumb enough to make a pile of laundry for myself to have to take home. Now, tell me why I just locked my door in Storm Carmichael's very angry face—in the middle of the business morning.''

''Becca,'' Tracy said. ''We should at least ask after her health first.''

''Are you kidding? I want to know the good stuff—'' The cell phone in Becca's hand rang and she checked the caller ID. ''Oh, wait. Don't say a word. I have to go let Sunny in. I mean it. Not a peep. I don't want to miss anything.''

''Why is Sunny here?'' Donetta asked.

''Because I called her.'' Becca gave Donetta a did-you-flush-your-brains-down-the-toilet? look.

When Becca jogged out of the bathroom, Donetta looked over at Tracy Lynn. ''I'm not having another conversation on a bathroom floor. Let's get out of here, okay?''

Tracy's blond eyebrows shot up. ''You're the headliner, sweetie. I promise, your faithful audience will sit anywhere your little heart desires.'' She helped Donetta to her feet. ''Although I'd like to know who you're talking to in the bathroom besides us girls.''

They nearly crashed into Sunny and Becca on their way out. Tracy still had her arm around Donetta as though she might faint dead away at any moment.

''Oh, my gosh. What happened?'' Sunny asked, out of breath. ''I had to stuff a poodle in a cage, but I got here as quick as I could. Are you hurt?''

''No,'' Donetta said. Since the veterinarian's office was just up the street, it had taken Sunny mere minutes to cover the distance.

Tracy Lynn herded her forward. ''Shoo. Give us room. We're not discussing Donetta's problems in the bathroom.''

Sunny and Becca reversed direction.

Donetta was getting that ridiculously weepy feeling

again, and it made her testy. "I can walk, Tracy Lynn. I'm not an invalid. I'm just pregnant!"

Tracy let go so fast that Donetta nearly fell face first on the floor. She was spared that indignity because Sunny and Becca skidded on their boot heels and whirled around, causing a four-way pile-up. A pile-up that turned into a silent group hug, arms linked waist to waist, heads bowed, foreheads touching.

For a long moment Donetta simply drew strength from her friends as a vibrant current flowed through their circle of four. Then, her head still bowed, she rolled her eyes upward, and saw that Becca, Tracy and Sunny were trying to see past their eyebrows, as well—all of them focused on her.

She bit her lip and grinned. "Hey. How are y'all this morning?"

Becca was the first to recover from their huddle. "All righty, then. We need tea. And biscuits. I'll brew. We'll sit. Donetta, you will spill your guts—*not* in the manner in which you just did," she said before Donetta could make a wisecrack.

Before Becca could move, her cell phone rang. She glanced at the caller ID, then at the front window, where Storm was standing, surrounded by Jack and Linc Slade, Gavin Hayes, Colby Flynn and Jerald Randolph.

"My Lord, there's a cowboy convention out on the very sidewalk," Becca said, and lifted the tiny phone to her ear. "Storm—"

Sunny plucked the phone out of Becca's hand. "Storm, this is girl talk. Why are you all pacing like—"

Donetta snatched the phone out of Sunny's hand. "Storm..." She turned her back to her friends and to the front window, as well. She felt silly talking to him on the phone when he was standing right outside.

"Are you okay?" he asked. "That's all I want to

know. And what the hell is wrong with Becca, locking the door in my face like that? And then my sister rushing in…''

''Sugar, that's more than one question.'' She smiled at his frustration and leaned against a shelf of children's books. ''It's just baby fits, and the bathroom's torn up at the salon. Honestly, y'all are going to draw a crowd and have the media here if you don't disperse. Tell Jack Sunny's fine. Becca decided we needed a Texas Sweethearts roundup.''

Through the phone she heard him talking to the men, lying through his teeth about Donetta and Sunny being late for a meeting they'd forgotten about, then telling the guys he'd see them back at the salon. Static crackled in her ear as he shifted the phone.

''Why did Becca lock me out?''

''I told her to.'' She waited out the silence, then faced him and walked toward the front of the store. He was holding a cell phone to his ear, scowling at her. The men had left. Only a locked glass door separated them.

She didn't know what imp got into her, but she couldn't resist poking at him. ''Did anybody ever tell you how cute you are when you're mad?''

He stared at her as though she'd lost her mind. Then his face relaxed into a really sexy, fun-loving, smile-with-me kind of smile. ''No, darlin', I don't believe anyone has ever told me that. Thank you. I would love to return the compliment, but somehow I think it'd get that temper of yours stirred up.''

''Mmm. I like intelligence in a man. Admirable trait. Nice gene to pass along, too. Now, go fix my salon.''

''I'd rather take you home.'' He didn't need to elaborate on what he wanted to do with her at home—his tone was suggestion enough.

She winked, even though her heart was thudding. ''I have my own ride, thanks.''

"Pretty brave with this glass between us, aren't you, Slim?"

She kept forgetting that her aloof seductress act was no match for his masculinity. Darned if she would let him know that. Her smile was sassy, still flirty. "Say goodbye, Storm."

"Wait!" He put his hand on the glass. "Will you be all right? They're going to ask questions, you know." His voice softened. "Do you need me?"

Do you need me? Oh, yes, she thought. In so many ways. She resisted the urge to fit her hand to his against the glass. So close, yet separated. That was how it would be for them. There had always been uncrossable boundaries between them, limits set by age or by distance or by her marriage. For her own peace of mind, the boundaries had to remain.

"I'll be okay. The girls know about the baby. Will it bother you that they'll know you're...you know?"

"The father? No. But I'd have preferred to have a better understanding of our plans before my sister and your pals do. Think about it, Donetta. I'm standing on a sidewalk, talking to you on a cell phone, and there's a plate-glass window and locked door between us."

She *had* been thinking about it. And now she also saw what a master he was at disguising his emotions, because his green eyes tightened at the corners, a hot lick of anger escaping before it was sucked back under strict control.

"Storm. You will be the first one I discuss plans with." As soon as she figured out what they were. "We'll talk when you get home, okay?"

He nodded. "You're going to go straight home and get some rest after this?"

She'd gotten out of the habit of accounting for her time, and for a hair of an instant, his question—which was part demand—made her spine stiffen. She shook away the defensiveness and nodded. Then her eyes widened.

''What?'' he asked, alarm in his voice.

''Hang up! Here comes Miz Lloyd in her Bonneville.'' She disconnected, reached for the roller shade hidden beneath the cabbage-rose Victorian valance and pulled the shade down right in his face. Tracy Lynn, Sunny and Becca must have seen the same thing, because they were also yanking down the shades of the front window. Becca got the Closed sign flipped on the door and the last shade drawn just as Millicent Lloyd wheeled her boat-size '65 Pontiac into her usual diagonal parking space directly in front of Becca's Attic.

''Well, that was close,'' Sunny whispered, brushing at the springy blond curls that had escaped her ponytail. ''Not that I have anything against Millicent, but after the commotion at your salon yesterday, you know Darla Pam will be racing here with her chops drooling as soon as she sees the Bonneville. She'll have to make sure Millicent doesn't know anything new that she hasn't yet heard about. She was in the café last night after you and Storm left—Darla Pam, that is—flapping her jaws. Mama wanted to knock her off the stool.''

Donetta bit her lip and looked around at her friends, who all sat slumped as if they'd just finished a ten-K run. They shared a smile. ''I say we lend Anna a hand—or some knuckles.''

''Let's not be bloodthirsty,'' Tracy Lynn admonished. ''Donetta, you gave up that behavior when you were twelve—''

''Fourteen,'' she admitted. ''Kate Brinn. And it wasn't a fight. I only bumped into her by accident and she fell head first into her open gym locker.''

''I knew it was you!'' Becca said, letting out a peal of laughter. Everyone shushed her and listened to see if Millicent was at the door. Not hearing anything, Becca motioned toward the small room at the back of the store, which boasted four bistro tables with wooden chairs, and a limited coffee and sweets bar, and they all filed in.

''Having the fire department show up in the girl's locker room to get Kate's hair unstuck was so priceless,'' Becca said, filling a plate with biscuits and scones.

Donetta gave an innocent shrug. ''She called you a flat-chested ho. What was up with that?'' Becca had a great body, but all four of the girls had still been virgins at fourteen. ''I offered to cut her hair loose for her. I *told* her I was going to go to beauty school, but she wailed like a baby.''

''You might have shared this with us,'' Sunny complained, laughing. ''Kate gave every girl in school dirty looks from then on and claimed someone was practicing witchcraft. And since we're on the subject of secrets...'' She pointedly looked down at Donetta's stomach.

''Yes, let's sit,'' Tracy Lynn said, ever the hostess. After nursing her mom through the final stages of cancer, she'd taken over as hostess for her father and his political entertaining. A position at which she excelled.

Becca put mismatched china cups and saucers on a tray, added the teapot that was steeping apricot tea and set the arrangement on the table they all sat around. Her short black hair fell forward as she bent over to pass out utensils. Maroon highlights sifted through the ebony strands, which slid perfectly back into place when she straightened. Darn good haircut, Donetta thought, admiring her own work.

Becca poured the tea, passed out the cups and sat. ''Here's to all four of us closing up shop before lunch. May Donetta make it worth our while.'' They lifted their cups.

''Here, here,'' Sunny said. ''I didn't think she could top Debbie Taggat's haircut, but I stand corrected.''

''*Debbie* Taggat?'' Tracy asked. ''Isn't that Drucilla's *dog?* The little mop that shivers incessantly?''

'''Fraid so,'' Donetta said, then glanced at Sunny. ''If she came in needing stitches, it wasn't from me.''

''No stitches. Worms. I just noticed the cute pompoms and recognized your work.''

''Gee, thanks.''

Sunny grinned and lifted her teacup. ''Okay, now that we've given you enough space so you won't clobber one of us for fussing, would you please repeat what we thought we heard you say?''

''You heard me. Otherwise we wouldn't be sitting here pretending to drink tea like civilized ladies. I'm pregnant.''

''Is this a good thing?'' Tracy asked quietly.

In other words, Donetta thought, well versed in reading her friends, how did she want them to react? Was this a commiseration party or a celebration party? They'd be on board for either one without a second's hesitation.

She swallowed against the ache in her throat, placed her hand at her stomach and glanced at the women, who waited without judgment. It had been Sunny's idea to form their Texas Sweethearts club back when they were nine, and Donetta had suspected it had been her friends' way of making her feel she *belonged* somewhere. That day had cemented a bond among the four little girls that was still as strong as ever in womanhood.

''It's a good thing,'' she said softly.

''Hot damn! We're going to have a baby to spoil!'' Becca rubbed her hands together.

''Is the daddy in the picture,'' Tracy asked, ''or are you going the single-mother route?''

Donetta shoved her bangs back off her forehead. The three women beaming at her had burst into celebration mode as one. Small wonder someone hadn't whipped out the knitting needles.

"This is the tough part. He's in the picture, but…" She glanced at Sunny, then back down at her cup of tea as though the bits of leaves floating on top would tell her what to say. "But I'll be going the single-mother route."

"Why?" Sunny asked, the light of battle sparking in her green eyes. "He doesn't want to step up to his responsibilities?"

"No, he *does* want to. It's me. I can't go through that again, you guys. I have my salon. My life was perfect—it can still be perfect with the baby, too. But I can't tie myself to another man." She wasn't kidding herself. Her friends were dancing all around the subject of the father, yet they were all speculating because of the scene with Storm.

She had to admit it flat-out sooner or later. Dropping her forehead into her hands, she said, "I can't believe I slept with Sunny's brother!"

Chapter Ten

The only sound for several minutes was the jackhammer two doors away at her salon.

"Well?" Donetta finally asked.

Becca shrugged. "I'm fine with it. I'm just trying to picture it."

"Same here," Tracy Lynn said. "I had a little trouble with the brother issue until I realized I was casting myself in the role rather than you. Now that I have it straight, I think it's absolutely perfect."

"It does take some getting used to," Sunny remarked. "Especially the way the two of you bicker."

"You guys. It's *not* perfect. And we're not going to picture it or get used to it. You three have been the sisters I never had. You even shared your families with me. We know one another to the core...." She shoved at her hair. Lord, this was difficult. She didn't know how to explain.

"Tracy, I know how desperately you want a baby." Her voice shook, and she cleared her throat. "This has got to be hard for you, considering the timing." Tracy had received the news two weeks ago that her in vitro procedure hadn't been successful. "I just want you to know, I understand."

"Oh, Donetta. No." Tracy leaned forward, snatched

Donetta's hand and held it in both of hers. "I don't begrudge you your baby."

"I know," Donetta assured. "I really do. You just want one of your own, too. And it'll happen. But you're going to torture yourself if 'why not me?' thoughts pop into your head, and you'll keep it inside and feel like a guilty traitor and not want anyone to notice because you think it'll make you look selfish or awful...and I'm trying to tell you to just *don't.* Okay? Just don't do that!" Donetta's eyes filled with tears. She wasn't sure who was more startled—her or the three women staring at her.

"Holy crud," Sunny whispered.

Donetta gave a watery chuckle. "Don't make a big deal. This hormonal thing is the pits, but you'd better get used to it. Tracy Lynn's going to be cryin' in her teacup before long." Starting a family before she turned thirty was a promise Tracy had made to herself, something she'd talked at length about to her mother before Chelsa Randolph had died. Since she'd be turning thirty on Christmas Eve and she didn't have a husband on the hook, she'd chosen to pursue her dream via in vitro fertilization.

She looked at Tracy. "I don't know why in the world I ended up pregnant first, but I expect you to catch up. We're going to throw you that baby shower on your birthday—regardless of how many stripes show up when you pee on the damn stick."

Tracy swiped at her own tears. "What would I do without you guys?"

"You *couldn't* do without us, so don't even think about it," Donetta said. "That's what I mean about knowing someone. Most men only let you see the surface of who they are—except for maybe Jack with you, Sunny." She glanced down at the simple wedding band on Sunny's finger.

"We use our judgment," she continued, "and intuition, and we usually figure them out sooner or later. But I'm a prime example that surprises can jump up to bite you on the butt. I can't take another chance on what I see or feel on the surface. I need ironclad guarantees—and sadly, they don't exist."

"Are you saying you think Storm is like Tim?" Sunny asked. "That he would hurt you?"

"No." She sighed. "That's not the point. He's a really strong guy, yes. And he's assertive. But I'm not afraid of him." Forgetting her up-do, she speared her fingers through her bangs and sent a bobby pin sailing. "I don't want to get married again. I'm happy with my life—"

"You said Storm isn't the problem," Tracy interrupted, retrieving the bobby pin from the floor. She glanced at Sunny, then back to Donetta. "Do you not...like him in that way?"

"No. I mean yes." She could hardly think straight. "It's not that—"

Becca pounced, clearly determined to get a confession before the moment was lost. "So you *do* like him."

Donetta slapped her palms on the table, rattling the teacups no one was drinking from. "Would y'all just listen? If anyone could change my mind about marriage, Storm would be the primary candidate. But Sunny just remarked about how we butt heads. We both want to drive the bus, and there's only one set of keys." She shoved the bobby pin back in her hair.

"Right now, our disagreements are mostly teasing. But what if we were together twenty-four/seven? Would the conflicts start to get old? Wear down our nerves and tolerance for each other? What if some weird deep-down trait surfaces that one of us decides we can't stand and it becomes an irreconcilable difference? All of you would be forced to choose between us."

"Like how?" Sunny asked, a frown of bewilderment marring her brow.

"Like Cindy did when I left Tim. You were there, Sunny. She couldn't maintain a comfortable friendship with me *and* her brother." The memory still had the power to sting. "Think about the strain it would put on the holidays. We've been one big happy family all these years. Friends. I don't know a quicker way to screw up a friendship than sex and love. How about you girls? Sunny, you're excluded from answering because you're incapable of seeing past the newlywed stars in your eyes."

Sunny rolled her eyes.

"Donetta has a point," Becca said. "Don't glare at me like that, Tracy Lynn. I didn't say it was the *right* point."

"So, what does Storm want?" Sunny asked.

"To do the right thing. But what *is* the right thing? A little over a month ago, I went to his place on an errand for your mom and somehow we ended up horizontal. The next morning, I said, 'Yikes, that wasn't smart. Let's keep things on a friends level.' He called me a few days later to make sure I was really serious about the 'just friends' part. Other than running into him on occasion at the café or the post office, I hadn't talked to him again until yesterday, when he came in and locked me out of my shop and my apartment. Now, is there anyone sitting at this table who wants to wage an argument for love over duty?"

No one made a peep.

"I don't need a man to do his duty by me. Especially a man I've loved all my life—as my friend," she quickly added, kicking herself for getting carried away. "I just want everything to go back to normal."

"Normal, except with a baby added," Sunny said. "Mama's going to be tickled. First Tori, now this baby. She can thumb her nose at Trudy Fay Simon, who's always going on about her grandkids, and do some more bragging of her own.''

Donetta bit her bottom lip. ''Can we hold off for a little while on telling your mom? Or anyone else, for that matter. I want to talk to Grammy before the gossips get ahold of the news, and she won't be home for another two weeks. Lord, I don't want to disappoint her. I was her second chance to get it right after Mom turned out the way she did. Now here I am, pregnant and ripe for another scandal in Grammy's life.''

''Betty can handle anything those old gossips and busybodies dish out,'' Tracy Lynn said. ''There's no shame in raising a child as a single mom if that's what it comes to, though I hope you and Storm can work something out.''

''Regardless,'' Becca said, ''we're behind you. If anyone so much as looks at you cross-eyed, they'll have us to deal with.''

''Absolutely,'' Sunny agreed. ''Becca Sue will hold 'em, I'll punch 'em out and Tracy Lynn will tell them exactly how the cow eats the cabbage.''

Donetta laughed. ''Well, we're a regular force to be reckoned with, aren't we?''

''I hope to shout.'' Tracy Lynn fluffed her blond hair, and the gold bracelets on her wrist jingled. ''However, you don't get off this easy, Donetta Dawn. Getting pregnant by accident is a definite panties-on-Bertha offense.''

Donetta's jaw dropped. Her friends were all grinning and nodding. ''Not so fast. We can't make any decisions without Tori's vote. What a shame that she's still in school.''

''As her mother,'' Sunny said, ''I have her proxy. Panties on Bertha, Donetta.''

She remembered Storm's claim of buying the Anderleys' place because of the panty tree. The view from his kitchen window was going to have some color added. She looked at Tracy Lynn.

"Well then, I vote that *intent* to get pregnant out of wedlock constitutes a trip to Bertha, as well. All in favor?" Becca's and Sunny's hands shot up.

"Closing the store during business hours," Sunny said to Becca. Tracy, Donetta and Sunny raised their hands.

"Stuffing Dru Taggat's poodle in a cage and leaving her alone with worms in her butt," Becca fired back. Donetta, Becca and Tracy Lynn's hands went up.

The tea was stone-cold, but the laughter warmed Donetta. "Since Storm shanghaied me to his guest room after padlocking my house, I don't have very far to go to reach Bertha."

"Don't gloat." Sunny dipped the edge of a scone in her tea. "You're handicapped, so we would have had to pick you up anyway. Now that I'm a married woman, though, I don't think I should be flashing my behind in broad daylight, so I'm voting for midnight tomorrow—"

"Wait a minute," Tracy said. "You mean we're not going to just bring an extra pair in our pocket?"

"Did you ever cheat and do that?" Donetta asked.

"No. But we were girls then."

"Oh, and I suppose we're ready for walkers and hearing aids now?" Sunny batted her lashes at Tracy Lynn. "I say midnight tomorrow. How about the rest of you? Anybody too old to stay up that late?"

Tracy Lynn crossed her arms and leaned back with a smirk on her face. "Look at your own self when you say that, Mrs. Slade. You and Donetta are the mothers in the group now—and have already hit the big three-O, I might add. Becca Sue and I are still spring chickens."

"Midnight it is," Donetta said, before anyone's claws came out. A mother. This was the first time she'd truly thought about herself as someone's mother. It was amazing. And scary as all get out.

DONETTA WAS BACK AT Storm's house before noon. With men crawling all over her salon, toting power tools, she'd decided they could do without her input today.

Juggling two grocery sacks, she let herself into the house through the kitchen door—and stopped dead in her tracks.

"Good night!" If Dixie hadn't trotted forward to meet her, she might have jumped to the same conclusion Storm had last night at her apartment—that someone had broken in and tossed the place. She set the bags on the counter and headed toward the living room, half afraid of what she would find.

It was worse. The bags of clothes she hadn't yet unpacked were strewn from the bedroom to the kitchen and all parts in between. Pandora streaked past her and leaped onto the back of the sofa.

"How did you get out of the bathroom?" Pandora ignored her, the tip of her tail swishing along the back of the couch.

Wonderful. She hadn't even been here twenty-four hours and his place was wrecked. She suspected this was Sneak's and Pandora's work.

Dixie leaned against her leg as though expecting she might need a little help standing. She glanced down at the shepherd, whose eyebrows shifted over velvety brown eyes as she divided her attention between Donetta and the two menaces in the living room.

"Don't look so upset, Dixie. I know you're not involved, and I don't hold you responsible. It would take a bigger woman than either one of us to sit on those two maniacs. I'm sure you did your best, girl." She patted Dixie and scowled at Sneak and Pandora. Without an ounce of apology, Sneak panted happily, her ears flopping as she whipped around to see what Pandora was doing. The spoiled cat was daintily grooming herself, causing the bell on her collar to jingle.

"As if you're too good to get down here and clean up your mess?" she said to the cat. "Storm is going to have a hissy fit if he sees this."

Sneak barked and snagged a pink tennis shoe with angora laces. Dixie shot forward, showing that she hadn't forgotten her assertiveness training, after all. Sneak wisely dropped the shoe and ran.

"I'm really not in the mood to clean up this mess, you guys." She stuffed clothes back into bags that weren't ruined by teeth or claw marks, noticing that the heavy-duty trash bags were the only things that had sustained any real damage. The clothes, shoes and hair accessories she picked up were wrinkled but unharmed. She dragged several bags to her bedroom, came back, frowned over a sack of old cosmetology books and supplies, and decided to shove those into the coat closet.

It hardly looked as if she'd made a dent in the mess, when she remembered the groceries and had to stop to put them away. She managed to stow the perishables, but when she unwrapped the butcher paper on the filet mignons, the aroma did something horrible to her system. She barely got the steak shoved in the fridge before afternoon sickness sent her racing for the bathroom.

THE SUN HAD ALREADY SET by the time Donetta climbed out of bed, feeling halfway human again. She splashed cool water on her face, ran a brush through her hair and slicked on nude lip gloss, then headed toward the kitchen to brew some tea. The house was dark, but the hallway was an unobstructed trek from end to end, so she didn't bother with the lights until she got to the dining room.

She groaned, remembered the mess and shifted her body into high gear. She had no idea what time it was, but she didn't want Storm coming home to this chaos—especially since he knew she'd been here most of the day.

Rushing into the kitchen, she hit the light switch just as the back door opened. Too late.

Storm stopped in his tracks—as she'd done earlier. His hat shot up a good inch as his hairline shifted. He looked around the room. His gaze finally came to rest on Donetta. "Was anybody hurt?"

She nearly laughed, but her heart was racing and she was half sick worrying about his reaction to the condition of his house.

"Not yet." She snatched up a black silk top and a purple sandal. "A certain little dog and sulky cat are dancing with the devil's girlfriend, though." She retrieved her contour eye shadow brush from beneath the chair and set it on the table. "My afternoon nap ran a little longer than scheduled. I haven't had a chance to get everything picked up."

He nodded and stepped right over a pile of shoes. He didn't kick them out of the way or get all torque-jawed. "You needed the rest. I'm going to grab a quick shower."

He seemed in an awful hurry to get away from her. And the kitchen and dining room were only a teaser compared with the rest of the house—unless she'd managed to gather up more than she'd realized.

He passed by her, and she fell into step two paces behind him, carefully moving with him, timing her footsteps with his. She peered around his wide shoulders when he flipped on the hall and living room lights. Yes, the front room still looked pretty bad. Her feet were already in forward motion, when he stopped abruptly and turned around.

"I forgot to—" His words slammed to a halt at the

same time her lip gloss wiped itself on the collar band of his T-shirt. His hands shot out to steady her.

And didn't she feel like the biggest fool? "Um...what did you forget?" She cleared her throat and nonchalantly tugged at the hem of her scoop-neck tank top as though she hadn't just stealthily crept behind him like Lucy Ricardo trailing Ricky. Storm followed the movement, his gaze settling on her breasts for longer than was strictly polite.

"Is there a reason I'm wearing your lipstick on my shirt—when I'd much rather have it on my mouth?"

"Can't think of one offhand." She looked away, partly because she was fibbing and partly because now he'd made her think about kissing.

"So, why are you nearly riding piggyback?"

"I was probably getting a peek at the living room... to see if it was as bad as I thought. I promise, I really did haul three or four bags out of here."

"Oh, I believe you. Especially since I don't see a single one of the animals."

"You're right. I didn't even realize. Where are those stinkers?"

"Probably hiding under the billiard table, thinking we won't see them even though they're in plain sight. Do me a favor? Next time you're clinging to the back of my shirt and there's a chance for one of these close encounters, could you aim a little higher with your mouth?" He winked, then headed down the hall toward his bedroom.

Her heart beat double time—and not because of worry over a messy house. She wanted to follow him right into his bedroom and give his suggestion a try. She figured he could take it from there.

And she was an idiot. That was how they'd gotten into this mess in the first place. A kiss. A really, *really* fabulous kiss. If she'd kept her lips to herself to begin with, they could have had a very nice friendship and she wouldn't be worrying about what might jerk his trigger finger, or which disagreement would be the breaking point that sent out wider shock waves, far past the two of them, and forced loved ones to take sides.

AFTER HIS SHOWER, Storm came out of his room carrying a pink bra, a silk pouch filled with makeup brushes and one black sandal with a five-inch stiletto heel.

"This could end up as an ongoing Easter egg hunt," he muttered, stepping into Donetta's room and distributing the items where he guessed they belonged—drawer, closet and bathroom. Some of her things had been put away and some were draped halfway over a hanger or drawer, as if she'd had to abandon the task in a hurry. Man alive, he didn't know how the woman was still standing. It was as though she had the walking flu.

He knew she'd had a rough day, and he didn't care if she left every article of clothing she owned hanging from the ceiling fans, but he couldn't help thinking she was testing him. Her comment about aligning the silverware with a ruler kept coming back to him.

He wanted to know more about that. Maybe his curiosity was morbid, but the sooner he had all the blanks filled in, the sooner he could figure out what the heck he was doing wrong with Donetta. Because right now he felt that he was missing the target completely, and he hadn't even gotten to the firing range.

As he walked down the hallway, he smelled food. The cat, he noted, was perched on his stereo in the living room—she must have felt safe enough to come out of hiding.

In the kitchen, Dixie was sprawled on the cool tiles, politely staying out of the way. Sneak dogged Donetta's every step, making herself a four-legged tripping hazard.

She scooped up the little dog and rained kisses on Sneak's head.

"Now, I don't go that far in spoiling her," Storm said.

She jumped and whirled around. "You scared the daylights out of me!"

"Sorry. You think that mutt deserves all that affection after what she did to your clothes and my house?"

"I don't hold a grudge. Besides, who could resist this face?"

"*My* face isn't so bad." He grinned when she rolled her eyes at him. "Are you cooking?"

"Not exactly. I'm warming a can of soup. There's salad and sliced fruit in the fridge, and if you'll take this menace, I'll get the bread out of the oven." She passed Sneak to him, her hands tangling with his as the dog wiggled in excitement.

"I had better intentions for feeding you after you worked at my salon all day, but me and that raw steak couldn't seem to get along. So you get soup."

"I didn't know we had steak."

"I stopped at the market on my way home. It looked innocent enough in the store. The trouble started when I unwrapped it. The smell laid me out flat for hours—and it was fresh." She donned oven mitts and removed a small loaf of steaming bread, then transferred it to the top of the stove.

Storm wondered if she realized she'd called this "home." He opened the door to the service porch and set Sneak down, snapping his fingers for Dixie, as well. "Look-a-here. Someone's already filled your supper bowls. You girls go eat, and then play outside for a while."

He shut the door, then went over and reached for bowls in the cupboard above Donetta. His body practically caged her against the stove. A scant inch and the sweet curve of her behind would be snuggled into his groin. That was one of the things he loved about Donetta's height. She fitted him perfectly.

She went absolutely still for a moment, then surprised him with a sharp elbow to his gut.

"Oof. All you had to do was say 'excuse me' and I would have moved," he complained, and backed away to set the bowls on the counter.

"Did I ask you to come messing in my kitchen?"

"Actually, darlin', I believe it's *my* kitchen."

"Not when I'm cooking in it. That falls under squatter's rights or something. So sit down while I'm in upright mode. You never know when that'll change."

"I have a better idea." He took the bread knife out of her hand and turned her toward the table. "Why don't I take back the ownership deed and you sit." He guided her to a chair and sat her down without giving her a chance to argue.

He dished up the salad and fruit, then stowed the leftovers back in the refrigerator before he ladled soup. Once he'd put the food on the table, he joined her.

"How'd it go at the salon this afternoon?" She started on her salad and fruit, waiting for the soup to cool.

"It went good. The extra help made a big difference. All the demolition work is finished."

"Demolition? You make it sound like they knocked down the building. Please tell me I'm not going to go in tomorrow and find the place gutted."

He grinned. "It's not gutted, Slim. But the floors and walls are opened up so the work can begin now." He pointed his fork at her bowl. "You're just playing with that. At least drink the broth."

She took a sip. "So, what do you think it'll take? A couple more days?"

He almost choked on a swallow of soup. "Uh, no. We're still looking at a couple of *weeks*."

Her stomach knotted, and she decided she'd had

enough to eat. She pushed her plate away, sipped at her glass of water and watched as Storm finished the rest of his meal.

''I told you this wasn't going to be a quick process,'' he said softly.

''I know. I'm just impatient. When I see that many men working on a construction project...'' She shrugged. ''I'm building it much faster in my mind.''

He scooted his chair back from the table. ''Come on, let's go sit someplace where it's more comfortable.''

She stood and picked up her plate. He whisked it out of her hands. ''You cooked. I'll clean. Later.''

He'd already put away the perishable food. ''That's a deal. I won't refuse,'' she said.

''Thanks for making dinner. You didn't have to.''

She shrugged. ''I like to cook. Even if I didn't, you can't do too much harm to a can of soup.''

''Oh, I've managed a time or two. When I went back to Houston to tie up loose ends, I sat down and started reading the paper, and burned the canned stew so bad I had to throw out the pan.''

''You threw away the whole pan?'' She picked up the rest of the clothes and shoes decorating the living room floor and stacked them in a pile. ''You should have called your mom. She'd have told you to fill the pan with hot water, toss in a used fabric softener sheet and let it soak overnight. Works like a charm.''

''It was a cheap pan. No big loss.''

But what he'd been through in Houston could have been a very big loss. To all of them. She sat on the couch, studied him as he prowled the room.

''Are you ever bothered by...'' She shook her head. ''Never mind. That's not a good subject.''

''The shooting? I don't talk about it a lot, but I'm okay with it. I wouldn't be eager to go deep undercover again.'' He moved to the large picture window that overlooked the backyard and the lake beyond. ''When you're pretending to be one of the scumbags, you don't get to bring the Kevlar with you."

"What possessed you to go in before your backup got there?" The image of a bullet ripping through his flesh actually caused her a physical pain. "Do you always take risks like that?"

He glanced over his shoulder, brows raised. "Which one of those questions do you want me to address?"

Her eyes snapped to his. She couldn't judge his mood or his tone. It was almost as if he was upset with her because she didn't *know* these details. "Look, if you don't want to talk about it, just say so."

He turned back to the window and was quiet for so long she thought he'd decided the subject was off limits. Then he began to speak.

"The arrest was scheduled for the following day," he said. "A big shipment of guns was coming in, and I still had some surveillance equipment to activate. The posse expected me to be there. Things were heating up, nerves were strung out, tempers nasty. It was hell-hot, muggy, with mosquitoes big enough to saddle and ride. I didn't have a good feeling. Roy didn't, either—Roy was my partner," he explained. "Ranger Sergeant Roy McCann. But the weapons bust was my assignment. I had to check it out."

He rubbed the back of his neck as though he could still feel the sixth sense he should have paid attention to.

"Roy's wife was pregnant with their first child, and I didn't want him in the middle of whatever might be going down. If it was nothing, I figured we'd laugh it off in a couple of days when the case was buttoned up. I knew Roy would give me grief. He'd stick to me like flypaper and watch my back whether I wanted him to or not. He would step in front of me and take a bullet. I'd do the same for him."

Donetta watched him pace. He still maintained his

slow-walking, slow-talking demeanor, but she could see the tension, the veins that plumped on his hands and forearms, the taut lines bracketing his nonsmiling mouth.

"I told myself it was just the heat making me jumpy." He shoved his hands in his pockets and gazed out the darkened window. "Dark as pitch, the blacktop still hot enough to fry eggs, heat radiating off it and burning straight down your lungs. The locusts and the crickets didn't seem to mind. They sounded louder than I remembered. A monotonous two-tone that droned on, as if they were singing *safety* over and over."

Chills tingled over her arms. She got up and crossed the room to stand beside him at the window. She couldn't say why she did it, just that she wanted to be close in case he needed someone or something to anchor him here—to remind him he was in Hope Valley, not in Houston bleeding on a hot blacktop. She was almost sorry she'd started this, wanted to stop him, tell him she didn't need to hear any more, but something told her he needed this, to get it out.

"I had a gun in my boot and one at my back, shoved in the waistband. I reached around and took off the safety. That's when I should have listened to my body. The hair on my neck was standing up stiffer than a cat's back. I got as far as the door of the warehouse. Tereso Pallenzia met me. He was the leader. I knew right then he wasn't going to let me in. Behind him, I saw why. An INS officer—Immigration. I'd hooked up with him on a couple of border cases. He was working on one of his own now—to the tune of sixty million. He was cutting Tereso in on the deal. He'd seen me leaving the warehouse that morning." Storm rubbed a hand over his stomach.

"I knew Tereso would plug me, and I figured my only chance was to make sure it wasn't point-blank. Instead of retreating, I went in aggressive, got in a good round kick. I was still airborne, halfway into the spin-around from the kick maneuver. I had my hand on my weapon when the first bullet slammed into my back.''

Donetta jolted, clutched the sleeve of his sweatshirt, smoothed it, then slipped her palm over his back and rubbed, soothing them both.

''My gun was aimed when the next slug got me in the stomach.'' His tone changed, his forehead creasing as though his concentration was painful.

''My body had completed the revolution, feet had touched the ground. I didn't feel the third shot because it knocked me back. I managed to squeeze off four rounds. Three subjects went down. Then three more fell right after that.'' He shook his head. ''But I hadn't discharged my weapon. My vision wasn't so good by then.'' He glanced down at her. Her hand had stopped directly over his kidney scar, as if she'd walked every step of the nightmare with him.

''Funny, I didn't know I remembered all of this. I thought my recall stopped at the first shot and picked up with Roy cussing me up one side and down the other, bawlin' his eyes out.''

Donetta was on the verge of doing exactly that. She'd never met the man, but she liked Roy McCann just fine. If she took a squalling fit, she'd be in esteemed company.

''Go on,'' she urged.

''Not much more. I saw this big ol' shadow come streaking by, blending in with the night. Couldn't see him, just the fire shooting out of the ends of his Colts. Humph.'' He nodded in approval, as though he was watching Roy sprint across the backyard toward the lake.

''That son of a buck should've had somebody filming him for the TV. Feels like I'm remembering an old shoot-'em-up. Two Colts spitting like dragons, ol' Roy leaping over a hedgerow, a trash can…my body.'' His jaw went slack. "Well, I'll be go to hell. I'm going to kick his sorry butt from here into next week." His dark eyebrows nearly met as he planned pain and mayhem on Roy's body.

"I don't think I'm going to let you do that," Donetta said.

Storm, still frowning, looked down at her as though he'd forgotten she was there.

"At least, not before I have a chance to kiss him," she said. His eyes were now remarkably clear of nightmarish images. "And then," she added, "I'm going to help Roy kick *your* sorry butt into next *year.*"

His smile grew slowly. He took his hands out of his pockets. "You figure you can handle that, Slim?"

The lust in his eyes made her think of a tiger ready to pounce.

Donetta wisely took a step back. She'd intended to tease, to accept his challenge. But she could see by the slight narrowing of his eyes and the muscle clenching in his cheek that he'd misunderstood.

"Storm—"

"Why didn't you come when I was laid up?"

The quiet words stopped her in her tracks. Her heart squeezed, and there was guilt.

Chapter Eleven

"I was there," she said quietly. "After you had the surgery. I stayed with you all night. I talked to you about the Mavericks and Spurs game, the NBA block-buster trades. And about Sunny because she was dating that guy Michael in Los Angeles and I was worried about it. She seemed to be letting him take over her life, and at the time, I was neck deep in what a relationship like that could become."

He sat down in one of the tapestry-upholstered armchairs that angled toward the fireplace and nodded for her to sit, as well. His silence was patient, but not altogether comfortable. He rested his elbows on his thighs and leaned forward slightly, his body turned toward her.

"Your mom and Sunny were exhausted," she said. "The hospital set up beds for them in one of the rooms, but Sunny wouldn't budge. When I got there, she was curled on her side, lying across two folding chairs pushed side by side, and she had her hand over yours. She was insistent that someone hold your hand at all times. I mean really insistent, like militant—'I'll knock your head off if you don't listen to me' type thing. Not to me," she clarified. "To the nurses who came in to monitor you. I thought maybe I'd have to dig in her bag for a cow tranquilizer and shoot her with it."

The clock on the round mahogany table between them ticked in the stillness, its rhythm reminding her of the trailer park she'd lived in as a child. Tap. Tap. Tap. The slow, steady drip of rain from the gutter spout onto the piece of tin sheeting Donetta had put half under the trailer by the steps to shelter the baby frogs Mama didn't know she'd kept.

"Sunny needed sleep, and when I told her I was free until morning, she handed you off to me."

Chills raced up her arms as the words echoed in her mind. Maybe it was the hush in the room, but until just now, she hadn't considered the profound significance of Sunny relinquishing responsibility of that vigil to her. She'd been part of the family, the only one Sunny had trusted with her brother's life.

Storm still hadn't spoken. He just watched her. She wasn't sure what he wanted from her, what he was thinking, what he was feeling or waiting for.

Perhaps he simply wanted to know what went on around him in the world when they'd all been so afraid of losing him.

Remembering brought an ache to her throat. She'd loved him then, as he'd lain in that hospital bed clinging to life. She'd loved him when she was ten, and twelve, all the years after and in between.

She loved him still.

She'd said the words to him only once. That night in the hospital, when she was still married to another man, she'd whispered it into the palm of his hand, rested her cheek there. She'd come so close to breaking that night, and that would have been so dangerous. She had needed all her strength and mental resources to deal with Tim. Because she had known he would find out that she'd lied to him. That she'd stayed the night at the hospital with Storm.

And that's where her guilt had come from. She hadn't returned to the hospital as a friend or loved one would have. Not because she didn't want to. Because she *couldn't.*

''That's the night I started thinking about leaving Tim. So I talked to you about it. I didn't tell you any of the bad things. The doctors didn't understand why you weren't waking up after the surgery. I didn't want to upset you, even though I wasn't sure if you could hear me. And I didn't want you to hear my shame.'' When his muscles bunched, she knew he was poised to lean toward her, and she lifted her chin, put up the shield that came so naturally.

Censure shadowed his eyes, but he relaxed, forearms dangling between his widespread legs, elbows still propped on his thighs.

''I planned my future with you—not *with*...I mean, not us together.'' He nodded and she took a breath and continued. ''I told you about the salon I'd someday have, and about my marriage being a mistake. I probably talked as much for me as I did for you. I even revealed some of our Texas Sweethearts secrets—which was very bold of me then. The girls haven't sent me out to Bertha to give up another pair of panties, so I feel pretty confident those secrets are safe—unless you undergo hypnosis and spill your guts. Then we might have a problem.''

His lips twitched, but his watchful mask remained. Now his silence was really beginning to unnerve her.

''What is it, Storm? I'm running out of subjects. You seem to be waiting for something in particular. I can't read your mind.''

His chest rose and fell. ''I didn't know you'd come. I thought...I'm surprised no one told me.''

''Did you ask?''

He shook his head. ''I didn't want to admit that I was disappointed. And I guess I was probably afraid someone would notice how much I wanted—*needed*—

to see you. I felt like an ass. You were married.'' He shrugged. ''Did you come back after that night?''

''No.'' She rubbed her fingernail along the seam of her capris, smoothing the snagged tip she hadn't yet gotten around to fixing. ''Tim didn't like me spending time with your family—mainly, he didn't want me to see you.''

''It makes my heart hurt to think about what you went through. I know my sister wasn't living here when you were married, but didn't Tracy Lynn and Becca suspect something wasn't right? Didn't they notice any bruises?''

''Oh, Tim was smart enough to make sure the bruises didn't show. And he didn't like for me to hang out with my friends, so I didn't see Becca and Tracy much those two years.''

''What made you finally leave?''

''*Finally* leave? Ironic word choice. Don't you really want to know what kind of woman stays in hell for that long without plotting an escape?''

''Donetta. Don't. I've seen more than my share of domestic violence. I'm not judging you.''

''Sorry. I thought I'd put most of this out of my mind.'' She took a deep breath. ''I didn't want to be a failure like my mom. I didn't want to disappoint Grammy.''

She looked down, picked at the chip in her fingernail, then began to speak, her voice so soft Storm had to lean in to hear.

''I made manicotti—Tim's favorite, set the table with candles. Everything was perfect. Nothing was out of place. The pans were washed and the sink was scoured. I just had to remove the bread and manicotti from the oven, take the salad out of the fridge. I had some stupid idea that at last things were going to get better, that we just needed something more to draw us together.''

She looked up and met his gaze with a steadiness that made his heart squeeze. "This probably sounds pretty pitiful to you—"

"No. Netta—"

"It does to me. I wasn't the same person then. I'd let him take away every bit of my self-esteem. Anyway, we'd never talked about having a family—Tim was busy positioning himself for promotions at the bank. That night I told him I wanted to have a baby, asked him how he felt about starting a family.

"He didn't say anything. He got up from the table to get the dessert out of the fridge. Apple tarts. I remember I'd run the first batch down the disposal because the crusts hadn't aligned perfectly."

Storm wanted to reach for her hand, hold her, but intuition told him she wouldn't appreciate the contact just now.

"I knew something wasn't right when he went quiet like that, when he *offered* to get up and get the dessert. Tim enjoyed being served. I should have run like hell. Instead, I jumped right up and raced into the kitchen when he called my name." She crossed her arms over her stomach.

"It makes me so mad now when I think of that night. The apple tarts were still in the fridge. He had no intention of getting them in the first place. He was standing by the stove. You'd have never guessed a meal had been cooked in that kitchen—the floors and counters actually gleamed. Then I saw what he'd been in there *searching* for. Two little dots of marinara sauce on the tile backsplash. He said how could I ask him to consider starting a family, how could he trust me to take care of a child, when I couldn't even wipe down a wall properly. He broke my ribs that night."

Storm swore and shot up out of his chair.

"The next morning, I had a miscarriage."

"Oh, my God. You were already pregnant?"

She nodded. "You asked what made me leave. That was it. I was still bleeding when I picked up the phone and called Sunny. I said three words—'I need help.' She didn't ask any questions. Told me to pick up my purse and drive straight to the airport. Like a puppet, that's exactly what I did. There was a plane ticket waiting at the counter."

"You didn't get medical attention?"

"Not here. They would have called Tim. Sunny drove me to the hospital as soon as I got off the plane in California."

He paced, raked a hand through his hair, then stopped in front of her and held out his hand. "I know you want to be tough—but I can't be. Will you come sit with me? I need to hold you."

She put her hand in his and stood, letting him draw her into his arms. They stayed that way for a long moment as he held her tight, rocked her, offered solace and heartfelt regret with the sketch of his lips at her temple. Donetta couldn't remember a time in her life that she'd felt so cherished…so safe.

He led her to the sofa, tucked her into the corner, then sat beside her and pulled her legs into his lap. Her eyes nearly rolled back in her head with pleasure when he began to massage her feet.

"Why didn't Sunny call me?" he asked.

"I made her promise not to. You were still recuperating from the gunshot wound. You didn't need any additional worries."

"I want to kill him, you know."

"Sometimes I think the same thing. But neither one of us will do that, because then we'd be in jail and he would win. And the 'Secret' in Donetta's Secret is truly what I told you before." She hadn't realized she was going to go into this, but he already knew about the abuse, so she could hardly be blamed for telling.

"I made a deal with Tim. His image and status are

very important to him. I could have let the whole town know who and what he is, but there was something I wanted more—my salon and the deed to Grammy's house.''

''The bank held the loan?'' he asked.

''No. Tim did. He gave Grammy a bunch of double-talk financial advice and ended up owning her house. Nice guy, huh? I wanted the title back, free and clear. I wanted a divorce settlement large enough to start my business, with the house as a separate package. I knew he'd fight me on splitting our assets, but I'd earned every penny of that money. At the cost of my self-esteem, maybe, but I got that back, too.'' This was the one part of her Tim episode that she was really proud of.

''I stayed with Sunny for two months. You were mending—I'd kept tabs. I called Tim from California, told him I wouldn't contradict him if he wanted to tell everyone he was the injured party and his beloved wife had gone off with another man and broken his heart. I did know that much about him. He wanted to save face at all cost, run with the big dogs. And he'd get more sympathy and pats on the back for holding up well if he was the victim.'' The rhythm of Storm's thumbs against the ball of her foot made her feel boneless.

''I'd come to the realization that *I* wouldn't be the victim. I had made my choices—bad ones—so I'd go on from there. And I promised to keep his dirty little secret. I'd taken pictures. I had evidence. Thank goodness I stuffed the photos in my purse before I went to the airport. I mailed him a very nice self-portrait a few days before I called him, so he knew I wasn't bluffing. He'd even left an incriminating paper trail by writing down one of his threats to Grammy.''

''People like that eventually do slip up.''

''I traded my silence for money, and my nightmare

for my dream. I've kept that secret—mostly. Sunny, Jack, Tracy Lynn and Becca know—and now you."

"Not my mom? Or your grandmother?"

"No."

"How can you still be loyal to a dirtbag like that?"

"I'm not being loyal, Storm. Rehashing all this with you is the most I've thought about that part of my life in almost two years. I just wanted to start with a clean slate. I didn't want people feeling sorry for me, or wondering how I could have stayed two years. Or comparing themselves with me, talking about what *they* would have done in my situation. If I'd been an outsider looking in at someone else's life, I would have believed what everyone else rightfully thinks. That there's no way I'd put up with that kind of crap. That I'd be out of there so fast the guy's head would spin." She gave a self-deprecating laugh. "People do talk a good game, don't they?"

"People also say don't condemn until you've walked a mile in someone else's shoes."

"Speaking of that, since you're not willing to take on these baby fits for me, weren't you going to try to work some magic on my brain and make it go away?"

"I don't plan to make your brain go away, darlin'. Just the baby sickness."

"Cute. If you can do it, though, you'll definitely be my hero."

"I like the sound of that." He squeezed her foot. "Hopefully, I won't have performance anxiety."

She laughed. "I'm not going to make the obvious comment on that one. I'll just warn you again that I'm not a good subject for hypnotism."

"Warning noted. Stretch out and get comfortable," he said, lifting her legs out of his lap and shifting so he was sitting on the edge of the couch, facing her. "Did the person conducting your previous session use a counting method?"

"Yes. And visualizing colors and warmth and pretty meadows."

"What did you feel?"

"Relaxed, but still distracted. Worried about being looked at when I wasn't looking back. Vulnerable, I guess. And I really wanted to get it right, but I felt I wasn't."

"The ability to concentrate is what allows hypnosis to work. Can you put yourself in my hands and trust me to keep you safe?"

"I hope so."

"Let's get a more positive dialogue going in your head, okay? The more your conscious mind resists, the more difficult it'll be to go under. I use a hands-on method, so I'll be touching you." He placed his palm over her forehead. "Like this. No farther down than your eyes. If at any time you feel scared, just raise your finger."

She tested her finger, then nodded. "Are we starting?"

"Not yet. I'll let you know when we're ready. You're not going to be in a trance or unconscious." He stroked the length of her arm, to her fingertips and back up, a gentle massage to soothe and relax. "You'll be able to hear everything I'm saying and whatever else is going on around us. And when we're finished, you'll remember everything that went on."

"If I'll be so aware, how do I even know if it's working?"

"You'll know. Close your eyes and relax for a minute, okay?" She felt the cushions on the couch shift as he got up. A minute later, the stereo switched on. The soothing sounds of the ocean's surf washed over the room as though replacing the very air.

She wanted to open her eyes, to see where he was. She experienced what a wild mustang might feel while lying down—vulnerable to predators.

Her eyes popped open. He wasn't staring at her. He was reading something on a piece of paper over by the oak bookshelves. She quickly shut her eyes so he wouldn't realize she'd been peeking. The sudden attack of nerves made her stomach churn. Well, at least she'd be able to tell if the experiment was working. If she didn't toss her cookies before the session was over, that would be a good sign.

She smelled the familiar scent of Storm's skin, felt his warmth an instant before the cushions by her elbow dipped. His palm rested across her forehead, growing hotter, an anchor of safety.

"Just relax," he said. "We're going to start now. Concentrate on my voice. Just my voice. You're safe."

His deep baritone calmed her. She tried to follow each of his suggestions, to visualize a specific time in her life when she'd felt unequivocally well.

She clung to his voice, and at times she was almost convinced she was feeling different, as though the hypnosis was working. So she struggled to examine the sensations with her fully conscious mind. Each time she did, Storm would patiently urge her to concentrate, remind her she was experiencing a peaceful easy feeling.

Storm eased the pressure of his hand on Donetta's forehead. He could tell she was resistant, that she was pretending. That was common—a patient wanting to please the therapist. But it wouldn't get her the healing she needed. And he couldn't force it. He brought her awake as though she'd been truly under, hoped that at least some of the suggestions he'd given her would help her to relax.

"Open your eyes, Donetta."

She looked up at him, and he smiled. "You did fine."

"But it didn't work."

He lifted her shoulders, scooted beneath her on the

couch, then laid her back over his lap, her head pillowed on the sofa's rolled arm. "What did you feel?"

"This is going to sound crazy. When you told me to relax and imagine a peaceful, easy feeling, the tune to an Eagles song popped into my head. You used to have their *Hotel California* tape in your truck, remember? It seemed to be playing every time you drove Sunny and me home from school. Weird association, I suppose, but I started humming it in my mind, and I might have been…distracted."

Storm didn't know whether to laugh or kick himself in the butt. He'd blown it. Next time—if there was one—he'd find different relaxation words. Words that weren't part of lyrics that worked a shared memory.

"What else?" He stroked her hair, watched the way the fiery red strands sifted through his fingers.

"I felt relaxed. A little dizzy. Scared. I kept wanting to examine how I was feeling, you know? Like part of me was standing off to the side, checking to see if I was really hypnotized or if I was faking. Am I your first failure?"

"No. My second." He felt her go still for a moment, then tense. "You okay?"

She moaned and sat up. "I really wish your remedy could have worked. Stay here." Her feet hit the hardwood floor and she was gone.

It was all he could do to keep from following her. And he couldn't help feeling as though he'd let her down. He was in the business of protection. Yet he hadn't protected Donetta from her slimy ex-husband. Or the contractor who'd taken advantage of her. And he couldn't protect her from the exhausting sickness of pregnancy.

He wanted to make it all up to her. But she was resisting him on every level.

He definitely had his job cut out for him. Teaching Donetta to trust wouldn't be easy. Nor would convincing her that her worries over having a committed relationship with him were groundless.

How could she think their twenty-five years together only made them skin-deep friends? Hadn't she remembered his Eagles tape? She'd told him Texas Sweethearts secrets—he was going to have to work on remembering that.

He didn't understand exactly what it was that she wanted. Did she think they could be close only if they'd lived in each other's back pockets the way she and Sunny did? Hell, that was what women had girlfriends for—the touchy-feely stuff.

He was scowling when she breezed back in the room. Then everything within him settled as though his world truly was in harmony. God, she was gorgeous. She held Sneak against her chest, her cheek rubbing the little dog's head.

The smile on her face captivated him. No matter what life had thrown her, she'd always bounced right back with a grin or a sassy remark. She kept her heartaches private. Never let them stop her from moving forward.

Hell of a woman.

He didn't want her to shoulder her burdens alone anymore. He wanted to be the man to share her load, ease her way, the one to put that sweet smile on her face every day for the rest of her life.

"What's up?" he asked when she still stood there grinning at him, her feet bare, her pants exposing tanned skin from her calves down.

"Sneak wants to know if she can sleep with me."

"Hell no." He bit the inside of his cheek, trying to keep a straight face. "Do you have any idea what that'll do to my ego if my dog gets to share your bed and I don't?"

Her grin turned playful, a hint of the seductress slipping in. Oh, man, he was a goner.

''She doesn't take up as much room as you do.''

''Want to bet? She hogs the covers. And she'll keep you up half the night.''

''And you wouldn't?'' she challenged.

''Only if you wanted me to, darlin'.''

The look in her eyes said she did. Yet she just picked up Sneak's paw and waved it at him. He had an idea he could change her mind with very little effort. And man, he wanted to. But that wasn't a good way to build her trust in him.

'''Night, she said softly. ''Thanks for trying with the hypnosis.''

He nodded and watched her disappear down the hall with his dog, wondered if he would manage to get any sleep at all. Checking the watch on his wrist, he noted that it wasn't quite ten o'clock. Roy ought to still be up. If not, he was about to be.

He punched in his ex-partner's home number. The phone barely gave half a ring before he was greeted by a surly male grunt.

''Sounds like your night's going worse than mine, pal.''

''Storm? Man, where've you been? You forget who your friends are?'' Roy paused for a moment. ''Uh-oh, hear that?''

''The baby crying?''

''Yeah,'' Roy said. ''Hold on, let me just sneak on out of the kitchen here like I got some serious Ranger business going on that needs doin' in the garage.''

Storm grinned when he heard Marnie call Roy's name, hollering that it was his turn with the baby when the phone rang at ten-damn-o'clock at night. ''Sorry. Did I get you in trouble?''

''Man, I'm always in trouble. That's just how I like it, too. Woman's got a lot of passion in her when she gets all het up. Tessa's sick with chicken pox, and she's one *very* cranky three-year-old. So, what's up with you?''

''I'm going to be a dad.'' Storm heard the sound of heavy plastic hitting concrete, then a string of curses. Trash can, he guessed. ''Stub your toe, pal?''

''What's wrong with you? Blurting something like that when a man's trying to tiptoe through the dark? You never said anything about a woman. Am I supposed to send cigars or black roses?''

''How about some of those wristbands Marnie used before she fell for my warm hands and deep voice.''

''Man, you better watch that kind of talk about you and my wife having a mind affair. I might have to mop up the floor with your white butt. And why do you want the bracelets? Your woman doesn't like your 'warm hands and deep voice'?''

''She's having my baby, isn't she?'' He let his tone speak for him. ''As for the hypnosis, she's a tough candidate. Way tougher than Marnie was.''

''Well, let's trot her past the Roy McCann test. What's her name? Can she cook? And is she smart?''

Storm smiled. Roy never asked about looks. His philosophy was ''You don't go by the outside package—but it's always nice if she's got a little meat on her bones.'' Donetta, however, was losing a lot of that ''meat'' due to morning sickness.

''Her name's Donetta Presley. She can cook—but that knowledge mostly comes to me secondhand, so it might not be admissible. She's very smart. Keeps me on my toes. Owns her own beauty shop. Five foot ten. Long red hair. I've known her since she was six—which would have put me at twelve and her definitely off limits. And she's anxious to meet you. She's got some notion that you're capable of kicking my sorry behind into next year, and she wants to partner up with you.''

Roy's booming laughter made Storm's grin stretch wide.

"Now, that is *my* kind of woman. So, how come you're not calling to invite me to the wedding? Man's gonna be a father he ought to marry the mama." There was the barest hint of censure in Roy's voice. He was a man who believed strongly in family and fidelity.

"It's complicated. But I'm working on it."

"You mean she's refusing the wedding ring? Oh, wait till I tell Marnie."

"Would you just get me the damn wristbands and put them in the overnight mail?"

"Hell, Storm. I might even drive them down myself."

"Not without your wife and kids, you won't. And as crazy as I am over my goddaughter, you're not exposing me to the chicken pox."

"I'm going to tell her you said that. Okay, I think Marnie still has a box of those bands she never opened after you worked your magic on her. I'll hunt it up and have it to you by tomorrow afternoon. And if you need a little help in the romance department, you just give me a call. I'll come show you how it's done."

"Over my and Marnie's dead bodies." He chuckled as Roy's laughter pealed again. "Thanks, pal. I'll owe you."

"Damn straight. And I like it when your account's heavier than mine—uh-oh. Gotta go. Mad woman heading this way carrying a crying baby. Later."

Storm disconnected. Roy and Marnie were like no other couple he'd ever met. The way they carried on, you'd think they were always fighting, yet one look and you could see how crazy they were over each other. For years, Storm had envied that relationship, wished he could find his match, as Roy had.

Now that he thought about it, he and Donetta had a few similarities to Roy and Marnie.

Had she been his match all these years and he'd never known it?

Chapter Twelve

"This isn't half-bad as a shampoo bowl," Katherine Durant commented.

Donetta directed the spray of water over the real-estate agent's hair, checking for inconsistencies in color and tone. With her friends' help, they'd managed to turn Storm's kitchen into a makeshift salon—although the project had taken them the better part of the day. The oblong kitchen table was pushed against the cabinets in front of the sink and padded with blankets and towels. She'd piled up pillows to form a slanted backrest and covered them with a plastic cape to keep them dry.

"Isn't it cool? I actually got the idea from Anna Carmichael. Whenever a bunch of us girls spent the night with Sunny on a Saturday, Mrs. C. would have us lie on the countertop with a towel rolled under our neck as a pillow, and she'd wash our hair in the kitchen sink. We all had to have clean hair for church."

"We were little girls, though," Tracy said, holding Sneak in her arms. Anna, Becca and Sunny had gone back to work, but Tracy Lynn had stayed all afternoon. Although she tried to hide it, Donetta knew darn well that Tracy was concerned over these frequent bouts of nausea. "I'm still worried about some of your older ladies climbing up on the kitchen table."

''The step stool works great,'' Kat assured her. ''Once they lean back with all these towels and pillows stacked under their neck and shoulders, they'll be in heaven.''

''That's good to know,'' Donetta said.

She tried to take shallow breaths because the smell of hair dye was causing her stomach to turn. For the hundredth time since last night, she wished that the hypnotism had worked. She felt as though she'd been put through the wringer and hung out to dry.

''I'd forgotten how close you are with Storm's family.'' Kat turned her head and nearly got an earful of water. ''Is that why you're living here with him?''

Donetta saw Tracy move in a step. She had to expect this type of question. Rumors were already flying around town, and now that she was doing hair out of Storm's house, there would be even more speculation. But she wasn't ready to discuss her private life. Granted, that was pretty much what went on in a beauty shop, but Donetta made a habit of listening rather than offering.

''Storm can be pretty bullheaded and protective about his friends,'' she said. ''Someone broke into my salon and now he insists I need a bodyguard. I guess that's the cynical nature of a cop. No big deal. Giving in was easier than listening to him predict horrible things that might befall me—or anyone else I stayed with. Plus, he doesn't trust Judd Quentin, my contractor.''

''I don't, either, if you want to know the truth,'' Kat said. ''I've had some deals fall out of escrow over permits that weren't recorded on structural improvements. I suspect Judd had a little under-the-table business going with our old fire marshal.''

''Storm thinks so, too. So here I am, all cozy in his guest room.''

Thankfully, Kat accepted the explanation. Donetta

knew the same question would arise time and again for the next few weeks. Her stomach pitched when she remembered that her living arrangements weren't the only thing that would be fodder for gossip in the coming months.

Lordy, the townsfolk were going to have a good old time speculating about her life. They'd have to hold a town hall meeting for this event, though. The salon was the usual spot to exchange gossip, but they couldn't very well dine on the owner in her own place of business.

"So who's your hot date with, Kat?" She shut off the water, wrapped a towel around Kat's hair and motioned for her to go sit back at the countertop bar, which she'd set up as her workstation.

Kat gave a wicked smile. "A broker I met at the real estate convention last week. I'm not sure if he's my type, but I thought I'd play with him a little."

"Girl, you're bad." Katherine Durant was only a couple of years older than Donetta. She was smart, gorgeous and seemed to have as much trouble hooking up with the right guy as Tracy Lynn did. It didn't make sense.

Kat sighed. "I talk a good game, anyway. Hopefully, this date won't conveniently forget his wallet the way the last one did. I don't mind paying my half. It's the whole pretense thing that gets to me."

"The financial adviser stiffed you with the check?" Tracy Lynn asked, aghast. She popped a Saltine in Donetta's mouth, giving her no choice to refuse since her hands were busy with the blow dryer. Tracy was determined to feed her past the morning sickness.

"Turns out he was actually unemployed," Kat said. "It's kind of tough to land a job when you've recently been in jail for running a telemarketing scam."

Donetta paused, chewed the cracker and swallowed.

''Advised people right out of their money, hmm? How'd you find out?''

''I put his name in a search engine on the computer.'' Katherine laughed at Donetta's widened eyes. ''Hey, you have to be careful these days. I want to know what's happened to all the good guys out there. I keep thinking about that song—'Where Have All The Cowboys Gone.' That's what I probably need.''

''The song?'' Tracy asked.

''No, the cowboy,'' Kat answered.

''Stop by my salon.'' Donetta took a sip of the sweet tea that Tracy offered, then picked up a round brush and directed the stream of heat to the tips of Kat's hair as she stretched and rolled the strands to give a smooth, silky style with a hint of curl at the ends. ''You'll find several cowboys there.''

''Oh, I drove by and peeked in. What an awful mess. I hope you're going to sue the pants off Judd Quentin.''

''I'm not thinking about lawsuits right now. I just want my salon put back together and open again.''

''It's a shame Judd did you dirty like that, Donetta. Speaking of construction, though. Have y'all seen the house Linc Slade's building out there next to Jack's?'' Kat asked. ''It's huge. And the horse stables look like something you'd see in a Kentucky horseman's magazine.''

''He breeds horses,'' Tracy said, flicking her blond hair behind her ear.

''And very successfully. Too bad he already owned property. That man has plenty of money to spend, and I'd have made a nice commission selling him a home. I wouldn't mind hooking up with him on a more personal level, either.'' Katherine Durant's graceful smile was reflected in the eight-by-ten free standing mirror Donetta had set on Storm's breakfast bar.

Donetta saw Tracy shoot a daggerlike look at Kat. What was up with that?

"You know what's really wild?" Katherine continued, oblivious to Tracy's glare. "He's building that huge estate and he's not even sure he's going to stay."

"Who said?" Tracy Lynn demanded.

"The man himself."

The back door opened as Donetta glanced up, shutting off her blow dryer. Dixie leaped to her feet and blocked the entrance, then wagged her tail and moved aside, deeming their guest welcome.

Donetta smiled. "Hey, Anna. I didn't expect to see you again today. Coffee's made if you want some."

Tracy let Sneak down and helped Anna with the sacks in her hands.

"No time, hon." Anna bustled in to load the refrigerator with food. "I'm on my way over to pick up Sunny and Tori, and I thought I'd drop off some supper so you wouldn't have to cook. I'm still worried about you pushing yourself like this when you've not been feeling well."

"I'm doing okay. Don't fret over me, Anna."

"Of course I'll fret. Honestly, *someone* has to worry about you. Now, if you change your mind and want to come with us to the picture show, just hop a ride with Tracy Lynn. Storm can pop this food in the microwave for his supper, and there will be plenty of leftovers."

"Anna, you're a sweetheart," Donetta said. "I'm still going to pass on the show. I've got too much organizing to do." Anna was taking Tori to Austin to see the new Disney film, and Sunny, Becca and Tracy Lynn had invited themselves, as well. Donetta had refused. She could just imagine smelling popcorn and spending the entire time in the rest room.

Sneak did her jumping trick, and Tracy scooped up the little dog again to coo and cuddle.

Someone knocked on the back door. "Trace, would you see who that is?" Donetta sprayed Kat's hair.

''Word must have spread if I'm getting walk-ins already.''

''Forget it,'' Tracy said, heading for the door. ''You're not doing any more clients today.''

Donetta had an urge to stick out her tongue, but she curbed it. ''You're all set, Kat.''

''I appreciate this. I didn't realize you weren't feeling well.''

''I'm fine. Tracy Lynn's just a nag.''

Donetta moved around to the sink, rinsed her application bottle, washed out the bleach bowl and threw away her used foils. When she didn't hear Tracy Lynn speaking to anyone, she glanced toward the door.

Lincoln Slade stood on the threshold, a large shipping box in his hands, his dark brown hat cocked slightly and tipped low on his brow. He was staring at Tracy, mute, and she was staring back.

A sense of dread washed over her for no reason. Her mind immediately jumped to Storm. The salon. Power tools and injuries.

''Linc?'' She was at the door in two seconds. ''Is everything okay?''

He tipped his head in greeting. ''Mighty fine. UPS dropped off this box for you. Thought you might need it.''

She let out a relieved breath and glanced at the shipping label. ''My product order from the beauty supply. Thank you. You didn't have to drive out here, though. Storm could have brought it with him. It's about time for him to get home, anyway, isn't it?''

Linc shrugged. ''Package came a few minutes after he left. He was over at the sheriff's office bird-dogging his deputies—somebody ought to teach the man what *vacation* means.''

Anna laughed. ''Well, if that isn't the pot calling the kettle black. I agree with you, of course, but you, young man, are even worse than my son.''

"Seems I recall you putting in some late nights at the café, Mrs. C."

Donetta laughed. "Come on in, Linc. You're not going to win that argument, so don't even try. Just set the box over there in the corner."

Linc followed her instructions, looked around the kitchen, nodding slightly, a half smile flirting with his lips. "You always were a resourceful woman, Donetta. I'm sure that's one of the qualities Storm appreciates about you."

Donetta's stomach lurched. Did he know about her and Storm? No. Even if Sunny had told Jack, neither one of them would have let the news go any further—even to Jack's brother. She had to calm down. Keeping a lid on this news until Grammy came home was going to be difficult. But she didn't want to tell Grammy over the phone, and she didn't want someone else blabbing the minute her grandmother stepped foot back in town.

"Do you think he'll mind that I rearranged the furniture?" she asked, tongue-in-cheek.

Linc ambled toward the door, glancing out the window. "Guess you'll find out in a minute. Looks like he just pulled up." He paused when he got to Tracy Lynn. Reaching out, he gave Sneak's ears a scratch, then winked and glanced toward the door that had just swung open.

Storm walked into his kitchen and stopped dead, feeling like a trespasser in his own house. Man alive. Boxes of hair dye were stacked on his countertop, the kitchen table was doubling as a recliner in front of the sink and the chairs to the dining set were lined against the wall. The air smelled of hairspray, perfume and his mother's chicken casserole.

He frowned, and his gaze went directly to Donetta's. "Did you move that table by yourself?" He hadn't meant to snap.

He saw her eyes dart down to Katherine, then back

up. Okay, fine. They were going to have to discuss this. He wasn't used to worrying over who he could say what in front of. Still, she was in no condition to move heavy furniture.

"Of course she didn't," Anna answered for her. "And do you always greet your houseguests with questions before you even say hello?"

He felt his lips twitch when Donetta batted her eyelashes at him irreverently. He'd known from the start she would always have more people on her side than he would—the majority of them *his* family and friends. Hell, even Roy had been charmed with her, and that had merely been from a description over the phone.

"Sorry, Mama. Hey, Donetta, Katherine, Tracy Lynn, Linc…Sneak and Dixie," he added, just to tease his mother. She whacked him with a dish towel.

"I've delivered the supplies," Linc said. "So I'll be on my way."

"Same here," Kat said, standing. "Just let me run down the hall to the ladies' room."

"Tracy, we ought to be on our way, too," Anna said. "You know Tori will want to go early."

"Well," Donetta commented, looking at Storm, "it's a good thing I was finished with Kat's hair. You sure know how to clear a room fast."

"Wasn't my fault. It was Mama fussing at me. Everybody's afraid it'll be their turn for a scolding next."

"Already had mine," Linc said.

"My condolences, man." He tried to keep his expression solemn, but he had an idea his eyes gave him away. "And, Mama, where are you taking Tori on a school night?"

"To the picture show, if it's any of your concern. And it's not a school night. Tomorrow's a free day because of a teachers' meeting and—"

The sound of Katherine's scream rang through the house.

Storm was out of the kitchen in a flash, Dixie at his side, Linc only a pace behind them. In the foyer, Katherine nearly slammed into his chest, her face as pale as a bleached sheet. In a single move, he steadied her and passed her to Linc. Heart pounding, he searched for the source of danger, hooking his hand in Dixie's collar until he was sure she would stay.

Katherine gave a nervous laugh. "Something fell out of the closet when I was reaching for my coat. I'm sorry. It was probably nothing. I couldn't find a light switch, and…gosh, I'm embarrassed. I was afraid to look."

The coat closet was open slightly, the foyer cloaked in the shadows of dusk. A black trash bag spilled out, along with a towel and the edge of a furry blanket. Storm didn't recognize any of it as belonging to him. He moved closer.

"Sorry," Donetta said. "I crammed a bunch of stuff in there when Pandora and Sneak played hide-the-panties with my things. It's a wonder you weren't buried by the avalanche, Kat." She started to pass by him.

Storm flung out his arm, stopping her. "Just in case the avalanche isn't finished—Linc, why don't you take the women back in the kitchen."

Linc complied and Katherine, Anna and Tracy Lynn went willingly. Donetta stood her ground, looking at him as if he were some kind of a nut.

"I'm cautious, okay?" he said in his own defense. Damn it, he'd stopped at headquarters to retrieve the package Roy had sent and hadn't kept up his end of the surveillance on Judd Quentin. "At least let me and Dixie go first."

The second Dixie heard her name, she charged forward and nosed open the door, then quickly backed out, growling and shaking her head fiercely.

His heart jumped right up into his throat and he

swore. Swiftly, he hooked his arm around Donetta's waist and shoved her behind him.

In her mouth, Dixie held the decapitated head of a woman.

"Oh, no, Dixie." Donetta slipped past him before he could catch her.

"Donetta, stop." His voice cracked out like a whip. He wasn't certain how Dixie would react. On the job, a dog's adrenaline flowed the same as any other officer's.

Trying not to look at the blond hair spilling over his wood floor from a bodiless head, he put himself between Donetta and the dog, his mind running through a list of procedures. Thank God the other women weren't present.

"Dixie hasn't been tested in a situation like this since she retired. At least not with me."

"A situation…?" Donetta frowned when he continued to hold her back. "What *is* the matter with you?" Then she looked from the dog holding a woman's head by the hair and back to him.

She chewed on her bottom lip. "Um…I guess I shouldn't have put Gloria in the closet."

"Gloria?" He jolted when Dixie trotted up and placed the decapitated head right into Donetta's outstretched hands. She lifted it and turned the open, lifeless eyes toward him.

"Gloria," she announced. "Goddess Gloria—the glamour girl of beauty school."

Storm reached over and slammed his palm against the light switch. Donetta was grinning like a loon, holding a heavily made-up mannequin's head, its stringy blond hair falling over her arms. Even in the light it looked like something from a gory crime scene. He felt like a fool.

"What the hell is that doing in my closet?"

"I don't know. *You* packed it. When you were

snatching stuff at my apartment, you must have scooped up a pile of towels and blankets and got Gloria, too.''

He shook his head, ran his hand over his face, then started to chuckle. His personal life, he realized, had been so dull without Donetta in it.

''Let me see her.'' He plucked the pitiful thing out of her hands. ''Come on.''

''Storm! Don't you dare go in there and scare Katherine again.''

DONETTA RINSED THE SPONGE and barely got the water squeezed out before Storm hooked it from her like the NBA's Michael Finley making a steal.

''Hey! I was using that.''

''You're going to scrub the shine right off the countertop,'' he said.

Despite the fresh orange scent of the all-purpose cleaner, the kitchen still carried the faint smell of hair dye and the chicken casserole they'd had for supper. ''You're the one who scared the bejabbers out of everybody and made Tracy Lynn knock over my peroxide.''

He grinned. ''Good thing she's an uptown girl, because she'd never survive out on a ranch with bugs and snakes and smelly animals. It doesn't take much to upset her sensibilities. Did you see how she climbed right up Linc's body?''

''I saw. And you've got no room to talk, Sheriff. You nearly peed in your pants when Dixie got ahold of Gloria.''

He stepped closer, his chest nearly touching hers. ''I might toss my cookies, darlin', but I assure you, I don't pee my pants.'' He brushed his thumb across her cheek. ''I have something for you.''

She could barely get her tongue unstuck from the roof of her mouth. When his eyes went all soft that way and his lazy baritone deepened, it just made her go stupid. "A—a healthy constitution, I hope?"

"Maybe." He set down the sponge and removed two stretchy wristbands from the boxes he'd laid on the countertop. "Roy mailed these acupressure bracelets. Normally, they're for motion sickness. But they're supposed to work on pregnancy sickness, as well. Marnie, Roy's wife, had good luck with them."

"I thought you used hypnotism on her."

"I did—after she got tired of smearing paint on the bands. She's an artist." He turned her hand over, gently held it in his palm, then placed three fingers over her wrist—right where her pulse was beating wildly, blaring her body's response to his nearness.

Donetta stared at the top of his head. Mere inches away, she could easily lean forward and rest her cheek there.

He glanced up at her, then carefully slid the elastic band onto her wrist as though it were a precious diamond bracelet. Emotion swamped her as he picked up her other hand and gently repeated the procedure, positioning the elastic so the small bead settled at the pressure point on the inside of her wrist. The drab gray color of the bands didn't do much for her skin tone, but if they worked, who cared?

"Maybe I'll start a new fashion trend." She could hardly draw a decent breath when he looked at her with such utter tenderness.

He brought her knuckles to his lips and kissed them, his gaze holding hers. "Maybe. I just want you to feel better."

She was incredibly moved by his concern, his gentleness, the quiet sincerity in his voice. He made her want. Desperately.

And she realized she was about to break her own rule about keeping their friendship simple.

She leaned into him, her mouth a breath from his. "Thank you."

She wasn't sure which one of them closed the final distance, but the instant their lips touched, her intended kiss of gratitude shot from platonic to erotic, all decorum abandoned.

Her entire body came alive. She tugged her hands from his, wound them around his neck and lost herself in the warmth of his lips, the sketch of his tongue, the utter skill he brought to a single kiss. She'd started it, but he'd taken over, and she was happy to let him, reveling in the press of his aroused body against her hips.

The pressure of his mouth eased, and he stepped back, leaving her dazed.

"Time's not moving any slower, darlin'. We need to get married."

It took a moment for her mind to snap back to coherency. When it did, she couldn't quite believe her ears.

"Time's not moving any slower?" she parroted. "If that's been your approach to marriage proposals, no wonder you're still a bachelor."

"You want romance? I can give you that, Donetta."

She shook her head. "You know how I feel about marriage."

"We're having a baby, in case you forgot."

"That doesn't equate to marriage." She sighed. "It's not going to happen, Storm. Don't make it any more difficult."

"Why does everything have to be your way?" he asked.

"Because I have more at stake."

His jaw went slack. "That's *my* baby, too."

"I'm not denying that, or suggesting you'll have limited access to your child. All I'm saying is that *I* don't come with the package. You're concerned about your rights with the baby, and that's not an issue. You don't have to take me to have your child.''

''So, you'll hand over physical custody to me?'' His quiet taunt held a suggestion of menace.

She gasped, clenched her fists. ''No. And don't even try to pull that crap with me, Storm. *I'm* providing shelter, nourishment and all the baby's needs these first nine months. *I'm* heaving up my toenails ten times a day. *I'm* turning into a raving, crying, hormonal lunatic—''

''Donetta—''

''Now, if you think *you* can lie in a room full of strangers with your feet up in stirrups and squeeze out a seven- or eight-pound baby through your penis, maybe we'd have something to talk about! If you could then place that child at your breast and provide life-sustaining food, well…well it would be downright petty for me to put up such a fuss, wouldn't it?''

He put his hands on her shoulders, bent his knees slightly and looked straight into her eyes. ''I apologize. That was a stupid thing for me to say. I'd never fight you for custody. I just lashed out without thinking.''

''Yes. That sort of thing tends to happen in the heat of anger, doesn't it?'' She immediately held up her hand before he could speak.

''Now it's my turn to say I'm sorry.'' She sighed, closed her eyes. ''Let's don't do this, Storm.''

He stroked the back of her hand, ran his fingers feather-light up her arm, then caressed her cheek. ''I don't want to fight with you, either. Can I ask you a touchy question?''

''Might as well. I've settled from a boil to a simmer, so if you're going to make me mad again, I guess this would be as good a time as any.''

He smiled at her. ''Did you and Tim fight? Have screaming-and-yelling kind of arguments?''

"Of course not. A bank manager is too civilized for that."

"That's what I figured. Keep that in mind, okay? His meanness, his need to control, was his own sickness. He *looked* for reasons to hurt you—you didn't provoke him. And just because you and I butt heads, that doesn't mean we're going to ruin our relationship—as friends or as lovers. You don't hold back with me, Netta. You say what's on your mind and get it out in the open. So there's nothing to build up into the kind of resentment you're so worried will tear us apart."

"Can you show me that in your crystal ball?" She saw the frustration and the sadness in his eyes. Bittersweet sentiments that she shared. Sentiments that made her want to keen like a wounded animal. "I didn't think so."

STORM WAS LYING WIDE-AWAKE in bed when he heard the back door open and close. He reached for his gun and his flashlight, not bothering to pull on pajama bottoms over his boxers. Nor did he turn on the flashlight. He had to get to Donetta.

The clock on the nightstand read 11:55 p.m. He scanned the hallway, his eyes already adjusted to the dark, and noted that her bedroom door was shut and the bathroom door was open. His adrenaline spiked, tightening his muscles even as his insides shook. Where was Dixie? If he'd heard the door so clearly, why wasn't either dog barking?"

He slipped across the hall into the bathroom, listened, then carefully, quietly, slid back the pocket door that led to the guest room where Donetta slept.

The wood slider was suddenly wrenched from his fingers and flew open. For an instant sound roared in his ears. His surroundings became surreal—a flash of white, the smell of hot asphalt. Then his mind and vision cleared in a blink.

Sneak jumped into his arms just as Storm thumbed the switch on the flashlight. He should have remembered that Sneak knew how to open the pocket door.

Donetta's bed was empty. His heart knocked against his ribs like the rapid-fire kick of an AK-47 assault rifle. Sneak's soft ears brushed against his chin and his neck as the terrier sniffed and licked and welcomed, vibrating happily in his arms as though nothing was amiss.

"Where're Dixie and Donetta?" he whispered. The little dog's head cocked, ears standing straight up, then flopping again as she wiggled to get down. He let her go, and Sneak bounded across the room to scramble up on the upholstered wing chair by the window, front paws on the windowsill.

That was when Storm heard a female giggle. More than one—an adult and a child. He shut off the flashlight, lowered his gun and moved to the slightly ajar window, absently scratching Sneak's velvety ears and soft head.

Donetta and Sunny, holding Tori by the hand as she walked between them, were heading down the gentle incline of the backyard toward the lake. Donetta wore a bulky sweater over a pale, ankle-length nightgown that glowed like neon in the moonlight. Sunny was dressed similarly, except she had on a man's hunting jacket over her granny gown. He had no idea what they were doing outside at midnight in their pajamas, but he was at least glad to see Dixie trotting along beside them.

Headlights arced toward his side yard. Nearly pressing his forehead against the windowpane, he strained to see. His jaw dropped. Tracy Lynn's convertible Mustang streaked across his grass as though it was burning rocket fuel. By damn, he was going to turn his deputies loose on her—regardless that her daddy was the mayor. The woman was a menace behind the wheel. She should at least have a care for the undercarriage and suspension of the car. He was surprised the stereo wasn't blaring. Then he remembered that Donetta was the one who didn't know how to turn a volume knob counterclockwise.

"What the heck is going on?" The flashy red car disappeared behind his barn and the headlights went out. More feminine giggling floated on the night air. "Stay here, Sneak."

He jogged down the hall and through the service porch, grabbed a pair of night-vision binoculars from the hook over the washing machine. Leaving his revolver on a high shelf above the dryer, he quietly stepped outside onto the porch that wrapped around three-quarters of the white farmhouse.

Chills pebbled his skin as he sat down in the wicker chair. Man, it was cold. And he was still wearing only his boxers. He wasn't going inside to put on clothes until he knew what those four women and his niece were doing. Through the binoculars, he saw that Tracy Lynn and Becca had teamed up.

Laughter carried on the night air. The full moon lit the yard, turning the bark on the naked cottonwood tree almost white. Their voices echoed off the water, but their words were unintelligible. The four women appeared to disagree about something.

Then, stunned, he watched as Donetta hiked her gown up to her waist, hooked her thumbs in the elastic sides of her panties, skimmed them down her legs and whipped them off.

"Well, I'll be go to hell." He snatched the night glasses down and stared with his vision unaided, as though that would allow him to see better. Realizing his mistake, he nearly blacked his eyes in a rush to get the binoculars back in place. The confounded woman had that heart-stopping scrap of fabric around one finger and was twirling it over her head like a rodeo cowgirl fixing to rope a calf.

Heat blasted his system as his body went steel hard. How much torture was a man supposed to endure in his own house? His body was telling him that striptease ought to have been a private dance for *him.*

Once before he'd watched Donetta Presley strip off her underwear out in the open beneath that old cottonwood tree—the day before her high-school graduation. Like now, she hadn't known he'd been there.

Man alive, that had been twelve years ago, but the image in his mind was still clear. It had been broad daylight, and she *hadn't* been wearing a granny gown. That day she'd worn denim shorts and a little shirt that left at least five inches of her belly exposed. And she'd had to take the shorts all the way off in order to remove the panties.

"Whoa." He quickly lowered the binoculars when he realized his sister and Tracy Lynn were about to lift their gowns. His initial astonishment turned to amusement and he found himself grinning like a fool. Leave it to Donetta to be the daredevil and lead the disrobing. And *what* he wanted to know, could they have done that would require the entire group to atone?

On second thought, he was probably better off not knowing that answer.

Although he was no longer cold—was pretty hot, to be honest—he went inside, stowed the binoculars, retrieved his gun and went back to his bedroom to listen for her return.

One way or another, he was going to prove to Donetta that love didn't need a crystal ball.

Love. His heart raced wildly, and he sat right down on the bed.

By God, the chances of getting any sleep were zip to none. And the blame rested squarely with the tall, stubborn, redheaded woman who was turning his life upside down piece by nerve-racking piece.

Chapter Thirteen

By Friday, the wristbands were working like a charm. Now that she felt human again, Donetta wanted to eat everything in the house. And evidently she had, because the refrigerator was looking pretty bare. A carton of eggs, milk, a couple of apples, beer and cheese. Not exactly dinner fare.

She smelled Storm's masculine, fresh-from-the-shower scent an instant before a bouquet of flowers appeared in front of her. Pink carnations, white mums and red roses. Next to shoes, flowers were her favorite thing.

"What's this for?" She plucked the fragrant blooms from his hand, buried her nose in them and turned. He hadn't been holding this showy burst of color when he'd passed through the kitchen door a while ago.

He reached around her and shut the refrigerator door. "In honor of your first visit with the baby doctor."

She shifted a few feet away from him and leaned against the counter. She'd waited for him to ask when he'd come home from working on the salon, assumed it would be the first question out of his mouth. She thought he'd forgotten, and it had bothered her. "It wasn't that big of a deal."

"Want me to take the flowers back?"

"Touch them and I'll break your fingers." She

grinned and retrieved a vase from the top cupboard. It dawned on her that she was as familiar with his kitchen as she was with her own. "How did you sneak these past me?"

"I left them in the truck when I saw the car in the driveway, figuring you still had a client. I didn't realize Trudy Fay was already on her way out. So, how'd it go at the doctor's office?"

"Good. We're healthy." She filled a cobalt-glass vase and arranged the flowers. "Lily gave me a bagful of prenatal vitamins and said I'm due around the fourth of May. I already took one of the vitamins and all I've wanted to do is eat. Before I know it I'll be big enough to shade an elephant."

"You'll be beautiful." He brushed his fingers over her neck, shifting her hair. "Let's go out for dinner tonight."

"You don't have to ask me twice." She stepped away from him and snatched her sweater from the back of the chair. He was in an odd mood…more hands-on touchy than usual. As though he'd suddenly taken lessons from his mother. "This kitchen is a bit of a challenge to cook in, anyway."

"What kitchen? It's a beauty shop."

"You're the one who locked me out of my salon. Don't start complaining now. So, where are we going? Friday night at Anna's?"

"I thought maybe someplace different—Angus Twins."

"Steak sounds good to me. Let's go before I starve to death."

"Can't have that." He held the door open as she gathered her purse and shrugged into her sweater.

Dusk brought the melody of tree frogs, crickets and the two-note chorus of cicadas. The air was chilly, carrying the scent of the lake. She glanced out at the water, which had turned gun-metal gray as the sun traded places with the moon, watched as a night bird took flight over the lake.

And there was Bertha, still decorated with four pairs of panties. Well, one of them was boxer shorts with red hearts on it—Sunny's contribution.

"I'm surprised to see the cottonwood still flying its colors," she said. "When the Anderleys lived here they used to take them down right away."

"The present owner likes the view." He grinned and opened the truck door.

When she looked back at him, his gaze was on her behind instead of the tree. His eyes lifted slowly, and Donetta nearly forgot to breathe. Heat shimmered across her skin, swam in her blood. It wasn't often that she had to look up at a man. The urge to stand on tiptoe and press her mouth to his was a fire in her veins that threatened to flash out of control.

"You keep looking at me like that, darlin', and we'll never make it out of the driveway."

She blinked. For one crazy instant, she thought about taking him up on the sensual threat. Thankfully, she regained her senses and climbed into the truck. "You promised to feed me."

He sighed, his mouth kicking up at the corner. "What could I have been thinking?"

ANGUS TWINS WAS A DIMLY LIT steakhouse a few miles outside of town that did a brisk business on Friday nights. A favorite of the locals, it was the place for dancing and socializing, and the food was legendary. Even though they'd arrived earlier than the party crowd, the only seating left was in the bar, and the hostess showed them to a corner booth close to the stage, where a three-piece band was setting up for entertainment.

Storm ordered two nonalcoholic beers, and by the time the waitress delivered the bottles, Donetta was already tearing off a slice of warm bread from the basket on the table.

"They make the best bread here. I'm in heaven."

After they ordered, Storm held up his bottle for a toast. "Do you realize we've never been on a real date?"

Her heart jumped into her throat, and she nearly spilled her beer. "Is that what this is?"

"I'd like it to be."

"Storm—"

He touched the neck of his bottle to hers. "How are the bracelets working?" He nodded at the elastic bands on her wrists.

Donetta sighed. Dates, in her opinion, involved a certain intimacy, and she was trying hard to avoid that, so she didn't further the debate.

She lifted her hands. "Amazingly well. The only drawback so far is getting the fabric wet when I shampoo a client."

"That was Marnie's complaint—getting the bands wet."

She remembered that Marnie had given up the wristbands when Storm had hypnotized her. Donetta felt bad that she couldn't let go with him enough for the hypnotism to work on *her.* After all, she'd given her body freely enough. Why hadn't she been able to give her mind, as well? "Dr. O'Rourke was interested in the bands. She's all for using natural products."

"It seems funny to call Lily 'Dr. O'Rourke.' I remember when she got stage fright in the high school play and ran off in tears. It was the *Wizard of Oz*—and she was Dorothy."

"I hope she had an understudy."

"She did." He took a sip of beer. "Are you feeling better about the baby?"

The switch in subject caught her off guard. Again. Nerves made her heart pound. The conversation was awkward. "I never felt *bad* about it. I was just…surprised. I needed time to adjust."

"And have you?"

"Yes."

"Are you hoping for a girl or a boy?"

"Either one. As long as it's healthy." She bypassed the faux beer and took a sip of water, surprised that her hands weren't shaking.

He leaned forward, ran a finger over the back of her hand. "Are we going to ask about the sex when you have the ultrasound?"

"Do you want to know?"

"Yeah. I think I do. It'll give us longer to fight over a name."

She smiled to cover her unease. She expected him to be involved with their child, but at some point they would need to ease off. Once her salon was up to code, they wouldn't be living in each other's back pockets. Maybe she was making too much of this. Friends could certainly discuss baby names and such.

"You think we'll fight? How about Storm Jr. if it's a boy?"

"Forget it. We're not naming the kids according to the weather."

"That's 'kid.' Singular. I never knew your mom named you according to the weather."

"That was my dad's doing. I should be thankful it was storming that night. I'd have hated being named Sunshine or Spring or something."

She laughed. "That probably would have gotten you in a few fights."

The waitress brought their salads, interrupting their discussion. Donetta told herself that the constant swarm of butterflies in her stomach was only because they were temporarily thrown together. Once she was back to life as usual, the relationship would sort itself out.

She dug into the salad. "Is Judd still working out

all right?'' she asked when she'd scraped the last bit of lettuce from her plate.

''He's getting the job done. Had to hire a couple more guys. Jack and Linc put in as many hours as they could spare, but they both have their own business to tend to. Same with Colby and Gavin.''

''I guess you were worried about Judd planning nefarious deeds for nothing, huh?''

''I never worry for nothing, Slim. I still don't trust him. Can't put my finger on anything specific, but the back of my neck is still itching.''

''You're a cynic.''

''Comes with the job.'' He leaned back as the waitress placed steaming plates of steak and potatoes in front of them.

Donetta slathered butter and sour cream on her potato, and as they ate, the conversation lulled. It was an easy silence, and that surprised her. Silence with Tim had set her nerves on edge, given her reason to angst.

''Does that ever bother you?'' she asked, picking up their conversation. ''Being so suspicious of everyone?'' They were alike in that respect, she realized. Even though she was comfortable enough to be herself, neither of them trusted easily.

''No.'' He seemed bewildered by the question. ''You get conditioned to people lying to you every day. If a cop's not suspicious, it puts him in danger. The crime and ugliness did get old, though,'' he admitted. ''Coming back to Hope Valley, I've realized there's more good than bad in the world. I'd begun to forget that.''

''But you're still cautious about Judd.''

''He's given me reason to be. The scam he pulled with you shows his true character. Only a fool would trust twice.''

Exactly. She met his gaze, certain her thought was blatantly clear, then laid her fork and knife across her plate to signal the waiter that she was finished with her meal.

"Don't be drawing the wrong conclusion, or making comparisons—between us," he said.

"I didn't say anything."

"You didn't have to. Your tone and your eyes said it for you." He pushed his plate away and sipped his water. "God knows you've got plenty of reason not to trust, but I intend to change that."

Before she could comment, he stood and held out his hand. "Dance with me?"

Her heart lurched. She hadn't even realized the music had started. Now she heard the sensual notes of a ballad—one meant for holding a partner close. "That might not be such a good idea."

"Afraid you'll want to jump my bones?"

Her eyes went wide. It was a dare, pure and simple. He knew she wouldn't—couldn't—resist. Especially when he wore that sexy, devilish smile.

"Come on, Slim. Have a heart. Don't leave me standing here looking rejected."

She put her hand in his, followed him onto the small square of wood flooring, where several other couples were swaying together or doing a slow two-step.

"I shouldn't let you have your way," she said against his neck as he drew her in. Her insides were jumping like frog legs in a skillet.

"Oh, you absolutely should. I can't seem to *get* my way with you. My ego is beginning to suffer."

Her lips curved. "I doubt that." She'd danced with him only once before—at Sunny and Jack's wedding. The press of his body against hers had set off an inferno inside her. Just as it did now.

Why couldn't she have been oblivious to the consequences of falling in love with Storm? He'd been out of her reach all her life, yet he'd still been her most cherished dream—a secret dream that she hadn't attached any hope to because it never occurred to her that he would even be interested.

Who knew they'd one day *want* with such fervor?

Would she have felt differently if this had happened before Tim? Before she'd learned an even harder lesson about pain and loss?

Speculating didn't do any good. It was too late for them. Because she *had* learned a lesson. And the price of repeating past mistakes—of possibly losing him—was too high.

She couldn't give him the ties that would take away her freedom. And those were the very ties he wanted.

"Relax," he whispered. He brought their joined hands to his chest, rested his cheek against her temple.

If a woman could relax while snuggled up against Storm Carmichael's wide chest, something was seriously wrong with her. His spicy aftershave teased her senses. Beneath her hand, the soft knit of his pullover sweater radiated heat from his broad shoulder. She felt his arousal pressing behind the fly of his jeans as their bodies brushed. It was like making love standing up.

Her libido shot into overdrive because she knew he could do just that. The night she'd gotten pregnant, he'd made love to her in ways that had stunned even as they had thrilled.

She needed to get her mind off sex. Pretty difficult in this position. At last, she just gave in to the sweet torture, because despite her brain's warnings, she was having a really good time.

"Thanks for suggesting this," she said against his ear.

"Dancing?"

"And dinner. It's been years since I've had a real evening out like this…other than with the girls, I mean." She didn't want to say 'date' because that made it sound too personal. Their relationship had already become *too* personal.

His hand slid up her back, beneath her hair, held her as though she was his most cherished gift. "It's my pleasure...literally," he murmured.

Lord, when he spoke in that deep, suggestive drawl, looked at her out of those intense green eyes, she wanted to pull his head down to hers, feel the weight of his lips, the hot liquid silk of his tongue against her, around her, in her.

Each time he moved forward, his thigh pressed between her legs, making her ache with longing in that vibrant, tender part of her body. A heart-stopping kaleidoscope of images flashed through her mind...a face so familiar...naked bodies straining...clever hands stroking, arousing enflaming.

He was her strongest weakness. And that was so dangerous.

When the song ended she stepped back, shaken by the emotions swimming through her veins. Did pregnancy do this to a woman? she wondered. Throw her hormones totally out of whack? Make her so sensitive, the least little friction could cause her to burn? Have her yearning to forget caution and ignore the consequences?

"We should probably get going," she said, surprised her voice didn't shake since her insides were quaking. "I have a client booked at eight o'clock in the morning."

He stared at her for a long moment, as though oblivious to the couples leaving the dance floor. "On the weekend?"

"Saturday's my busiest day."

He followed her back to their booth, placed several bills on the table and helped her on with her sweater, pulling her hair out from the collar. "Sure you don't want dessert?"

"*Now* you ask me after you've already paid the bill."

"I'm having a little trouble reading your signals, Slim. Won't take but a second to call the waitress back."

"I'm teasing. Dr. O'Rourke won't be happy with me if I gain sixty pounds."

He put his hand at her back as he guided her through the restaurant. "You've got a long way to go, darlin'. Did you tell her about the weight you'd lost these past few weeks while you were so sick?"

When he asked these personal questions, showed this compassionate side, it gave her a giddy jolt. "She knows."

They were nearly to the door when they came face-to-face with Tim. The surge of fight-or-flight adrenaline hit her fast and hard. He had the deceiving blond good looks of an Adonis…and the black soul of a predator.

"Hello, Donetta."

In a subtle move she wasn't sure he was aware of, Storm stepped a half pace in front of her, shifted her slightly behind his shoulder. Protecting her.

"Tim," she acknowledged.

Storm paused just long enough to meet Dilday's gaze, his own deliberately intimidating. Typically, the scumbag wouldn't hold his stare. The pretty boy was only brave enough to pick on women. Shoving him back out the door, giving him a taste of his own medicine, would be so easy.

He resisted the temptation. "Excuse us," he said as he maneuvered Donetta out the door. The nicety galled him, but he didn't want to provoke a fight and upset Donetta. She'd been through too much upset where Tim Dilday was concerned. One thing was sure, though. There wasn't room enough for both him and Dilday in the same town. He would have to remedy that.

When he had Donetta in the truck and was settled

behind the wheel, he looked over at her. "Sorry about that. Nothing like a creep to spoil a nice evening."

"Oh, I wouldn't say it was spoiled. Seeing him caught me off guard for a minute, but I actually enjoyed watching Tim sweat when you gave him your dangerous-cop look."

"If I'd been alone I would have done more than that."

"Don't try to fight my battles, Storm. Tim's history."

"How can he be if you keep running into him?"

"That's just it. I don't run into him."

"It's a small town. Pretty hard to avoid him."

"Yes, it is. But you and I didn't run into each other until Sunny came back and gave us a reason for our paths to cross. It's a matter of where you hang out. People can go months without speaking to their neighbor if their schedules don't mesh. I make it a point to see that mine doesn't coincide with Tim's."

He started the truck and put it in gear. She had a point. They were supposed to be such close friends, yet in the two years he'd been the sheriff of Hope Valley, he'd hardly seen her.

Part of that, he realized, was his own avoidance. After the shooting he'd felt numb, alienated because he'd been forced to retire from the Rangers…not whole. And he'd felt betrayed by Donetta because he'd thought she hadn't been at the hospital when he'd needed her. Now, of course, he knew different.

He turned on his high beams as they traveled down the nearly empty highway. He hadn't realized how late it was.

The smell of alfalfa wafted through the cab from the air vents. Up ahead he saw movement and automatically let off the gas. Senses alert, he observed a lone pedestrian weaving along the shoulder. The person stumbled and fell into the ditch at the side of the road, then jackknifed to a sit and attempted to climb up the two-foot slope. He rolled back down like a turtle flipped over on its back.

"Oh, my gosh, Storm. Did you see that?"

Storm blew out a breath and tapped the steering wheel, the speedometer needle falling rapidly as he braked. He didn't need night-vision glasses to ID the subject.

"Gus Sackett," he said. "One of my regulars, who spends a few nights a month at that fine bed-and-breakfast known as Hope Valley Jail's drunk tank."

"Poor guy. He can't even get out of the ditch. We've got to help him."

"Darlin', Gus isn't one to appreciate folks helping him." He slowed the truck to a crawl and shut off the headlights, mentally tossing coin. The muscular 260-pound man operated the junkyard out on Stoddard Road, and when he was drunk, he was meaner than the dobermans that guarded his gate.

Storm wasn't in the mood for a fight. At least, not with Gus Sackett.

He didn't want to expose Donetta to that kind of a scene. Especially after she'd just seen her ex-husband.

"What are we going to do?" she asked.

"I can leave him here, and hope he sleeps it off and doesn't get himself killed by a wild animal or a semi. Or I can haul his sorry ass in."

"Can't we just give him a ride home?"

"Tried that before. When he's this bad, he won't stay put. There's no telling where he left his truck or how he ended up out here. Besides, he's got two other pickups. If we take him home, he'll climb into one and try to find his way back to the bar."

If Sackett wanted to drink himself to oblivion and step in the path of a freight train, that was one thing. But Storm was worried about the unsuspecting citizen who might swerve to miss a drunk passed out in the middle of the road.

He flipped on the radio. "I'll call it in, have a couple of the deputies swing on out here and wrestle with big Gus." He checked his watch. "It's nearing shift change. Skeeter's not going to be thrilled. When I was starting out in police work, the senior officers always handed off these calls so they didn't get stuck staying late."

"Then why do that to Skeeter? We're here anyway. Do you need help getting Gus in the truck or something?"

He frowned at her. "You said that on purpose, didn't you? I'm not crazy about having nasty bodily functions stinking up my truck. That's sometimes a real problem with these drunks. Besides, you've had a pretty weak constitution lately."

She held up her arms. "Got my magic bracelets on. Come on, this is silly. The station's not that far from the house. Beth has her hands full with the new baby, and she counts on Skeeter getting home at a reasonable hour to help her out."

"How do you know about my deputy's home life?"

"Duh. I own a beauty shop in a small town. Around here if you don't know what you're doing, someone else surely does."

"I'll have to be sure and tell the chamber of commerce to add that to their brochure," he said dryly. "'If you lose your mind, mosey on over. We'll keep track for you.'"

She laughed. "Come on. I've never seen you at work."

"I'm not at work now." Like that had ever stopped him. He blew out a frustrated breath and picked up the mike. "Dispatch, this is Sheriff Carmichael. Margo? You still awake?" One thing about working in a small town where crime hovered in the single digits was that their rules on radio transmissions for the swing and graveyard shifts ranged from lax to none.

"This is Dispatch here, Sheriff. You're breaking up and I didn't copy the last part of your transmission. And that'll be a negative on your ten-nine," Margo added with a good amount of sugary sarcasm.

Storm chuckled and looked at Donetta. "Translated, she just told me that she didn't catch the question about being awake, and no, she doesn't want me to repeat it."

"Ha! Way to go, Margo. You guys need someone like her to keep you in line."

True. He couldn't imagine how they would get along without her. At fifty-eight, Margo Reed had the reflexes of a cat, could field six calls at once without dropping a single stitch in her knitting, knew the position of every unit and officer in the field and still ran roughshod over everyone at the stationhouse.

He keyed the mike again. "I'm out at mile-marker three on Old Bird Creek Road, Margo. There's a man in a ditch and I'm fixin' to extend him a polite invitation to occupy our guest suite for the evening in our fine county establishment."

"Sheriff, I'd like to know what you're doing on this radio in the first place. I surely recall you informing the entire department that you were helping yourself to some vacation days. You've got no business taking intoxicated subjects into custody on your own time. Just tell me where to send the limo, and I'll have Skeeter hop right on out there and bring in our boarder."

"No need, Margo. I'm already here. Tell Skeeter I'll come in hot and just to open the back door of the cab. If we time it right, old Gus'll roll right out and put himself to bed without an escort." He winked at Donetta when she sucked in a breath of disapproval. It sounded like a good plan. Too bad it wouldn't actually work.

''Did you say Gus?'' Margo asked. ''Now, you just sit tight, Sheriff, and let me get you some backup. No reason in the world for you to spend your vacation nursing cuts and bruises—I'm counting on you to get that beauty shop open again. Steve brought Sackett in last time, and he had to get four stitches in his ear—Steve, not Sackett.''

''What is this?'' he muttered, glancing at Donetta. ''Step on Storm's Ego Night?''

''Oh, I think you can handle it,'' she said.

''Margo? You wouldn't be insinuating that I can't hold my own against an intoxicated citizen, would you?'' He grinned, kept his thumb on the mike button so Margo couldn't come back at him. ''Advise Skeeter I'll be en route in three.'' Before he could replace the mike, he heard it key, heard Margo clear her throat. He actually laughed.

''Sheriff, I don't think I copied that last transmission. Did you say you'll have your subject in custody and be headed into the station in three minutes?''

''That's affirmative, Dispatch. En route in three. And unless there's an emergency, be advised this channel is now code ten.'' He knew Margo would be perturbed over his command, but radio silence was imperative if he hoped to get big Gus to the station without a messy brawl.

''Copy that. Code ten at 2202.'' As soon as Margo stated the official time, all that followed was silence. He muted the radio, but wouldn't turn it off completely. That open line of communication was his safety net.

One thing the shooting had done to him was make him more cautious. He still experienced times when approaching a subject in dimly lit areas caused his gut to tuck right up under his rib cage. He didn't like to associate the word *fear* with those incidents, even though the department shrink had hammered that angle ad nauseum.

"Seat belt on?" He saw that it was. "Hold tight, then. As soon as I'm out of the truck I want you to climb over here on my side and get out. Stand by the front fender on this side and don't move until I tell you. I'm hoping I won't end up in a fight with big Gus, but if it comes to that, I don't want you caught in the scuffle. Are we clear?"

"As crystal. I'm timing you."

He turned his headlights back on and hit the gas, racing the last fifty feet and coming to a nose-diving halt.

Leaving the truck's motor running, he snagged his handcuffs and high-powered flashlight from the glove compartment, got out of the truck, jogged around to the passenger side and opened the back door of the crew cab.

By now, Gus was half sitting, half lying at the edge of the ditch. Turning on the flashlight, Storm shined the beam right at Gus's forehead. He didn't want to blind the man and end up having to guide 260 pounds of drunk male across the shoulder of the road. All he needed was enough strategically placed light to keep Gus from seeing him.

"Hey!" Storm hollered. "Are you the guy who called for a cab?"

He heard Donetta choke on a muffled laugh.

"Huh?" Gus seemed to think about that for a minute.

"Come on, buddy. My meter's running and I've got another fare in a half hour. It's a good one, too. Did you call for a cab or not?"

Gus stumbled to his feet. "Damn straight, I did."

As Storm held open the door, keeping the flashlight steady, Gus made his *un*steady way across the grassy shoulder of the road and started to crawl into the back seat.

"'Bout time ya got here," he mumbled, falling face

first against the leather seat. Storm cringed, knowing the stink of alcohol and foul body odor would seep into the leather and linger like week-old garlic and onions. He'd have to scrub down the whole interior.

"Scoot on in, pal, and I'll have you all cozy in a jiff. Here, let me give you a hand." He stood on the running board and urged Gus in farther. "Why don't you just lie down and get some shut-eye while I do the driving."

In a matter of seconds he had Gus's arms positioned behind him, gently closed the handcuffs around his meaty wrists and tucked his legs in so the door would close. By the time he crisscrossed the seat belts over Gus in a way that would prevent him from rising up, the man was already snoring. Wasn't that convenient? He didn't even have to knock the guy out.

"Get in," he said to Donetta. "Quick." Shining the flashlight on his watch, he grinned, jogged around the truck, jumped in and put it in gear. Donetta was already belted in. The oversize tires spit rocks and dirt as he hammered down on the throttle. No sense spending any more time than necessary cooped up in a vehicle with the likes of big Gus Sackett.

"A *cab?*" she whispered, her voice alive with amusement.

He shrugged. "Seemed like a good idea." He lowered both side windows just enough to get a stream of fresh air and lifted the mike.

"Dispatch, three-Adam-one. Be advised that my last transmission was incorrect. I'm en route at 2204. ETA seven." He replaced the mike and grinned like a fool.

"Took me two minutes to get Gus Sackett handcuffed and secured in the vehicle. Seven minutes and we'll be at the station. You got anything else to say about my male prowess or sheriff abilities?"

"At the risk of making your head swell to twice the size of this cab, yes, I do."

He'd only been teasing, but she sounded serious. "Well?"

"I think what you did was sweet."

"Hauling old Gus off to jail is *sweet?*"

"Sure it is. You could have been rough with him. But you were resourceful, gentle, allowed him to save a little of his dignity. It hasn't been easy for him since Leona died."

Storm shrugged. He was aware of that. Gus was a likable guy when he stayed away from the bottle.

Still, Storm didn't feel all that charitable toward the man who'd put a kink in his first real date with Donetta. He'd intended to woo her, ease her into trusting him, into realizing that they had something worth pursuing.

He should have known better than to make plans. She had a way of surprising him, trashing all his good intentions.

Then again, maybe he should be thanking Sackett.

By damn, she'd been downright excited by the drama, goading him, even...impressed. Hell, he ought to deputize her.

On second thought, maybe not. Every man in Hope Valley would probably try breaking the laws just to get her attention.

He intended to be the *only* man entitled to that charm. He just had to find a way to conquer her resistance.

And in the interest of his aching body, he needed to accomplish that in a hurry. He'd been hard for days. All he had to do was be in the same room with her and his heart pumped the better part of his blood south of his belt. Add that erotic kiss the other day in the kitchen, and the mind-numbing press of her sweet body as he'd danced with her tonight, and he was seriously worried that particular part of his anatomy was going to sustain permanent damage.

He wanted her in his bed, yes. Knew he could seduce her there if he put his effort toward that end.

But that wasn't all he wanted.

He wanted her total surrender.

Chapter Fourteen

"I can't believe nobody's taken our underwear off that darn tree," Becca said, using her foot to keep up the soothing motion of the wicker glider. "It's been over a week."

Donetta stared out toward the lake, the sway of the glider nearly putting her to sleep. The raised porch on Storm's old farmhouse was her favorite place to relax—although technically she was still working, since they were waiting for the color to process in Becca's hair. She could barely make out the cottonwood as the evening sky darkened.

"I've been tempted to take them down," Donetta said, "but we never determined what the rules were about how long they had to stay."

"I suppose we should call for a vote."

"Do you really believe Sunny's going to care about Jack's Valentine boxers flapping in the breeze?"

"If we tell Jack she hung them there, she will." Becca used the towel around her neck to wipe away a drip of color at her hairline and flipped one of the tin foils back from her face. "If you ask me, though, I think Storm likes looking at your drawers from his kitchen window."

"He's getting an eyeful of yours, too," Donetta reminded.

"As if he'd know which are mine. We should have penalized Sunny for blabbing that summer." Becca turned slightly. "Did you ever find out if Storm saw the whole thing? Bare butt and all?"

Donetta groaned. "I haven't asked. I figured it's best just to let sleeping dogs lie. Lordy, even at seventeen I'd have been mortified."

"How's it going between the two of you? Have you given any more thought to making these living arrangements permanent?"

"You know I won't do that, Becca."

"You've got willpower, girl. Living with a hunky guy like that...well, you're a better woman than me."

"You have trouble with your willpower around Storm?" The zing of jealousy surprised her.

"No, silly. Not Storm. It's just so obvious that you're attracted to each other."

"Being attracted to someone and losing your freedom to him are two different things."

"Not all marriages are like the prison you were in with Tim," Becca said softly. "What if you just...you know, live with him."

"I am."

"I meant as a couple, dimwit."

"Because if it didn't work out, someone would get hurt. And that's the pits because you're right. I am attracted to him. *Really* attracted. I want to be with him, but I know I'll be going back home in a few days." She smoothed her hands over her skirt. "Don't you ever wish you could just be like a guy and have sex without thinking it to death? I mean, what's the big deal about enjoying someone without having to worry about expectations or living in each other's hip pocket."

"You haven't slept with him since...?" Becca's voice trailed off in surprise. "Good grief, you've already done it, and it's not as if you can get pregnant again."

"Tell that to the man. He walks around without his shirt and I nearly run into the walls. But every time I send out sexy signals, he just pecks a kiss on my forehead and disappears into his room."

"So, follow him."

Headlights arced around the corner, shining on the barn, then disappearing along the S-turn of the lane leading to the house. Sneak, who'd been chewing on Dixie's bone, scrambled off the porch, barking like mad, and cut through the flowerbed on her way around the side yard to meet Storm's truck. Dixie followed—probably figuring she ought to keep an eye on Sneak.

Donetta stood. "Maybe I will. Meanwhile, why don't *you* follow *me* back inside so I can check your color."

"Ah. Eager to get rid of me, hmm?"

"Actually, I thought I was being a pal. With all that tin foil sticking out of your hair, you look like a Martian hoping to get a signal from the mother ship."

"I'm not trying to impress anybody."

"I figured that out when you peeled off that white granny underwear to hang on Bertha. I don't understand how you can wear something so huge with such a skinny butt."

"Not everyone's comfortable wearing butt floss like you do. Besides, nobody's going to be looking under my dress."

The back door opened and Donetta's heart did a little dance that had her fingers trembling as she pulled the foils out of Becca's hair.

Before Storm could hardly remove his hat and hang it on the peg by the door, Sneak pushed in past him, spied the cat, and both dogs took off in hot pursuit.

"Hey, Becca Sue...Donetta. Don't mind me. I'm just passing through with the dogs." He grabbed a beer out of the fridge and turned to Donetta, his gaze skimming her from head to toe like a caress. ''I'm going to hit the shower, okay?''

''Sure.''

Becca raised a brow, waited until Storm had left the room. ''That sounded pretty cozy to me. Asking permission to shower. Just like an old married couple.''

Donetta pinched the next foil and yanked, smirking when Becca yowled.

FEELING BETTER NOW THAT he'd washed the construction dust off, Storm wandered back to the kitchen. There, he took a moment to appreciate Donetta's long legs, which her miniskirt nicely showcased. He was getting used to coming home each night to the smell of perm solution, bleach, shampoo and hairspray. He liked it, because that meant Donetta was still here. But time was running out, and so far he hadn't had any luck convincing her they were right for each other. Convincing her to stay.

Becca was laying money on the counter, her short black hair sporting three different colors of streaks. The highlights were subtle and intriguing instead of garish, proving Donetta's talent as a colorist.

''Looking good, Becca Sue,'' he commented, taking a seat in the chair she'd just vacated.

''Why, thank you, sir. So, how's that salon coming? And please tell me it's almost finished. With Donetta's Secret closed, my business is suffering. People used to at least stop in for coffee when they came into town to get their hair done.''

''The salon's about ready to reopen.''

''Really?'' Donetta asked, excitement ringing in her voice. Her wide smile transformed her beautiful face, lit her amber eyes, socking him right in the gut.

''Yeah. Blane's due out tomorrow to do a reinspection.''

"And I can move back in as soon as he's done?"

"That's what I've been busting my butt for. To get you back up and running."

She raced around the table, threw her arms around his neck and kissed him full on the mouth. Stunned, he didn't even have a chance to capture her face and prolong the excited kiss before she danced back to Becca.

He knew he must look like a lovesick sap, but he couldn't take his eyes off her. The soft fabric of her miniskirt flirted with her thighs and flared when she skipped. Her breasts were growing fuller due to pregnancy, the plump mounds teasing the scoop-neck tank top she wore beneath a sheer black blouse.

"Is he the best, or what?" she said to Becca.

Becca's gaze met his, softened. "Sure is. It's a wonder he's still on the market."

He saw Donetta's hands falter as she placed a bottle of shampoo in a plastic sack. During the past week, her friends had been subtly letting him know they were on his side. Their support hadn't done a whole lot of good. Her excitement over moving back to her apartment told him that.

"Okay, I'm out of here," Becca said, and hugged Donetta. "Bye, Storm. You be good, now."

He kept his gaze on Donetta's skirt as she shut the door behind Becca and came toward him.

"I like what you did with Becca's hair," he said.

"Becca's a hairstylist's dream. She's not afraid to experiment."

She moved around behind him, and the next thing he knew she was running her fingers through his hair.

"How come you've never let me do your hair?"

He shrugged. "I've been using a barber over in Austin. Guess I felt a certain loyalty to him."

"I think it's time you pledged your allegiance to me."

Lulled by the exquisite feel of her hands, he was caught off guard when she stuck a piece of foil against his scalp. Before he could stop her, she'd dipped a small brush in the bowl of goop sitting on the counter and painted it on his hair.

He jerked. "What the hell...?"

Her hands pressed against his shoulders, keeping him in the chair. "Hush up and be still."

"You just put dye crap in my hair."

"You said you liked Becca's color."

"On Becca!"

She laughed and draped a towel around him. "Relax, would you? I know what I'm doing—just a couple of subtle grape highlights. You'll hardly even notice them."

"Grape? I'll look like a fruit. And if I'm not going to notice, why put them in?"

"Oh, stop it. The grape will complement your skin tone, break up the solid black. And it won't compromise your masculinity in the least. Besides, I wouldn't wreck your hair. I have to look at you every day."

It was the "every day" part of her statement that had him settling. He damn well intended for her to see him every day. "I'll never live this down with my deputies," he grumbled.

She laughed, patted his cheek, then dabbed more of that gelatinous-like smelly stuff on another foil.

"Did you think those highlights in Skeeter's hair came from Mother Nature?" she asked.

"Skeeter gets his hair colored?"

"Yes. And don't bother trying to get a rise out of him. If you ask him about it, he'll hand you one of my business cards. He's sent me quite a few clients over the years."

"Well, I'll be damned."

"Mmm-hmm." She worked quickly, then dragged a

chair up in front of him as they waited for the dye to process.

"Hopefully I won't have chunks of hair falling out because of this."

"O ye of little faith—I'm not using bleach. Have some trust, why don't you."

"I will if you will."

She brushed back her long bangs—a gesture of hers when she was uncomfortable or wanted to change the subject.

"So, why *hasn't* some smart lady snapped you up before now?"

"I'm trying to let you."

She rolled her eyes. "Let's concentrate on the past fourteen or so years, okay? Tell Dr. Donetta all your problems."

He remembered her comment that hairdressers were like therapists. "Well, it's like this, Doc. There's a gorgeous, sexy woman who's having my baby, and I can't seem to—"

She whacked him on the leg. "Further back, clown. Tell me why you're thirty-six and still single."

"I've never been tempted to take a walk down the church aisle. I suppose you could say my job has been my wife. I did date a woman for about six months in Houston, though."

"What happened?"

"It fizzled out when she got tired of me not calling or showing up for a date because of work. Crime doesn't stop for love."

"Did you love her?"

"No." Looking at Donetta, he now understood why. He'd rated every woman on how she stacked up against Donetta. Especially her hanging her panties on Bertha the day before her high-school graduation. That image was burned in his mind. He'd taken the panties that day.

He still had them.

"I need to check your color." She hopped up, stepped between his legs and leaned forward to unwrap one of the foils in his hair. Her sheer blouse was unbuttoned, and the upper swell of her breasts spilled out of the scooped tank top. Two inches and he could press his lips to the plump mounds he knew would be soft and perfect. Her floral vanilla scent, warmed by her skin, drenched his senses, making him yearn.

Keeping his hands off her was becoming sheer agony. What was that noble crap he'd told himself about needing her surrender? Man alive, he didn't know how much more restraint he could dredge up.

He reached out and wrapped his hands around her rib cage, his thumbs just below her breasts.

She looked down at him, her amber eyes direct and heavy with sensual invitation.

"I think we can rinse you now." She stepped out of his loose hold.

He didn't say a word, just followed her over to the sink and leaned back on the table she'd turned into a fairly comfortable reclining chair. With the sink counter at his back, the setup was a little like being propped up in bed.

Warm water cascaded over his scalp; the slow, gentle scrape of her sculpted nails followed. He'd had his hair washed by women before, but it had never been such a sensuous experience. As she leaned over him, Donetta's breasts kept brushing his shoulder, while her hands caressed his head and neck, squeezing, stroking. His back teeth ground together so hard it was a wonder they didn't break.

She *was* purposely taunting him—with her movements as well as the tight nipples visible against her tight tank top. Ever since the night he'd taken her dancing, they seemed to have reversed roles. He'd been resisting the sexual aspect of their relationship, and she'd clearly conveyed to him she was good to go.

Damn it, nobility could stretch only so far.

She shut off the water and ran a towel through his hair. Every muscle in his body was knotted. He reached for her waist again, held her steady. Before, his fingers had been loose; this time, they were not. She could neither advance nor retreat unless he let her.

Her gaze snapped to his, and the look in her amber eyes severed the last thread of his control.

Before he could talk himself out of it, he lifted her and aligned her body on top of his, holding her firmly against his groin with one hand while his other hand angled her head for his kiss. Her breasts were pillowed on his chest, and her hips shifted restlessly against his erection, driving him mad.

He kissed her until he couldn't even remember his name, then buried his lips in her neck, nipped at the soft skin.

"Tell me to stop now, Donetta." Even as he said the words, he begged her to do just the opposite, his hand sweeping her back, her behind, the top of her thighs.

She sucked in a breath when he slid his palm beneath the hem of her short skirt, cupped the naked cheeks exposed by incredibly skimpy thong panties.

"I don't want you to stop." Her breath was unsteady, her lips roaming his face, his neck, her hands reaching down to the sides of his hips, heading inward.

He swung his legs over the side of the table, set her on her feet between his spread thighs, pulled her tight against him.

HIS STRONG HOLD on her was unbreakable, but Donetta didn't feel threatened or trapped. The last thing she wanted was for him to let go.

This man, who'd brought her soda crackers and held her when she'd been sick, teased her when she got riled and laughed with her when she acted crazy, had gotten under her skin. He made her remember why she'd had a crush on him when he was sixteen and she was only ten. A crush that had smoldered all these years, before igniting into a love she was unable to deny.

Lord help her, she couldn't refuse either of them for another second.

"I want you," she said. "Now. Inside me. Storm..."

He made a feral sound deep in his throat and slid off the table. "We need a bed." He lifted her in his arms, strode over to twist the lock on the door, then carried her to his bedroom.

It was times like this, when he held her with such little effort, that she realized what an incredibly big man he was. She clung to his shoulders; brushed her lips against his neck; inhaled the spicy scent of his aftershave, the clean smell of laundry detergent on his clothes.

The golden glow of lamplight gave his bedroom a seductive atmosphere, spilling softly over the wine sateen sheets of the unmade bed. Anticipation stole her breath as she remembered the last time she'd been in this room, in this bed...with Storm.

He set her on her feet, tenderly cupped her face and kissed her until her soul sang. He kissed her with reverence and gentleness, as though she were made of delicate, irreplaceable china that might shatter if not handled carefully.

She was on fire, burning from the inside out, yet he took his time. He undressed her as though he was unwrapping a treasured gift. Her sheer blouse fell off her shoulders, caught on her wrists. He unbuttoned the sleeves, bent to kiss her breasts above the neckline of her tank top. By the time she stood before him wearing nothing but the elastic bands at her wrists, desire was pulsing through her so hot and heavy she thought she'd faint.

As he pulled his shirt over his head, she reached for the snap of his jeans, hoping to hurry him along. Fingers fumbled and tangled until at last she was able to get her hands on warm, bare skin.

"Let's take it slow, darlin'."

Cool sheets caressed her back as he eased her onto the bed, followed her down and stroked her body with exquisite patience and thoroughness, as though learning every curve, freckle and indent.

A scream of frustration built within her.

What she couldn't get out of her mind was the uninhibited, wild way he'd made love to her before.

She wanted that again.

She hooked her leg around his thigh, gripped the back of his neck and arched her hips against him. "Quit pussyfooting around." A wash of heat stained her cheeks. She hadn't intended to verbalize the thought.

He looked down at her, arousal and amusement in his eyes. "You don't like my technique?"

"I just meant…I won't break."

He studied her for a long moment, his breathing as unsteady as hers. "I don't want to dredge up any bad memories."

"The memory I'm wanting you to dredge is just a little over two months old. I want what we had last time. I need…"

His eyes flared, and he rolled with her until she lay on top of him. "Then take it. Whatever you need. All of me, or as much as you want. Show me how you want to be touched."

And she did, blanking his mind, sending him right to the edge of madness, nearly making him regret his suggestion.

Skin to skin, their bodies pressed from chest to toes.

She writhed against him, never still, her hands and lips racing over him. He felt as though the top of his head was going to come off, held on to his control by sheer will.

She continually surprised him. She was so sensual. A man would be lucky to have this woman in his life. Forever.

He didn't know how much more of this achingly erotic torture he could stand. Her breasts slid against his belly as she moved lower on his body. He read her intention and rolled her onto her back.

"My turn now."

"Oh, no you don't." She flipped him back over and took him in her mouth before he could even think.

His hips shot up off the bed and he groaned, part shout, part prayer. He reveled in the feel of her slick tongue against him for just a instant or two more, then he swept her beneath him and covered her mouth with his. Maybe she needed the control, to prove something to herself, but she'd just have to hang on a little longer—at least until he took the edge off this mind-blowing desire that had built to an inferno inside him.

He filled his palm with her breast, kneed her legs apart and worked his way down her body, nipping, tasting, toying until he'd reached exactly where he'd intended to go.

Cupping her hips in his palm, he tilted them and made love to her with his mouth, determined to wring every drop of pleasure from her.

Donetta fisted the sheets, arched right up off the bed. The orgasm that ripped through her was incendiary. She screamed. Begged. With an utter loss of control, her entire body jerked with spasms that went on and on.

And then, while her womb still squeezed and pulsed, he shifted and thrust inside her in one long powerful stroke.

Colors burst behind her closed eyelids. He didn't move, just pressed, pressed, pressed…harder, higher, letting her ride the crest to completion and beyond.

And then he pulled back—slowly, oh, so slowly—and thrust again, setting a tempo that took her right back over the top. Heat scorched her. She couldn't draw in a deep-enough breath.

He snatched her legs up and around his waist, reached beneath her and supported her hips with his forearm and let go. She felt him swell incredibly hot and hard inside her. The room narrowed to just the two of them, as their bodies strained to appease and be appeased. And this time, when he shot her over the edge, he followed, soared with her, held her within the safety of his powerful arms and caught her as she fell through the exquisitely, mind-numbing freefall of bliss.

DONETTA AWOKE TO BIRDSONG. She lay quietly and listened as the birds announced their presence to the world, boasting of their status, impressing their mates.

She glanced at Storm's beautiful face, relaxed in sleep. He'd definitely impressed her. Time and again during the night. Her body felt both exhausted and renewed, tender and strong.

Carefully slipping out of bed so she wouldn't wake him, she went into the bathroom across the hall and brushed her teeth, finger-combed her hair and donned the silky robe that hung on the back of the door.

The building inspector was supposed to give the final okay on her salon today, which meant she'd be moving back to her apartment. Why did that thought cause her heart to sting? Last night she'd had another taste of what her life *could* be, yet she was still terrified that something would happen to change the closeness she'd shared with Storm and his family for nearly as long as she could remember.

A failed relationship headed that list of "what if."

Couples always started out with good intentions. But too many times, when passion dimmed, troubles brewed.

If she could just see into the future...

But she couldn't. She only had the past to guide her.

She went back across the hall and had barely crossed the threshold when she ran smack into Storm. Her hands shot out and connected with his bare chest. Without her shoes, the top of her head barely came up to his chin.

He swept her all the way into the room, backed her against the wall and kissed her, bringing alive the exquisite rush of sensations and recall of everything they'd done during the night.

When he lifted his head, they were both breathing hard.

"I thought I'd have to send out a search party for you."

She shook her head, her heart racing. "I'm still here."

"Are you okay?" His hands smoothed over the silk of her robe, inflaming her anew.

"Much better than okay. If there was a guarantee we'd have that kind of intensity for the rest of our lives..." She nodded toward the bed. "I'd be a happy woman. And we'd both be dead."

He grinned. "I feel pretty healthy. You look pretty healthy. We've got a good seventy years' wear-and-tear left in these bodies."

"You think so? Didn't you pay attention in Sunday school? God's got a book of names up there. If He's accurate enough to know when to expect us, then you can be darn sure we were each assigned a carefully calculated number of heartbeats. I don't know about you, but I used up an extra two years of my supply in that bed last night. And that's not counting what we did to each other early this morning."

"Well, now you've got me good and depressed. All I have to do is look at you—hell, just thinking about you gets my heart pumping overtime. Add the couple of times I've had a little flutter or two on the job and I figure my clock's running backward and I'm living on borrowed time."

He hooked his arm around her waist, and she shrieked when he tossed her on the bed. He landed beside her and soul-kissed her until her heart was as tangled up as their limbs.

Sobs gathered in the back of her throat, but muffled laughter escaped. "Is that any way to treat a pregnant lady?"

She might as well have poked him with a hot curling iron. He sprang off her in an impressive move that didn't appear to have any help at all from his arms and legs. His deep green eyes were full of remorse and concern as his hand immediately covered her stomach.

"Are you all right? Did I hurt you? Man, I can't believe I forgot." He pressed his ear to her stomach.

Just that quickly, everything inside her melted.

The familiar sting of tears flooded her eyes, accompanied by the ache in her throat that wouldn't let her swallow. She loved the baby growing in her womb, was even fascinated and awed by the changes in her body.

But she hated these unpredictable hormonally induced mood swings that were merrily having their way with her emotions and laughing in her face because she couldn't stop them.

She scrubbed the sleeve of her robe over her cheeks, then indulged herself for a few moments, spearing her fingers through Storm's thick, silky hair. She meant to steal only a moment, but instead of sliding out from under him, she wanted to bind him to her, hold him just like this for as many heartbeats as they each had left.

''He's a tough guy,'' Storm said, his breath warm against her stomach, his sensuously soft baritone causing her skin to vibrate, the sensation spreading through her body in ever-widening circles like ripples on a glassy lake.

''He's laughing. Either that, or your stomach's growling... His head jerked up. ''I didn't make you sick, did I?''

She lifted her wrists. ''The bands are still doing their job, thank goodness.''

''Maybe you're past the morning-sickness stage.''

She sat up. ''We'll see after breakfast. I need to run them through the wash. So far, every time I've done that I've been pea green by the time the dryer stopped. But hey, who knows. Maybe these little acupressure things have got all my chi flowing on course,'' she said flippantly.

''Now, look-a-here. Don't be knocking something that's clearly working. I'm a guy who sees things in either black or white. If I can get on board with misaligned cells and blocked chi, a flashy, damn-the-torpedoes trailblazer like you can, too.''

''I'm not knocking them.'' Trailblazer? Oh, she liked that. ''I might not understand the process, but that's okay as long as they keep doing their thing. We need to find out where Ray got them, though. I could use a couple of extra sets.''

''We could try hypnotism again.''

She gave him a bright smile, patted his cheek, then attempted to slide out of the bed. ''No sense taxing your strength. These are fine.''

Storm captured her wrist before she could get away. ''Marry me, Donetta.''

She closed her eyes, took a deep breath.

He knew he'd made a big mistake even before she opened her eyes. Achingly bittersweet sadness radiated back at him, along with resistance and unshakable resignation.

"No," she said softly.

He erupted in white-hot frustration. "So, what's your plan? You go your way and I go mine, and when one of us has an itch, we fall into bed and scratch it?"

"You don't have to be ugly."

"Damn it, Donetta. We're having a baby, and you're being totally irrational about the whole situation."

"No. I'm not. *You're* the one who's not seeing clearly right now because you want your way, and that's all you can focus on." She snatched her wrist out of his hold, jerked the lapels of her robe closed and tied the belt at her waist. She crossed the room and sank onto the chair by the window, dropping her forehead into her hands.

"Netta—"

When she lifted her head, tears were tracking down her cheeks. He swore and went to her, knelt in front of her. "Come on, darlin', don't do that."

He cupped her face in his hands, and the tear that dripped onto his wrist was like a splash of acid stinging his heart. He kissed her eyelids, her cheeks, the corners of her mouth. "I'm sorry. Tell me what to do. Tell me what you need."

"I need to be free," she whispered. "You have to let me go, Storm. If I married you…" She shook her head, tears still spilling over her lower lashes. "All I've ever wanted is the freedom to be myself, to have a home and a family to love. I thought I had that once, and went into the marriage trusting the way any other normal person would. Maybe…maybe if it had been you, things would have been different. I would be different. But it wasn't you."

She skimmed her fingertips over his face, pulled back and swallowed hard. "I love you, Storm." Saying the words to him nearly sent her over the edge. She took a breath.

''But if I allowed myself to have what my heart wants, I'd be taking the chance of losing it, as well. And I can't do it. I just can't do it. Please,'' she begged softly. ''Please try to understand.''

Chapter Fifteen

"I *don't* understand, Donetta."

"That's because you're reacting to the chemistry between us," she said. "As am I. It's new and different, something we haven't experienced between us in all these years. But the heat of desire can cloud issues, Storm. It doesn't last forever. The fire burns down—believe me, I've had countless clients in my chair reiterating this very thing. So, what happens between us when the flame goes out? Would we have anything left?"

"Of course we would."

"You say that now. But you can't promise. It's too risky to put our friendship on the line. Anything that affects us negatively will ripple down to too many others."

"You want an escape route," he said. "To share our child and our family, yet for each of us to keep our own space."

She nodded. "I'm sorry."

"Yeah, me, too." His voice was like sandpaper on a rough board. He stood up and jerked his T-shirt over his head, tugged on his jeans.

"Storm—"

"I'm not like him, Donetta. I don't have a deep dark side I'm hiding, waiting until I have you legally bound to me to show it.'' He raked a hand through his hair. ''Hell. I hate the fact that I halfway *do* understand where you're coming from. I've been blown away more than once when I've found out a guy I knew and liked was actually a sick creep behind closed doors.''

He turned and looked at her, flinched when he saw the near relief in her eyes, knew he'd hit at least part of the mark.

''That newsclip that played over and over on TV, which made it look like I was roughing up a citizen, left a powerful image in a lot of people's minds. I didn't use excessive force on Shantelle Kingsley, Donetta. The woman had an accomplice standing by with a video camera. The confrontation was staged, and the film was altered. It could have happened to any of the officers on the force, but I was the one in the wrong place at the wrong time. She wanted to sue the state in a big splashy trial, cash in on some easy money. Thank God the case didn't go that far. Roy exposed the evidence before I'd even completed two full days of suspension, and I was fully exonerated.''

She sat silently, listening to him. He doubted his explanation would change her mind. But he needed to tell her anyway.

''I have proof—and it's over there in my computer if you want to see it.'' He went to the table and scribbled a sequence of numbers on a pad of paper, ripped off the page and handed it to her. ''This is my password and access ID number.''

''I don't need to look at it, Storm.'' She tried to hand the piece of paper back to him, but he wouldn't take it. ''Why didn't the news stations tell the real story?''

''Because I asked the department not to release it. I was back to work and I didn't want any more attention drawn to the whole fiasco. I just wanted to forget it. The department handled any inquiries that came in on an individual basis. A couple of the channels gave a five second sound bite when additional charges were filed against the Kingsley woman. That information in the computer is as much proof as I can give you—other than my word."

"Thank you for telling me, Storm. You didn't have to."

"Maybe not. I can't imagine ever getting to the point of irreconcilable differences with you, but I know that's a genuine worry of yours. You can at least rest easy that any disagreements between us would never involve violence." He had to get out of this room. He could only be noble and self-sacrificing for so long before he put his fist through a wall and scared the hell out of her.

Because he knew there was nothing he could do to give Donetta the peace and emotional safety she sought. Except to let her go as she'd asked.

"I'll help you get your stuff back in your apartment as soon as Blane gives the go ahead."

HE HADN'T SEEN Donetta since he'd moved her back to her apartment three days ago. It was all Storm could do not to go to her, to demand that she come to her senses and acknowledge that they belonged together.

Sitting at the counter in his mother's café, he laid his fork down and pushed away his uneaten meal. Sunny, who'd been helping out with the customers tonight, poured herself a cup of coffee and leaned against the wall, obviously taking a break. He went over to her.

"Hey, big brother." She reached out and gave his arm a compassionate squeeze.

He shoved his hands in his pockets, unsure how to formulate the questions he wanted to ask. "Do I know you?"

She gaped at him. "Did you have a lobotomy you forgot to mention?"

"Not like that. I know you're my sister. But do I know *you.* If we went on one of those family game shows—how would we do?"

She grinned. "Because of your gender, I'd have the advantage over you."

"I'm not real happy with women-versus-men stuff just lately," he warned.

She set down her cup, touched his arm, then pulled him farther toward the kitchen, away from listening ears. "This is serious, isn't it."

"Yeah."

"Okay, I can only speak for myself here, but if we were on a game show, and I had to answer questions about you, I'd probably get around seventy-five percent right." She shrugged. "You keep a lot to yourself and we were apart for a number of years—"

"But we've always been a *close* family. You can't deny that, or the love."

"No. The love was never in question. But that's a different subject. You can love someone for years and not know what's buried deep." She gave him a shrewd look. "Donetta had no idea Tim was an abuser. She dated him close to a year. Saw him every day. Kind of scary when you think about it."

His eyes narrowed. "I'm getting pretty sick of being compared with that son of a bitch."

"I'm not comparing you, Storm. And neither is Donetta. After she stayed with me in California for a while, when she was ready to face things, we flew to Dallas to see Tim's mother and sister. They're nice people. Normal people. They seemed totally surprised by Tim's abuse."

He folded his arms across his chest to keep himself from punching the nearest wall. He didn't doubt the Dildays' shock. His own mother didn't know what Donetta had gone through, and Donetta was as close to Anna as her own daughter.

''I probably shouldn't be telling you any of this,'' Sunny said.

''Please, Pip. You're not breaking a confidence. I know about the baby she lost—*how* she lost it.'' His hands fisted. He uncrossed his arms, tried not to show his knotted tension. ''And the perfection Tim expected. I know how he broke her spirit—at least she *thought* he broke it. I've never met a stronger woman.''

Sunny nodded. ''We felt the strain the minute we walked into Cindy's house. It had been almost two months…Donetta still had the bruises, Storm. But it didn't seem to matter. Even with proof of Tim's culpability in the breakup staring Cindy in the face, she asked Donetta to leave and to not come back. Cindy had chosen a side. Her brother's.''

Bruises after two months? ''I should have killed the bastard,'' he muttered. ''Guess it's a good thing I was in a marginally better mood when I saw him yesterday. Looking the scum in the eye, knowing what I did then, was hard enough.''

''Why did you go see Tim?'' Sunny inhaled. ''Storm—you didn't do anything…*painful,* did you?''

''Shouldn't that answer fall into your seventy-five percent knowledge of me from our hypothetical game show? The guy's a dirt bag.'' He kept his gaze on his sister's, letting her draw her own conclusions. ''Dilday took a flight out of Austin last night. He'll probably be back in town in two, maybe three weeks. And that will only be to pack up his belongings and move. He doesn't work for Hope Valley bank anymore, either.''

Sunny laughed. ''I know what you're trying to do, and it won't work. I think you might have wanted to, but I don't believe you roughed up Tim Dilday. All the same, good riddance to him.''

''Why can't Donetta believe in me that easily?''

''Here's another sage piece from your smart sister. You're too impatient.''

"You just lost points, Pip. I've been more patient than a saint."

"Two weeks elevates you to sainthood? If you believe that, you sure don't know the basic difference between males and females."

Jack Slade walked up, caught the tail end of his wife's words and held up his hands. "Whoa. Private conversation. I'm outta here."

"Stay," Storm said.

"Man, I don't want to cause you embarrassment. Besides, I already know the lesson about girls and boys—"

"Just shut up and let my sister talk."

"The floor's yours, sugar babe," Jack said, grinning. "Be gentle."

Sunny smiled as she stood on tiptoe and smacked a kiss to her husband's cheek. "Remember when you flunked math class because you wouldn't show your work in long division? You just wrote down the answers?"

"Every one of those answers were correct," Storm defended, wondering what math had to do with him and Donetta.

"*You* knew that. But your teacher had no way of knowing if you were cheating, because she couldn't see all the numbers. Unless you consistently proved—in her presence—that you weren't hiding a cheat sheet, she had no choice but to flunk you. And since I happen to have insider information to both sides of *this* equation, I can tell you, you're repeating an old pattern."

"How?"

"You're in love with Donetta, and you figure that's all you or anybody else needs to know. *You're* confident that your solution is the correct one, that there are no hidden mistakes in your calculation. But Donetta won't look at your math answer and simply fall in line as you expect her to. She's worried about a possible decimal point you forgot to include that she can't see. And that upsets you because you *know* you're right, and you're used to getting your way."

Anna, obviously realizing something was amiss with her children, came to stand silently beside them. Storm barely noticed. He wasn't sure he understood his sister's analogy, but she'd just echoed words similar to the ones Donetta had said three days ago: *You want your way, and that's all you can focus on.*

"Donetta has a very good reason for not falling in line, Storm." Sunny's voice softened. "As long as you keep pushing, she'll have to push right back. And she knows from experience that pretty soon, a person gets tired of the strife. And when that happens you divide up the families, the cars, and the animals."

"But—"

"Picture it, Storm. Christmas arrives and the two of you have verbally pushed and shoved long enough, so you've split up. You're a little awkward with each other. You're our family, you know you're expected for Christmas dinner and you show up with gifts. But Netta is family, too. She's always been to Christmas supper. Now what? Do we ask her to stay home? Does she come? Should y'all bring gifts for each other, as well? Do you get mad because we're all so distraught over hurting one or both of you that you say 'To hell with it' and spend Christmas somewhere else?"

"Damn it, Pip, that's not going to happen." His outburst drew the attention of several diners.

"You're legitimate; she's the figurative stepchild," Sunny continued, hammering away as if he hadn't even spoken. "Mama and I love you both equally. These are the things Donetta is going to think about. But not for herself, Storm. It will be for the worry and heartache you, me and Mama will go through. She'll sacrifice *her* needs before she'll put us through that."

His chest felt ready to explode. The scenario his sister painted was intolerable. "I'm not listening to any more of this. You're all borrowing trouble where there isn't any."

Sunny snagged his arm. "Donetta loves you, Storm. She's always been in love with you. If that wasn't the case, none of this would be an issue. I'm on your side. I really am. I'd give anything to see the two of you together..."

"But?" he prodded, aware his tone was surly, yet unable to temper it.

"But she was mine before she was yours," she whispered, her eyes filling with tears.

The stark words knocked the breath out of him. Unbidden, an image of nine-year-old Donetta sitting on the front steps of his mother's house flashed in his mind. The stoic little girl trying to act as though it was no big deal that her father was gone, that he wasn't even her father at all. That her mother was a drunk who didn't even care enough to come home at night. People she should have been closest to, should have been able to trust, had shown that appearances could easily deceive, that nasty surprises lurked beneath the surface, hidden by false smiles and false words.

"She's been through more than any one person should ever have to go through," Sunny continued. "If she decides that loving you is too big a risk, she'll still have my support. We made a vow when we were nine. I can't explain how that's different from the husband-and-wife love, or the brother-and-sister love—but with Donetta, Tracy Lynn, Becca and me, it just is."

Storm swallowed back his own emotion. He noticed that Jack was paying close attention to Sunny's declaration, wondered if the other man had known just how strong that bond was.

A part of him noted that the café had gone unusually silent, but he didn't care if every busybody in town was eavesdropping.

He finally understood. They were lucky, Donetta and the other three Texas Sweethearts. To have a friendship and bond so strong was priceless. They'd been together all their lives, proven that they were unshakable, secure that there were no surprises.

Storm had been away for fourteen years, didn't have the day-to-day track record that could speak for him, substantiate the level of ease Donetta needed in order to trust him as she trusted his sister. He could only *tell* her how he felt. How he'd always felt.

But he'd just realized that he *did* have proof.

He scooped Sunny off her feet and twirled with her. "Thanks for doing my math, Pip." On the second revolution, when he was in the process of setting his sister back on solid ground, his gaze skimmed over Millicent Lloyd's shocking blue hair, the two grandmas…and collided with Donetta's amber eyes.

DONETTA'S WHOLE BODY was shaking with joy, with love…and with nausea. Why hadn't she *seen* how lucky she was?

Grammy Betty stood on one side of her and Storm's Grandma Birdie was on the other. Both women had their arms around her waist as though they expected her to keel over any second now—mainly because she'd taken off her wristbands and morning-noon-and-night sickness was clawing at her insides. As a precaution, Millicent Lloyd stood behind her.

"Well, Betty," Birdie said, leaning around Donetta. "Want to put some money on which one of our grandkids comes out of their stupor first?"

"Why, that would be like knowing both sides of the poker cards," Betty said. "Where's the challenge in that, I ask you." She squeezed Donetta's waist, whispered lovingly, "Take the step, hon."

The grandmothers had been home two days, and Donetta couldn't get over the drastic change in

Grammy. She was no longer the reserved, quietly proper woman Donetta had grown up with. Birdie's doings, she imagined. She'd intended to prepare Grammy for the gossip that would soon be dished out like potato salad at a Fourth of July picnic, but Birdie had been at the house, too, and somehow things had gotten completely out of hand. The next thing she knew, the women had cornered her, and even dragged Miz Lloyd over, determined to set Donetta straight on life, family and love.

She felt as though she'd been legally blind up until now, and was seeing the world through a new pair of special glasses.

She'd set the bar for normal human behavior based on her mother and Tim. The grandmas and Millicent had helped her see that those standards were an exception, *not* the rule.

Donetta took the step. And so did Storm.

''Dang,'' Birdie said. ''Wouldn't you know. It's a draw.''

Storm's hands went immediately to her face. They brushed back her hair, skimming down her arms to her wrists. He wore the type of panicked ''guy'' look she would have never associated with a man like Storm Carmichael.

''What's wrong? Did something happen? You've turned pale again—'' He stopped, frowned. ''Netta? Darlin', where are the bracelets?''

''Grammy has them in her purse. I want you to hypnotize me.''

Now it was his turn to go pale. ''Damn it, Netta. I can't just—'' He bent his knees, stared into her eyes, placed his palm over her stomach. The intensity in his green eyes was so powerful.

Why hadn't she ever realized before that she could *see* this man's heart?

Without breaking eye contact, he said. ''Betty, would you pass me those elastic bands in your purse?''

Before she could object, the elastic bracelets were dangling over her shoulder.

''Storm. No. I need to show you that I trust you. This is the only way—''

''I don't perform well under pressure, darlin'. And you caught me on the way out.''

''Excuse me?''

He chuckled at her incredulous tone. ''There's that fire I'm so crazy about.'' He slipped the bands on her wrists, pressed softly against the pressure point for several seconds, then kissed her with a tenderness that penetrated clear to her soul.

By the time he lifted his head, Donetta decided she *did* need a little support to stand. He handed her back to the grandmothers.

''Stay right here. Don't move. I have a quick errand to run. I'll be right back.''

She'd just told the man she was ready to surrender her body, soul, and mind to him...and he was going to run an errand? They were having a baby, for crying out loud. Shouldn't they be finding a quiet corner to discuss their future?

''This better be important, young man,'' Millicent said, with a disapproving sniff.

''Yes, ma'am, it is.''

He dashed out the door, and Donetta shook her head. She was crazy about the man, and absolutely bewildered. She cringed when his truck roared to life and slammed into gear before the pistons hardly had time to pump oil. He smoked the tires in reverse and left a good portion of rubber down Main Street as the beefy truck shot forward with a total lack of regard for the health of its transmission.

She turned back and met Sunny's eyes. Within seconds, she was hugging her friend, so incredibly moved by Sunny's summation of their friendship, because it matched her own.

"I've been an idiot," she whispered.

"Baby hormones," Sunny whispered back. "I'd have slapped you out of it sooner or later."

The door burst open and Becca and Tracy Lynn raced in. "What's going on?" Tracy demanded, looking around wildly. "Storm just peeled out of here like a madman." She saw Donetta and grabbed Becca's arm, hauling her through the café. "Hey, Grandma Birdie, Grammy Betty," she said politely in passing.

"Miz Lloyd," Becca added.

Donetta smiled. "I think I might have finally driven Storm past the point of salvation," she said to Tracy and Becca when they halted in front of her. She was dying to know where the heck he'd gone and why he'd had to leave right that minute.

"The grandmas look like they wish they were holding shotguns," Tracy whispered. "Do they know about the…you know?"

Donetta nodded. "They've had me holed up at Grammy's all day, and they even called in Miz. Lloyd. Lordy, I felt as though I'd been accosted by the Ya-Ya Sisters. Did y'all hear that Tim's been transferred to another bank in Northwest Texas?"

"I didn't know it was a transfer," Sunny said. "Storm tried to make me believe he'd beat the whey out of the guy."

"Did you believe him?"

"Of course not. I gave him a math lesson."

Donetta nodded. As did Becca and Tracy. It was a girl thing. "Miz Lloyd told the grandma's and me about Tim," Donetta said. "There was no mention of punches thrown."

Storm had quietly dealt with two bullies in her life. He hadn't caused a fuss or drawn attention. He'd shown his goodness by giving the men alternatives—

another job for Tim, no arrest and another chance for Judd.

Although she'd handled Tim by divorcing him and she *would* have handled the contractor on her own if Storm hadn't jumped the gun and gotten there first, his sweetness touched her. He didn't want her to hurt or feel sick, and he would move heaven and earth and *people* to make sure she was safe.

That's when she'd realized that she *did* know him. With every touch, every glance, every deed, he'd been trying to show her that. And she'd been too blind to see.

She'd been hiding, determined that there would be no more men or relationships in her life. But Storm was a detective. He found people who were hiding—exposed them.

And he'd found the key to her hideaway...left a part of himself there so that he could always come back again, so that he could always find her. Through their child. A forever tie.

And oh, how she wanted that tie.

Every eye in the café turned toward the front door when the white pickup squealed into the parking space.

"Somebody ought to give that boy a ticket," Millicent commented.

Donetta's heart pounded as he came through the door and headed directly for her. She was instantly wary of the sexy sparkle in his eyes.

He stopped in front of her and pulled a pair of red bikini underpants out of his pocket.

"Do you remember these?"

Horrified, Donetta tried to snatch them from him. "Storm!" she hissed. "Have you lost your mind? You're flashing my underwear in public!"

"What's so private about them? You left them hanging on Bertha twelve years ago for the entire town to see."

"Twelve—" For a moment, Donetta was speechless. Sunny had told her Storm had only *seen* her decorating the panty tree. There'd been no mention that he'd actually taken them. She'd been eighteen that summer, and he'd been twenty-four, home for Sunny's high-school graduation. "You *kept* them?"

"Yeah. I always wondered why. I finally figured it out. You said I had commitment phobias because I haven't had any lasting relationships. That's not the case. Turns out, I'm a one-woman man. My heart has always known what my brain didn't recognize."

His big palms were so tender as he cupped her face. "I love you, Donetta. You can't doubt a man who keeps your underwear for twelve years. That's got to prove something. You should be cherished, and I want to be the man to do that. For the rest of our lives. Please marry me."

At last she'd understood. Marrying Storm wouldn't take away her freedom.

His love and devotion would set her free. *Had* set her free.

This time, she knew her dream would come true.

"You're making me a pretty good offer. I've always wished I could call Anna 'Mom' for real."

Anna put a hand to her bosom, right over her heart, then snatched up the hem of her apron to wipe her tears. Grammy smiled and, with Birdie and Millicent trailing, went to stand next to her.

"I've heard of marrying for money," Storm said, "but for a guy's *mother?*"

"Well, I suppose you have other attributes that are enticing." She gave him a smoldering look that made his eyes flare and his chest rise and fall with desire.

Oh, yes, she thought. They were going to have a *very* good life together.

"I happen to love you with all my heart, Storm Carmichael. And since we're going to be parents," she said quietly, ''I suppose you ought to make an honest woman out of me.''

He hauled her into his arms and kissed her. When he came up for air, he grinned at the beaming crowd.

''Hey, everybody, it's time Donetta's secret came out. We're getting married—and Mama, you're getting another grandbaby.''

Darla Pam Kirkwell, who'd plopped herself front and center at the counter so as not to miss any juicy gossip, sucked in a scandalized breath.

Anna promptly dumped a pitcher full of cold milk in the woman's lap. ''That ought to give you something to gasp about.'' Her eyes scanned every corner of the café that now bore her name. Surrounded by her friends and family, she perched her hands on her hips.

''And that goes for the rest of you. I defy anyone to make a peep about Storm and Donetta announcing my next grandbaby before the wedding!''

Darla Pam huffed and marched toward the door with as much dignity as a woman could muster while wearing milk on the front of her skirt.

Storm didn't give her a second glance. He had eyes only for Donetta.

All his life—and for the rest of his life, this Texas Sweetheart was his.